The Dark Tide
BOOK THREE
of the
WEREDING CHRONICLES

Christian Boustead

DISCLAIMER

This work contains violence and sexual scenes so be warned.
No person living or dead is described in this book and all events are of a
fictional nature.

Published by Christian Boustead
Publishing partner: Paragon Publishing, Rothersthorpe
First published 2019

ISBN 978-1-78222-726-7

Book design, layout and production management by Into Print
www.intoprint.net
+44 (0)1604 832149

CHE DARK CIDE

To Joseph and Alex.

ACKNOWLEDGEMENTS

I must thank the people at *Books Go Social* for editing this book!
I must also thank Anne and Mark at Into Print for all their help in getting it published!
If I have forgoton anyone, I apologise!

CONTENTS

Prologue 7

A ROSE ON THE WIND 9
WAKING UP TO A NIGHTMARE 16
FIRE AND WATER 21
KAIN 25
THE ROBIN AND THE DRAGON 27
SABLE AND ROSE 30
PLUMBING THE DEPTHS 34
RIDING THE LIGHTNING 41
THE REPOSITORY 46
THE CARETAKERS 57
ON THE WINGS OF LIGHTNING 67
FIRETHORN 82
SWORDS AND SADDLES 86
AIR DEFENCES 96
FINALLY GOING SOUTH 101
THE ROAD SOUTH 106
THE RUINS FROM DRAGON BACK 115
THE MIND OF A WOLF 121
THE BIRCHES 124
TALL TREES 130
THE KINGS 136
THE WHITE WOLF'S JUDGEMENT 148
THE STUDY OF THE BOW AND THE BLADE . . .157

THE VOICE OF WAR. .161

DRAWING LINES 167

CATCHING HOLD OF THE LIGHTNING. 175

THE PASSING OF A MANTLE 181

CHESS AND WAR. 186

THE FIRST BLOW 189

A DRAGON EYE VIEW 194

THE BRIDGE OF TEARS 199

WASHING AWAY THE DARK TIDE 205

HOLDING ACTION .209

FIRE AND LIGHTNING 217

THE DYING OF THE LIGHT 221

THE FLIGHT OF THE EAGLE 225

THE RIDE OF THE WHITE WOLF 231

THE FALL OF THE DRAGON 240

THE SILVER FLAME 246

THE TURNING OF THE TIDE. 251

EPILOGUE 255

ABOUT THE AUTHOR. 257

BOOK EXTRACTS .258

PROLOGUE

"The tide rises darkly, its bladed waves lapping at the Wereding's shore, and like King Canute, the Warden of the North bid them turn back."

Lea's record of the siege of the Kings from the Wereding Chronicles.

The being called the White Wolf, Tristian Silverbrow, stood on a high place and looked out to see the dawn. The wind whipped his long, snowy mane about his bestial face, making it flow across his dark green eyes, which in the right light occasionally gleamed a feral yellow, as though their colour was fluctuating. He gazed down from his eyrie in the citadel of the Twins and looked on the wasteland, which was his duty to protect and guard. As his eyes changed and his large nostrils flared, an angry expression flashed from behind his impassive mask. "The Darkling tide is rising to beat upon our shore," he said, in a whisper of a voice that yet rang through the stillness of the predawn like the rumble of thunder far off.

From behind him there came a deep purr of a voice, sounding like a cat. "And will they sweep us away, or break upon our shores?"

An animalistic snarl broke from his lips and his eyes blazed with a yellow fire, as if a flame had flared up inside him. "The storm is gathering, and we must stand to meet it."

"The storm is gathering, my love, because I summoned it," said the purr, as a tall woman with waist long white hair stepped into the light, her eyes flashing like lightning against black thunderheads.

The glimmer of a smile might have curled his lip at this, and then his face returned to its stern mask. "As I was saying, the storm is coming, and we will meet it if I have to draw the Kings myself!"

"And will we stand or fall, my love?"

"Only time will tell."

"I will be beside you," the woman said, stepping up behind her lover and throwing her arms around him.

"In that case I shouldn't worry!"

"Then there is still hope?" Her whisper in his ear forced a deep growl from him, though whether it was an expression of anger or lust was hard to tell.

Kye stared into the misty valley of the Sabrina and listened to the long, blood chilling howl of his father, Flash's, wolf voice. As the cry died away he waited for the mist to clear, so he could shoot an arrow at the horde of Goblins he knew were beyond the narrow span Flash was guarding. He had a shaft on the string, as did the thirty or so other members of the Silver Shield. Though he watched for the white curtain to move it did not, and he was left without a target, and for a moment nothing to do but wait. As he waited, he reflected on the events leading to this place and time. He had known this war would come, but even with his power of second sight he had not foreseen the strange happenings which led to this spot. As he stood there waiting on the weather, his mind went back to the night he ran from the lake at Care Diff to stop Rose Canduss from going north.

A ROSE ON THE WIND

"A rose's scent lingers on the air, its call a wordless cry to follow, but to where and to what?"

Kye's Journals.

Kye dropped to one knee on the steps to the Tower of the Eagle, and after a moment to regain his breath he proceeded to hammer on the door of the building belonging to Rose's family, and where she would have gone after the Moot. For a long time nothing happened, so he drew the short sword Great Mother had given him. The beast hilted blade was possessed of a spirit, and as Kye slammed the silver wolf's head against the wood, the yellow stones which were its eyes flashed, a snarl echoed in his mind and seconds later a voice spoke into his thoughts. If you want to knock down doors use a hammer, not me!

Forgive me, Kye thought back, My need is great.

The sword (Wolf's Fang), did not respond to this in words, but a low growl may have forgiven him. His knocking was eventually answered by a voice calling down from one of the high arched windows piercing the tower's upper levels. "Where's the fire?"

Kye recognised the voice, it was the soft, but powerful voice of Takana the Harpy.

"Takana, where is Rose?"

"Heading north with Lightning to see Firethorn."

"By the Black moon!" Kye cried in despair. "Goddess forgive me, I am too late!"

"Kye, what is wrong?"

"How long have they gone?"

"Maybe half an hour, but Kye, what is wrong?"

"There may still be time to catch them," Kye snarled and was turning to go when Takana's voice called him back. "Kye Silverbrow, if you do not tell me what is wrong I will burn you where you stand."

"I have seen a vision. Rose must not go north, it is a trap." With these words Kye turned and hurling back his head gave a long howl, soon answered by other Werewolves. Seconds later, through the magic links of blood, his siblings Silver Skin, Lea, and Lor reached out to him with their minds. Kye, what is it?

Meet me at the north gate, Kye thought back, running flat out for this gate.

Another voice reached into his thoughts, the purr of his lover, Eloo. Kye, are you all right?

Rose and Lightning are in danger.

Neither Eloo nor the other Werewolves asked more questions, but they all appeared at the north gate where Kye questioned the two giant guards. "How long ago was that?"

"An hour," said the giant, his voice a low rumble like an earth tremor felt far away.

"By the Blood Moon!" Kye snarled and turned to look along the arrow straight stone road leading north. "There may still be time to catch them."

"Kye, what's wrong?" Eloo asked, touching his arm.

Kye might have answered the short girl with the cat's eyes and ears, but before he could a great shadow passed over them, and the feathered form of Takana dropped out of the sky to land before them. Her great red wings raised a cloud of dust as they beat around her.

"Kye Silverbrow, you tell me what is wrong before I do something you will regret," she demanded, her feathers shrinking back into her flesh, so now instead of huge wings she had lots of small quills protruding from her arms.

Kye stared at her, his eyes flashing yellow before becoming blue and hooded. "Takana, can you reach Lightning's mind with your ring?"

Takana's eyes narrowed, and she tapped a talon on the stone. "It might be possible, he could still be in range, but why do you want him?"

"He and Rose should not go north; they are heading into a trap."

"A trap! What do you mean, a trap!"

"I cannot tell you details, all the vision showed me was them being consumed by black lightning," Kye snapped, tossing his short sword from hand to hand, an act that made the blade growl in annoyance.

Takana hissed, and raising the taloned foot that wore her ring she concentrated on the ruby set into the gold band. Her eyes turned a flaming red and her lips moved soundlessly, but after a moment she hissed and stamped the foot on the stone road.

"No luck!" Eloo guessed.

"Then we shall have to go after them," Lor said in his deep voice.

"And at once," snarled Kye, and he began to pull his tunic over his head as he strove to strip so he could change into his other form.

"Kye, wait!" Silver Skin, his silvery haired sister snapped, reading his intention from his actions. "We have not prepared for a journey north, but south, and we came here without the packs. At least wait until we prepare."

"No time," Kye said, flinging his tunic to Lor and strapping his sword belt around his naked chest.

Eloo turned away from Kye's wavering form to face Silver Skin. "I will go with Kye, and bring Rose and Lightning back. You can follow with the supplies and we can turn south from there." Without waiting for a reply she turned back to leap high, landing astride the back of the black wolf as tall as a horse, who had replaced the man known as Kye.

"Good hunting," Lea said, as the huge, sable Werewolf raced along the road in Rose's trail.

"Has Hunter given his permission for you to go south?" Takana asked, watching the huge wolf dwindle to a dot in a heartbeat.

"He has given his consent for us to go as far as the Kings, but he says it remains for Grandfather to decide whether we can go further," Silver Skin said, staring after Kye and Eloo even though they had vanished from sight.

"So you could turn south if Kye can catch up with them in time?" Takana asked, and plucked a quill from her arm.

"Yes, if Rose is alive when we find her," Silver Skin said, her voice full of concern.

"Well, whether you do or not, I would have you turn south," Takana said, and made a mystic pass with one hand over the feather, even as she held the conversation with Silver Skin.

"And why is that?"

"Because I believe the Darklings will attack the Kings and I believe Tristian will need all the help he can get."

"I hear you," Silver Skin said, and touched the silver disk hanging about her neck.

"But the White Wolf might be helped by the might of the Fire School."

"That he will have, as soon as I can gather my students," Takana said, and blew upon the quill which suddenly shot from her hand, and like a tiny arrow flew into the city.

Seconds later, Tor, the short but broad Minotaur, and a pair of tall girls appeared about her, materialising out of thin air.

"You called us, mistress?" asked one of the tall girls, whose voice echoed as if it came from a great distance, her form flickering as if she was a candle in the wind.

"Yes, Cora, we are needed at the Kings, pack our belongings and be ready to move out in an hour or so," Takana said to the tall woman, who could have been related to her. She had the same copper skin and hair, though she had none of Takana's feathers. Cora bowed and the three figures faded like the morning mist.

"I didn't think you could teleport in and out of the city?" Lea said, and considered Takana.

"Nor can you," Takana said, growing her feathers into the huge red wings of a bird. "Tor and the sisters sent mental projections of themselves."

"Say what?" Lea asked, but was greeted by a beating of wings and the dust storm they caused.

"What you saw were illusions," Silver Skin said, stepping back from the cloud.

"What now, Silver?" Lor asked, watching Takana fly higher until her red wings caught the sunlight and she appeared to ignite in a burst of flames.

"What Eloo said. We return to the den and pick up our packs."

* * *

Kye ran North at a great pace, not even some horses could have matched his stride. All this time Eloo clung to his back, her long hair flying out in the wind of his passing and the air full of her joyous laughter as she revelled in the delight of speed. Even when they left the stone road and travelled the deer tracks Kye ran as if a whip was behind him.

Only when they came to a shallow valley did his incredible pace stop as he stood on a ridge above it, his head held high, sniffing the wind.

"What is it, Kye?" Eloo whispered in the huffing Kye's ear. "Has the scent gone cold?"

Kye lowered his head to the ground and slowly moved into the valley. At the bottom of the dell he stopped, and Eloo slid down from his back so she could look around her. As soon as her feet touched the ground Kye went through the fluid change from beast to man, his yellow eyes scanning around him.

"What is it, Kye?" Kye did not immediately reply but knelt and stared at the hard ground. "What is it you see?"

"Use your magic," Kye croaked. "What do you detect?"

Eloo closed her eyes, summoned up her mystic power and reached out with her magical perceptions.

"There are echoes of magic," Eloo whispered. "Strong energy has been spent here."

"A spell battle," Kye said, pointing to where the ground was charred and blackened.

"But there aren't any bodies, no scavengers," Eloo said, and opening her eyes scanned about the dell and the sky above it.

Kye grunted and bent back to the ground, searching the human sized patch of burnt ground. When he stood back up, he held out several objects for Eloo's inspection. Eloo took the blackened and broken pieces of a wand, a twisted chain with a lump of metal hanging from it, and the broken hilt of a sword.

"These could have been Lightning's," she said, thoughtfully turning them in her hands. "But where is he? Where is his body?"

Kye pointed to the blackened ground, which could have been a body.

"Disintegrated?" Eloo asked, following his pointing finger. "I don't think so; a great amount of energy has been unleashed here but not enough for that!"

Kye grunted and turned back to the burnt ground. He moved to where a scattering of ash lay and inspected it.

"Anything?" Eloo asked, and sprinkled some powder over the broken items.

"A body was dragged away," Kye said, and stared at where a large clump of boulders stood.

Eloo chanted over the broken items and a red glow spread from them to the ground, where the man shape was burnt. There a figure formed, growing into a large winged form, and flew into the sky where it hovered for a moment before shooting north towards the mountains.

"It looks as if we know where Lightning went," Eloo said, and slid the remnants into her satchel. "But what of Rose?"

Kye reappeared from behind the boulders holding up a familiar shield, the winged wolf of the Silverbrow clan.

"Wasn't that the one you gave to Rose?"

Kye nodded, and walking back to Eloo pointed at the fly covered corpse of a horse lying before the burnt man figure.

"Rose's or Lightning's?"

Kye shrugged, and turned to look back towards the rocks.

"They were attacked from there?"

"Then they dragged Rose there and stripped her of anything they thought useful."

"Not the shield?"

"It could identify her," Kye said, and placed the shield on top of the boulders. Clutching his silver medallion, he cast a spell and the shield vanished.

"What did you do?"

"Marking the path for Silver."

"Okay, I'll ask you to explain later, for now I think we must go north."

Kye grunted, and a second later the great sable wolf with the silver flash at his brows stood before her. Its yellow eyes still held a spark of Kye's mind, but even as Eloo clambered onto his back he flung back his head and gave a huge, blood chilling howl that echoed off the rocks. Eloo clung with long fingers to his pelt as he sprang away and ran out of the low valley, towards the knife ridge of the mountains.

WAKING UP TO A NIGHTMARE

"On waking you may find yourself in a dream or a nightmare, but
both waking and dreaming are a reality."

From the Chronicles of the Grey Pilgrim.

Rose slowly swam up out of the darkness of unconsciousness, to find the world spinning around her. She was moving, she could feel this, but what she could not understand was why the ground was above her.

When she managed to get over the pounding headache clouding her mind, she realised something was immobilising her and her wrists and ankles were bound.

She managed to raise her head and look along her body to see the sky where her feet should be. Dropping her head back she saw the ground rushing up towards her, but she was not falling towards it. She slowly became aware she was slung like a sack of potatoes over the shoulder of a large man. Where was she, what was she doing here? Before she could answer her own questions, the creature carrying her came to a jerky halt, and Rose was flung to the ground where she lay shivering, stunned by the sudden stop. Then her view of the grey clouded sky was blotted out by a horrible face which pressed close to hers. The face was grey and rocky and Rose realised it must belong to one of the stone like Troll people.

"Awake, are we?" rasped a voice, as harsh as nails scratching on slate. "Thirsty?"

Rose realised she could not speak. Her throat felt dry and cracked, and nothing but a whistle came from between her lips.

The Troll face grunted and seconds later a water skin was held to her lips, and Rose gratefully gulped down brackish water. The Troll moved off and spoke scratchily with someone else. As she lay there the events of the last few days slowly returned to her. She had followed her father's killer through some kind of magical doorway and had ended up in the world of the Weredings where the Silverbrow Werewolf clan and Eloo the elf had taken her to their royalty, and while waiting for permission to go through their lands to the south to find her sister, Lightning, her new friend, had received a summons from a dragon to go north. It was while travelling to meet the dragon Firethorn that they had been ambushed by unseen attackers. Rose cried out as she remembered her last sight of Lightning. He had been defending her with a shield of magic when she accidentally cast a spell at him. Her last memory was of her power consuming him in a blast of red fire.

"I've killed him!"

Rose's plunge into an abyss of fear and despair was interrupted as a huge wooden figure loomed over her. Its face was a crude carving, its eyes shallow scoops in the wood. It was one of the tree men who had attacked them in the valley. What had Lightning called them? A Homunculus, was that it? As she remembered the creature's name the Homunculus reached for her with long branch like arms. Then she was dizzily twirling through the air as she was slung over its shoulder, and they were on the move again. At least this time she was the right way up, and she felt the headache lesson with the blood no longer flowing directly to her brain.

This allowed her to try to think straight. Her hands were bound tightly, but she could still feel them. Rubbing them together she realised not only was the magical ring which would have allowed her to communicate with Lightning or his mistress Takana gone, but one hand did not feel the same as the other. As she experimentally felt at her left hand, she found not skin beneath her fingers but the smooth scales which had begun to spread over her fist ever since she first used magic. The red scales had appeared after she unknowingly used magic, and she realised now it had spread again to cover her entire left hand after she unleashed the fire on Lightning. This reminded her of the fire and Lightning, and made her clench her fists in anger and frustration, making the cords bite tighter, but she only felt pain at her right wrist. The left, the one covered by scales, resisted the bindings. Rose realised they were stronger than the cord. She also realised the scales resembled those of a Fire Drake, and she remembered Lightning explaining how such dragons could change their bodies and shape their scales into blades and sharp edges. Could she do this with her new skin?

She focused her mind's eyes on an image of her wrist, red scaled, and imagined the scales there shift and change so their edges stood out like razor like blades, cutting through the cord, but nothing happened and the binding just bit harder into her right arm. Rose sobbed as the cord cut at her and she felt her head ache like a heartbeat or a painful drum. But she clenched her teeth and tried again. This time she thought she felt a strange tingling vibrate around her wrist, in a bracelet of tingles. Could she be doing it? She tried to rub her left wrist against the cord and she thought it loosened a degree, but before she could dwell on this she was swung down from the giant's shoulder like a bundle of dirty washing, on a hard stony surface. When she had recovered from the dazing force the wooden Troll had used, and the change from the dizzying swing through the air, it was to realise she was lying at the feet of three figures. They were shrouded in grey robes, but the faces glaring down at Rose were stony, and crystal like nodes glistened on the face of one of them. Like the one who had given her water, they were Trolls, and when they spoke to one another it was in the grating voice of cold emotionless beings.

"Strange that such a small and fragile creature can cause so much trouble," rasped the one Rose thought had given her water.

"Nevertheless," grated another, the one with sparkling crystals glittering about her eyes. "She is a threat and that is why Kain wants her."

Rose's ears pricked up at this name, could they really be talking about the assassin who killed her father?

"He had better pay us what he promised," rasped the third she Troll, the one with the black misshapen look of coal about her features. "We have risked much to get her; she had better be worth it."

The water Troll opened its hole of a mouth to respond, when its voice was cut off by a long, blood curdling howl.

"Where came that?" the crystal Troll asked, as it cast about. Its grey hands clenched on a long, gnarled staff, which it leaned on.

"From the south," the black Troll said. "On the trail, behind us."

"A simple animal of the mountains?" the water Troll asked of her sisters.

"Or one of the cursed Silver Shield whelps," snarled the black Troll, and spat in Rose's direction.

"Either way," broke in the glittering Troll, "we should be moving on."

She made a beckoning gesture to the Homunculus, and before Rose knew what was happening she was swinging through the air, one more slung over the creature's shoulder, and they were bumping along again at a great pace.

Rose would have liked to try shaping her scaled wrist, but there was no way she could concentrate on the act while bouncing at the wood giant's shoulder. She snarled at every jerk, and tried to think of some way to slip her bonds, but she could not think while bouncing up and down. So she tried looking about her at the passing countryside. This was not easy either, for the giant moved so swiftly and Rose swayed so much, she could only grasp at fleeting images. The country was mountains, and large grey stone walls rose around them or fell away. Rose realised they must have entered the Roaches, the mountains Lightning had been making for. From what she could make out these Troll women were making for a different part of the mountains. Rose was wondering darkly if she would get the chance to attack Kain before she died at his hands when she noticed a flash of bright colour out of the corner of her eye. She craned her neck and saw it again. It was a bright red bird, wheeling above them. It stooped and Rose's heart leapt, for it was a tiny dragon, could it be Flint? The little Fire Drake had brought them the message to go north and had been with them when they were attacked. She desperately wanted to cry out to it, but she did not speak the dragon tongue. Besides, if she did she might call the Troll women's attention to the wheeling dragon. She decided to risk it, but as she drew breath to call out the tiny creature stooped and disappeared behind a ridge. Rose nearly sobbed at the sight of the dragon disappearing. It felt like with its vanishing her hope had gone with it. But she had no time for despair because they had arrived at their final destination. The Troll women and their Homunculus servant had stopped in a shallow valley, scooped out of the mountains. Tall walls of stone rose around them, forming a shallow bowl in the rocks. At the middle of this plateau was a small, dark lake and to one side of this the remains of a ring of standing stones, and one set formed a stone door. Rose took all these details in as she was swung from the tree giant and set on shaky legs. As Rose squinted around her she got the strangest feeling she had been here before. However, any feelings of nostalgia vanished as from among the ruins there stepped an all too familiar figure sporting a wolf helm and glinting black blade.

FIRE AND WATER

"Witches used to be tried by fire and water, now I test them with fire."
Eloo to the Red Wizard, the Wereding Chronicles.

The fire of anger and revenge smouldering in her heart blazed up, and with a wordless cry she flung herself in his direction. Her legs, however, were not up to her heart's desire and the terrain betrayed her. She stumbled, to fall face first onto the hard ground. She was dragged to her knees by her long, red hair and gazed up into a black face, glaring at her with obsidian eyes.

At first Rose did not understand what she was looking at, then as her senses gathered themselves she realised she was looking into the masked face of a short figure, and a woman's voice hissed with blood chilling malice from behind the dark, wooden mask. "A sharp little flower, isn't she? It is time, perhaps, she was clipped."

Before Rose realised what the words meant, a dark blade flashed before her eyes as the masked woman flourished an obsidian knife, only inches from her face.

"Not yet, Sable," hissed one of the Troll women from directly behind Rose. "Not before we get our payment."

The woman, Sable, snarled and turned away and spat a word into the ruins from where there came grating sounds. Rose was dragged to her feet, to see emerging from the shadows a gang of about ten of the rat like Goblins, and behind them two hulking slate skinned Trolls.

They appeared to be carrying several sacks which chinked and rattled as the small rat snouted Goblins approached. Several of the sacks were dropped before Rose, and she watched as the black faced Troll woman stepped forward and upturned one of the bags to tip a spill of glittering gold coins. "Her weight in gold," Sable snarled, pointing at the gold with her black knife. "Just as you requested. Are you satisfied?"

What the Troll woman's answer might have been no one ever found out, because floating on the wind came the long, haunting cry of a wolf. This time, however, it was joined in its beautiful, if mournful song, by several more voices. Rose watched Kain closely, and marked it when he flinched and spun towards the call, his head cocked as if listening. The howls came again and appeared much closer.

"We have company!"

"Werewolves?"

"Worse," snarled Kain. "Kye is on the way."

Rose's heart leapt at the news, but she had no time to appreciate the feeling for she was heaved to her feet by the iron hard hand on her hair.

"Take her, our deal is over," said the Troll woman.

"Take your gold and go," hissed Sable, stalking around Rose.

"Take her," snapped the Troll woman, and Rose was flung to land at the dark woman's feet.

Rose was yanked to her feet and dragged to where a tall dead tree loomed blackly over the dark waters. There, her hands were freed from their bindings, but only for a moment before they were rebound so Rose was now bound to the tree trunk. One of the Goblins grabbed hold of Rose's shoulder length hair and yanked her head back, so she was looking up through bare and gnarled branches at the low grey clouds scudding across the sky. As she stared, she heard the harsh voice of Sable begin chanting beside her, and she began to sweat. She had a horrible feeling she would at any moment feel a glass blade slice her throat.

Rose was about to close her eyes, when the small valley was filled with a bestial roar that shook the stones beneath her feet, and the Goblin's grasp on her hair was gone. Rose looked forward to see Sable spin around to curse something above her and she gazed up to see wheeling above the lake a great red beast.

This scarlet creature, spinning above her on smoky wings, resembled a great red cat, but a cat covered in scarlet scales. It had a pair of long, curving horns protruding from the back of its head. At first Rose thought it was Flint — after all, this creature was almost a twin — but as she looked more closely at it she realised this monster was many times larger. She momentarily wondered if this Fire Drake was the same one she had faced before at the mausoleum, but that dragon had a skull like head. This one had the long feline head of a cat. As Rose watched, the great feline beast turned, and opening its long jaws unleashed a dazzling gout of flame, hitting the cowering group of Goblins and sending them flying in all directions, their small bodies flaring like tinder as the fire set them alight. The two Trolls roared a response and lifting huge crossbows to their stony shoulders fired spear long bolts at the flying attacker. Rose gasped, as she watched the javelin like bolts fly at the dragon, fearing he-she would be hit, but the drake beat its wings and was carried high into the air. The arrows missed it to fly across the valley and crash back to earth unseen. At the same time the powerful pounding of the dragon's wings caused a downdraft which fanned the fires breaking out in the small brush. Rose craned her neck to see where the dragon had gone, but he had flown out of sight and her attention was drawn by Kain's harsh snarl. "Sable, finish the sacrifice, I will deal with the dragon."

Rose looked for the short woman and saw her standing a few feet away, her hands weaving in the gestures of a spell. As she watched, the woman's form blurred as if Rose were seeing her through smoke or murky water, and she realised the woman was trying to make herself more difficult to be seen by the dragon. Then the woman was rushing at her. Rose suddenly realised that although her legs were tied together they were not tied to the tree. So as Sable's dark form rushed her, Rose pulled her knees to her chest and kicked out. Her boots smashed into Sable's blurred face and flung the woman back. As Rose did this, she felt the branch supporting her bound hands break and she slid down the trunk till she was sitting. This saved her life, for if the branch had not broken her face would have been where a bolt of black energy slammed into the trunk, leaving a charred hole in the bark. Sable, Rose realised, had hurled a killing spell at her, but missed, though she would not miss next time. Rose gathered all her strength and tugged at the ropes, and to her amazement they broke. She rolled away from the tree which was engulfed in black flames that burnt with a chilling cold. Rose looked desperately about for something to use as a weapon, but all she could find was a large broken bough which she grabbed, and standing, faced Sable with her makeshift club. Sable stood before her, her obsidian knife in one hand and a globe of black fire in the other.

KAIN

"Kain is wolfs bane to the Wereding's!"
Cole to Halmer, the Wereding Chronicles.

Kain strode across the hollow to where Goblins were running in every direction. Kain hissed, and shouted at them, "Spread out and get ready for his next attack."

A large Goblin turned to face him and stabbed at him with a spear, but Kain grabbed the shaft just behind the head. In one smooth motion he drew his great blade from its back sheath and brought it down on the spear arm, severing it at the shoulder.

The Goblin screamed and fell to its knees, and in a heartbeat its head flew from its shoulders, which made the silver wolf's head pommel of his black blade growl with satisfaction as it drank the blood covering its edge. "More!"

Kain ignored it and raising his voice snarled, "Do as I say, or I'll have all your heads."

"But lord, he can see us!"

"I will take care of that, just get ready."

Kain raised his sword before him, and falling into a kind of trance he called up the magic which coiled within the great black stone sitting between the silver fangs of the wolf's head. Calling upon this magic, he summoned a cloud of darkness that billowed forth from the blade and hung above them like a protective shield. Once he had conjured the cloud he delved into the gem's heart and drew on more of the magic reservoir to conceal within the cloud of darkness a web of dark strands, which would act like a net. Finally, he cast a spell protecting him from the dragon's fiery breath. His spells were only just in place when the Fire Drake plunged through the cloud and crashed into the web's sticky strands, thrashing as it tried to free itself.

"Fire," cried Kain, and fired a black lightning bolt into the ensnared dragon which made it roar in pain and rage. Twisting in the strands it hissed words of power, and the web vanished. Quick as a striking snake the dragon breathed a gout of fire that engulfed Kain in its flames, but he stood untouched. Kain spat a second black bolt at the dragon and with a roar of rage and pain the drake flew up out of the cloud. "Quick, he will attack again."

These words made some of the Goblins turn scaly tail and run, but the rest quailed beneath Kain's chilling gaze, and stopped where they were. Seconds later they were flattened by a great burning log the dragon dropped from above the cloud.

Kain began to hiss the words of another spell when a bolt of lightning streaked past him to impale one of the great Trolls aiming its crossbow at the sky. Kain spun around to find a huge black wolf with a Goblin between its fangs, a small figure crouching on its back. A long rod pointed at him. Kain flung himself to one side, just avoiding the next stroke of lightning. He rose to one knee and fired a bolt from the sword tip towards where the small figure crouched, a long mane of black hair swirling around it. Eloo, however, had somersaulted off the wolf's back to land in front of a pair of Goblins. The two squat creatures snarled and thrust at her with spears, but Kain did not pay her any attention for the horse large wolf, Kye, had flung the luckless Goblin to one side and was coming for Kain.

THE ROBIN AND THE DRAGON

"Sometimes pearls of wisdom fall from dragon's lips, instead of flames."
Luna to the Red Rage.

Sweat rolled off Robin's face as she concentrated on the large wooden shield floating before her. She was using her mind and magic to keep the shield hovering. The shield had felt light in her hand when Luna handed it to her, but now, fighting gravity with only magic and the strength of her mind, it felt like it must weigh several tons. A snort came from behind her and broke her concentration. The shield fell several inches and swayed to a stop as Robin attempted to recapture both her concentration and the shield. Then it was snatched away by another's invisible will, and magic. Robin spun, to find towering over her a mountain of red scales, the Fire Drake Tahane.

"You are not trying hard enough," snarled the dragon, its skull like mask flaring its nostrils, its eyes glowing with red fire that pinned Robin to the spot, as his will floated the shield high over her head.

"You keep distracting me!"

"And that is the point, my little red breast," purred the giant creature, fluttering his bat like wings, and curling his long tail around him. "How will you survive your first spell battle if you can't cast spells because you are distracted? You will be blasted to ash before you can even cast your first incantation."

"She will survive," purred Luna, and glared at the dragon, "because I will not allow any harm to come to her."

This only made the dragon snort, sending small daggers of flame lancing from his nostrils. "How very touching. If you are so protective of her, Luna, why am I wasting my time trying to teach her magic?"

"Because you persuaded me that you could teach me more than the Crimson Circle could," Robin spat at him.

This made the huge, reptilian creature rear back. Its wings spread out to block out the sky, and Robin was overwhelmed by a searing wind stinking of hot metal and sulphur as the ground vibrated with a deep volcanic growl. "More respect, little one!"

"Once you treat me so," Robin spat back, not at all afraid. With an angry flex of her mental muscles, she wrenched the shield from Tahane's grip and, spinning it onto its side, flung it spinning like a discus. The shield fell with a clang to the ground as its metal rim slammed into the iron hard scales of the Fire Drake's hide.

Luna chanted words of power, and a lash of lightning uncoiled from her hands. Tahane, however, did not strike at Robin or breathe killing fires over her, but instead proceeded to make a great ground shaking sound like boulders falling in a landslide. It took a long time for Robin to realise the dragon was not growling at her, but laughing. "So, it seems all we have to do to defeat the Weredings is make you angry."

For a long moment, Robin stared disbelievingly at the mountain of scarlet flesh, and then she too could not help but snort a brief laugh as she realised just how close she had come to evoking the dragon's terrible rage and power.

"I would prefer she had more control than that," Luna said dryly, the whip of lightning fading, her lips curling into a grin. "Let us try again."

Tahane sighed. "If I thought you have perfected this, I might, *might* teach you something special."

Robin sighed and lowering her gaze to the shield bent her will on it, and it leapt from the ground to hover level with the dragon's eyes. Robin's lips were forming a slight smile as she thought she detected a look of surprise in the almost expressionless mask when the world around her changed, and she was no longer standing in the twilight of the woods where she was training, but somewhere cold and filled with murky light. Her lungs were full of water, and her world was filled with pain. Without knowing how she knew it or how it could have happened, Robin knew she was experiencing the same event

Rose was. She was in Rose's body, and was drowning with her sister. Robin-Rose felt the darkness of unconsciousness clutching at her mind, and the world exploded in flames.

SABLE AND ROSE

"Sometimes, no matter how much magic you think you hold in your hand, you must stand alone, helpless against a foe, knowing that you are in trouble."

Lea to Dove, the Wereding Chronicles.

Rose crouched, her branch held up before her in an en garde position, its gnarled length her only shield and weapon against Sable who stood snarling before her, a black blade in one hand and the other holding a growing ball of dark fire. Rose wondered if there was some way she could level the playing field, and then she remembered the battle with the Homunculus. In the battle with the wooden men she had used the one spell she learnt from Lightning, and she decided to use it now.

"Insendium!" Rose cried, a coppery taste filling her mouth and making her wonder if she had bitten her tongue. It vanished as quickly as it had come and as if she had flicked a switch the end of her branch burst into flames, her red flare striving against the black fire.

Sable snarled in rage and hurled the black fistful of fire at Rose, and it splashed over her. Rose felt not heat as the dark flames hit her, but a bone chilling cold, which burnt her like a gnawing chill. The dark fire snuffed out her brand and melted away half of her branch. Where it touched her leathers, smoke rose and the hide became brittle, as if it had been frozen rather than burnt. As Rose danced back from Sable's first knife stroke her sleeve crumbled away, leaving her forearm exposed to the biting cold. She blocked another slash of the knife with the six inches of wood remaining to her, and as the blade sliced into the branch again the black blade shattered, sending long, dark, glittering shards flying in all directions. One of the shards sliced Rose's left cheek though she did not feel any pain. The breaking of the knife left Sable grasping a hilt with a jagged stump of volcanic glass. It was still a nasty weapon, but like Rose's dwindling branch, was not very large. Sable hissed as she regarded the broken stump. At first Rose thought she was simply upset, but as the hiss rose she made out words among the snarl, and realised the short woman was casting a spell on the stump. As Rose watched a long shadow grew from the shattered dagger to form a long narrow blade, which looked sharp enough to cut the air Sable flourished it through.

As Rose stared at this blade of darkness, she felt the embers of the magic which dwelt in her blood begin to awaken and raise their fiery head, as if a dragon was waking within her. She knew the burning sensation building within her chest was the magic gathering itself to lash out. She should have been afraid as she knew the scales which covered her would, after such a summoning, spread further over her body, but she was jubilant at the fact that the magic was rising to defend her against this dark woman. Whether the magic would have lashed out at Sable with destroying magic or not was never resolved, for as the fire within her was kindled, the black masked woman was plucked from the ground. Rose stared for a moment, not believing what had happened. She might have believed the woman had used magic, but Sable's long cry of surprise told Rose she was equally taken aback. She glanced up to see Sable struggling in the huge claws of the cat like dragon, carrying Sable away from the battle. As Rose watched, Sable slashed at the talons holding her with her one free arm, but even as she did this her voice cried out in great pain. Rose saw the dragon's claws flicker as if they were covered by heat, and Sable's robes burnt where the claws held her. Rose watched with a guilty joy as the dragon carried the woman out of sight over the edge of the cliffs surrounding the valley.

"I hope he doesn't choke on her," she muttered under her breath, leaning against the tree which was now flameless but charred, as she took a moment to gather her breath and strength.

She might have been killed in this moment by the Goblin creeping towards her, but as the rat like creature cocked its arm to strike at Rose with its club a voice rang out in command. Rose recognised the voice as belonging to Silver Skin, and spun around to find the tall Werewolf standing only a few feet away, her yellow gaze transfixing the dwarf like man. The words of her spell froze the Goblin to the spot. Silver Skin spoke more words, and Rose felt the air vibrate as power was drawn from it. The Goblin turned, its long scaly tail tucked between its legs as it scuttled away.

"Thank you," Rose breathed at her saviour. "I wasn't sure if you'd reach me in time!"

"If Kye was not such a good tracker, or driven by the goddess, we probably would have not."

"Where is he?"

Silver turned to point and gave a cry of fear, rage and despair. On the other side of the dell Rose saw the huge black wolf she knew was Kye tussling with the black clad figure of Kain. Even as she watched, there was a flash of light and Kye was no longer the huge wolf, but a naked man facing Kain who stood above him, black blade raised to finish him off. Silver Skin was suddenly a silver furred blur as she changed from human to wolf form and leapt in their direction. Rose watched, as Kye snatched from nowhere a short blade which glittered silver and suddenly the short sword was a burning brand sheathed in flickering blue flames, which looked more cold than hot. The blazing sword blocked the downwards stroke and as the two blades clashed blue flames were sent flying in all directions. Kain danced back snarling, and in the next instant his long sword was sheathed in black flames. Kye leapt to his feet, and circling Kain stabbed at his chest. Kain's sword, which gave him more reach, knocked the shorter blade aside. As the two blades met black and blue-white strove and mixed, as they appeared to grapple as much as the wielders. Silver Skin was suddenly slamming into Kain and Kye's striving forms, and all three were sent flying. The Trolls loomed over the tangle of bodies, and might have turned the battle, but as they raised huge clubs there was a rapid beating of wings and the two Trolls reeled back as they were bathed in the dragon's flaming breath. The flames blinded Rose with their glare and the smoke which rose further concealed her sight, but suddenly Kain was running across the tarn as if the dark water was glass. Rose realised too late that he was coming straight at her. Before Rose could react, his gauntleted hands grabbed her up and with inhuman strength lifted her bodily into the air and hurled her into the tarn. The freezing waters closed over her head. Rose had no time to react before the icy water filled her mouth and lungs. She struggled frantically to swim up so she could break free, but as she looked up at the surface it was to see the water inches from her freeze solid. Now a wall of ice stood between her and life.

PLUMBING THE DEPTHS

"Looking afar does not always help you to know the truth. After all, knowing is only the first step to wisdom."

Great Mother to Kye, his journals.

Robin was dying in the arms of an ice giant, his arms an embrace of freezing death, crushing her lungs and bursting her heart. She thought her life would end, when a voice reached out of the murk to pull her from the dark.

"Robin, come back to us!" Luna's voice filled Robin's world, and when she cracked her eyes to the painful light she felt the small woman's welcome presence clinging to her.

"Rose?" croaked Robin, lying on her back, staring unseeing at the first stars of the night.

"Robin, can you hear me?" Luna asked, stroking Robin's brow with a damp cloth.

"What happened?"

"You lost consciousness." Tahane's head blocked out the night sky like an eclipsing moon, his red eyes staring down at her. "Then after a moment you invoked a flame skin, and almost burnt Luna who was attempting to wake you."

Robin turned startled eyes on Luna, and drank in every detail of her small, perfect form. Her red hair glinted like a flame, and her dark green eyes flickered back at her. Luna appeared unharmed, if alarmed, and smiled at her.

"I'm sorry! I didn't mean to hurt you!"

"I know, kitten, you weren't in control at the time, but what happened? You called out your sister's name!"

"I was with her somehow," Robin said haltingly. "She was drowning!"

"Drowning, but you were not near water," Luna exclaimed.

"A joining," Tahane growled, low in the back of his throat.

"Tahane, you know what this is?"

"Don't take that offended tone with me, Luna," Tahane hissed. "I have a guess, not knowledge!"

"Stop it, both of you. Tahane, what happened? What do you guess?"

"That you and your sister both used magic at the same time, and somehow were linked by the magic."

"Can that happen?" Robin asked, suddenly hoping she could reach out to Rose again.

"You said she was drowning?"

"Yes!" Robin gasped, remembering the feeling of Rose's desperate struggles against the water in her lungs. "Rose. Luna, could I contact her again?"

"I doubt it, kitten," Luna said soothingly in her deep voice.

"I doubt it is possible," rumbled the deep, gravelly voice of Tahane, lowering his great head to stare at Robin with one of his large eyes, at least five times the size of her own.

"What do you mean?" Robin asked, staring into the glowing coal of his cat's eye slit of a pupil.

"Robin, look away," Luna snarled, glaring at Tahane.

"What?" Robin asked, feeling the great, black, vertical, slit of his pupil gaping open to suck at her.

"Tahane, stop it at once," Luna snapped, her voice suddenly as cold and cutting as a blade in winter.

Tahane snarled, his voice hissing like a kettle. Smoke escaped from his nostrils as he broke his gaze and turned his head towards Luna. "I meant no harm!"

"Your gaze is a weapon nonetheless, and you know it," Luna snapped, turning Robin towards her, and staring up into her dazed face.

"What just happened?" Robin said, blinking, feeling her world swimming around her.

"Never look a dragon directly in the eye," Luna said angrily. "Their gaze can be hypnotic, look at them directly and they can ensnare your will."

"Not my intention," Tahane growled from behind them.

Robin shook her head, as if fighting off the day, and then she remembered what they had been talking about. "Why can't I contact Rose again?"

"Because the reason I suspect you were able to link with her was that she was near death and so her magic reached out for help. The need to survive drove her to reach for you and strengthened the bond between you, but if she is safe or dead..."

"No!" Robin interrupted on the verge of tears. "That can't be."

"Calm yourself, kitten," Luna purred, trying to soothe her taller lover. "I am sure she is safe now."

"But how can you be so sure? How can we be sure?"

"I do not hold out much hope of it working," Tahane growled from behind Robin's back, "but you could try scrying for her again."

"It almost killed her last time, Tahane!" Luna protested, glaring at the dragon.

"Please, Luna, let me try," Robin said, holding Luna's hands, staring pleadingly into the smaller woman's liquid green eyes. "I have to try, Luna, I have to know."

Luna, who had been tense, her jaw clenched, melted under Robin's imploring gaze. "Very well, but I and Tahane will link with you to bolster your magic."

There was a warning snarl from Tahane. "I humbled myself in agreeing to teach you magic, and even more so to be a mount! But no one said anything about spell binding."

"What's up, Tahane?" Luna asked, her voice suddenly brimming with amusement. "Frightened I'll charm you?"

"I will not be linked," Tahane growled, and Robin heard a snap of his wings.

She turned to see the great dragon swing away from them, its long tail snaking out behind it as he padded away to interest himself in the small lake at the other end of the clearing.

36

"Dragons!" Luna muttered under her breath. "Very well then, we will have to make do with just us two."

"What do we do?" Robin asked excitedly, wanting to get this over and find out what had happened to Rose.

Luna did not answer for a moment, looking up to the now dark blue sky as if seeking Robin's answer from among the pinpricks of stars. Luna drew a deep breath, centring herself, and drew from her belt pouch a slender silver chain. "You will attempt to scry like you did at the tower, but before you do, I will link us magically so my magic empowers your own."

"Will it be dangerous for you?"

"Possibly," Luna admitted, and wrapped the chain around first Robin's waist and then her own. "But it will protect you against any magic that might try to prevent you scrying."

"But that could hurt you," Robin said reluctantly. "I don't want you hurt, because of me."

Luna smiled grimly and purred her response. "Little one, what hurts you, hurts me. If I can protect you, I will. Now, begin your scrying."

With tears of gratitude and love in her eyes, Robin began to chant over the pool. At her side, Luna was chanting her own spell, her hands casting powders around them both as her voice growled words of power. As Robin watched the waters take on an image not her own, she felt another presence. She knew it was Luna's presence, and she felt it surround her like a cloak of protection and power, gentle as silk but as strong as steel.

"Rose, where are you?"

As she uttered these words under her breath the pool rippled as if something beneath the water had disturbed it, and an image began to take blurry form in the water's mirror. As Robin watched, a fiery star appeared in the water. She blinked, and saw the fires wink out and a form fall from the dark sky. She knew it was Rose falling, possibly burnt. Robin gasped, realising Rose was falling to the ground, but even as she fearfully watched a huge red form (similar but not the same as Tahane), swooped down on Rose's tumbling form. Catching her in its claws, it flew off into the night sky.

"No!" Robin's denial filled the woods with its cry as the image exploded in ripples.

"Peace," Luna panted at her side.

Robin turned to see Luna at her side, on her knees, her body covered in sweat.

"Luna, what's wrong?" Robin asked in concern, helping her lover to her feet. Her concern deepened as she felt how alarmingly high Luna's temperature was.

"I put much into the spell of linking and it has drained me, that is all," Luna said, though her face was darker than Robin had ever seen it. Her pupils had become cat's slits, and her teeth when her lips curled into a grin were too long.

"I am sorry," Robin said, realising her need to see Rose had hurt her friend. "I did not mean to cause you harm, but I needed to see Rose was safe."

"And are you any the wiser," broke in the deep rumble of Tahane. His huge scarlet head swung to hang over them like a red thundercloud.

"You were watching?"

"Yes, my little Robin."

"But you did nothing to help?"

"It is not my duty to interfere in all your undertakings."

"Did you recognise the Fire Drake?" Luna asked, accepting a drink of water from Robin who had collected it in a leather bag, now empty of rosemary.

"He was not clear in the vision," Tahane said hesitantly, as if he was reluctant to admit something.

"But did you recognise him?" Robin snapped.

"I do not know him personally, but if I was to make a guess, I would say he was one of Firethorn's whelps."

"He will be a thrall of the Weredings," groaned Luna.

"No!" Robin cried, feeling despair sweep over her. "What will he do to her?"

"The Fire Drake?" Tahane asked, appearing unconcerned by Robin's despair. "If your sister is still alive, he could eat her or rape her."

"Tahane!" Luna snapped, seeing the look of fear twist Robin's features.

"Would you hide the truth from her, Luna?"

"No, but I might couch it better."

"There is, of course, a possibly worse thing this young dragon might do with your sister," Tahane carried on, as if he had not heard Luna. "He might charm her. He might enslave her to his will, and then she would be his slave."

"How can I save her?" Robin said, turning her full attention on Luna. "Can we use magic to save her?"

"Robin, I am not sure we could do anything even if you and I were up to it. Besides, to use more magic would not be good for you at the moment."

"Why not?"

"Robin, have you not realised what has happened to you?"

"What do you mean?"

"Look at your arm," Luna said.

Robin looked down at her bare arm. To her horror, her brown skin was now bright red and covered by the scales. They were spreading across her body every time her magic got out of control.

"No, not again," Robin moaned, and cradled her arm against her body as if it were broken. "Is this ever going to stop!"

"I am trying to help," Luna said, wiping a tear from her eye.

"But what am I becoming?"

"I don't know, kitten," Luna said her voice almost breaking.

"You must learn to control your magic," Tahane growled.

"How? It keeps going wrong."

"You must continue training."

"No," moaned Robin.

"Not now, Tahane."

"*Yes*, now," snarled the dragon. "If she wishes to stop this curse, she must harness her magic."

Robin turned teary eyes on the huge dragon and gathered her strength.

"What must I do?"

RIDING THE LIGHTNING

"Sometimes to know the truth is to ride the lightning!"
Silver Skin to the Red Wizard, the Wereding Chronicles.

Rose came out of the darkness slowly, and when she came back to the world she found it a grey misty one. She gazed about her and saw she was standing on top of a high flat hill. At first she thought, as she looked at the many taller peaks which like a ring of teeth encircled her flat eyrie, that she was alone, but as an unfelt wind moved the mists she realised she shared the plateau. She moved closer to see a huge form glistening bright red in the dull land. For a moment Rose could not understand what she was looking at. Then drifting closer, she realised she was seeing the huge bulk of the red dragon who had been at the pool. What was he doing here, and what, for that matter, was she? Where was here? As she watched, the dragon began to hiss in a sibilant voice and sway its head and great wings. Rose realised it was casting a spell. She watched as the huge monster cast, and the dragon's throat swelled as if it were about to unleash its fiery breath. An exhalation did emerge from its mouth, but it was not its usual fiery burst of flames that could cook a horse, but a lighter cloud of gas which washed over something lying between the giant monster's feet. Rose was drawn, as if by an invisible force, towards the bundle. Drawing closer, she saw it was the naked figure of a woman whose bare flesh was scarlet. Her body must be red hot, for the shallow pool she lay in was steaming around her form, obscuring its shape. Whatever the dragon had tried, it appeared it had not worked for the beast flung back its head and let loose a roar of anguish, which seemed to shake the mountain peaks.

"Who is she?"

"Can you not guess, child?" said a new voice from behind Rose.

Rose turned to find standing behind her a tall woman, wrapped in scarlet robes. Her long mane of sable hair flowed out behind her, in a wind Rose did not feel.

"Who are you?"

"My name is not important. What is, is what I can give you."

"And what is that?"

The woman held out a hand and uncurled her long fingers to reveal a large, glistening pearl cupped in her palm.

"What is it?"

"A pearl of wisdom," the woman replied in her deep purr of a voice that reminded Rose of Eloo. "Take it, child, it is yours. It and I have been waiting for you for a very long time."

"Waiting?"

"Don't question it, just accept it."

Rose reached out her hand, but as the tips of her fingers nearly touched it she drew back, feeling a quiver in the pearl as if it vibrated.

"That's no pearl."

"It is and it isn't," the woman whispered. "Take it, child, it will not hurt you."

Rose hesitated again, but after a moment's pause she reached out and grasped the pearl between finger and thumb. As she grasped the jewel it turned from a solid stone to vapour that swirled around her and then appeared to flow into her hand, and suddenly Rose was clutching her head as her mind was overwhelmed by a tidal wave of images. She saw a fireball explode around her, its heat flowing through her without hurting her. She felt lightning explode from her hands and impale a half seen giant. She felt the wind around her as she hovered hundreds of feet above the ground, and through all these images she felt rather than saw the hooded and cloaked figure made of scarlet scales.

"Rose, come back to me, child." The woman's purr cut through the whirlwind of images and pulled her back to the plateau.

Rose found to her surprise she was still standing before the woman.

"Are you all right?"

"What have you done to me?"

"Given you what you need to survive, in the days to come."

"Which is?"

"Wisdom." With that the red woman disappeared, leaving Rose to turn back to find a new person had appeared on the hill.

Rose blinked as she saw the small form of Moonstone, Kye's shy little sister. Her black head bent over the burnt woman, her tears splashing onto the charred form. As Rose watched, the great head of the dragon moved over the small woman and the burnt form.

"I have tried healing her," snarled the dragon, and as it spoke Rose shivered. She felt she knew the dragon's voice, but how could this be? She had never seen this beast before the pool.

Moonstone gathered herself, and holding up her necklace began to chant over the burnt form. Rose glided towards the three figures and as she drew nearer, she noticed things which appeared strange, and in ways she could not define, wrong. The mist appeared insubstantial, and the forms of the three figures so bright, but when Rose looked down at her own body it seemed almost as insubstantial as the mist. As if she was not real. Her confusion was interrupted by another ground shaking roar of the dragon, and when Rose looked back to the trio it was to see Moonstone sink to her knees at the figure's side, her head bowed, her shoulders shaking from grief and despair.

"Please, Rose, don't leave us," growled the dragon, and with the words Rose experienced the thunderbolt of realisation.

"No, it can't be me!"

But as she denied it to herself, Rose saw and recognised the long tresses that had not been burnt, but lay spread like a red cloak. Rose leaped across the space between her and the body, which appeared to be hers. She was suddenly standing over the long naked body, steaming as its crisped flesh cooled.

"It can't be," Rose moaned, looking down at her own unburnt face. "But if that is me, then what am I?"

As she asked this, Rose looked down at her own body, and saw it was misty. As if she were little more than a wisp. A thought made solid, or at least nearly solid. The dragon's great glowing eyes appeared to look straight through her, without seeing her.

"Am I a ghost?"

But as Rose asked the question, something told her that was not quite right. She was a spirit or something, not dead, and yet separate from her damaged body. As this realisation solidified in her mind Moonstone looked up with teary blue eyes and looked straight at Rose. It was as if she saw Rose, or did she, for she looked away and then as if realising what she had seen stared at Rose. "Rose?"

"What is it, Moon?" asked the dragon, whose sensitive hearing had picked up her whisper.

"I can see something, it might be Rose's spirit."

"What can you see, Moon?" asked a new voice, and the small girl and the dragon looked to one side.

When Rose looked in that direction, she thought she saw Takana the Harpy, but then Rose looked again and realised she was mistaken. Yes, this tall woman flexed large wings instead of arms, and walked on taloned bird's feet like Takana, but this harpy had night black feathers instead of Takana's fiery red plumage.

"Lady Stormstrider," Moonstone said, bowing. "I think I can see Rose's spirit."

The tall bird woman stalked up to stand beside the short girl, and with a flick of raven's wings and a muttered word the woman's azure eyes turned as black as a thunderhead. Within their night black depths lightning appeared to flicker and those dark orbs were locked with Rose's.

"You can see me?" Rose exclaimed.

"Yes lady, that is where I saw the disturbance."

"You are quite correct, girl," the harpy said, staring unblinkingly into Rose's shock widened eyes.

"You can see her spirit?" growled the dragon in its tantalisingly familiar voice that Rose still could not place, despite her best efforts.

"She is standing at her head," the harpy replied, lifting a finger tipped wing to point.

"Then she is dead," moaned Moonstone.

The dragon flung back its head and roared a cry which must have reached the heavens with its anguish.

"Peace," the harpy admonished, beginning to weave the gestures of a spell. Rose watched the woman's wings move through strange patterns, as the bird woman began to dance on the spot. Her taloned feet and hand like wings crafted the air as if she would sculpt clay. At the end of the spell the woman pointed at Rose and Rose heard a scream of wind and felt a great gust of air gather up her mist like form and blow it to her body. Then Rose was screaming, as all at once she was back in her body with all its wounds and burns.

She was not aware of the harpy weaving above her, until a wave of warm air washed over her and the pain went away. Rose found herself looking up into the three faces.

Then the dragon spoke. "Rose, you have come back to me."

"Lightning," Rose groaned, finally recognising the voice despite its animalistic growl.

When she looked up into the cat like muzzleand glowing, green eyes she saw the young man's face mirrored in the red scales and long twitching ears. The great Fire Drake was somehow Lightning.

"Lightning?"

"Yes, Rose, it is me," growled the dragon in a low thrumwhich might have been tinged by fear, if such a huge and powerful creature could be fearful.

"No, it can't be," Rose said, her mind reeling at the idea, and she rolled onto her front and was on her knees ready to fly when she saw her reflection in the water.

THE REPOSITORY

"People are not as easy to read as books."

A saying from the Druid Handbook.

Rose groaned in utter despair as she saw her reflection mirrored back at her as if she was looking at her body from without again. The Harpy's magic had healed her burns, but whether her magic had also changed her, or whether her own body had reacted to her magic Rose did not yet comprehend. But what she did perceive in the mirror was where her flesh had been kissed by fire it had transformed from pink skin to the bright reflective scales. They had begun on her hand, and now covered most of her body in a lacework of red plates. As if this wasn't bad enough, the scales had completely covered the left side of her face. So now it appeared as if she was wearing a mask over one side of her head, and her dark green eye was no longer a flawed emerald, but a baleful ruby.

"No, it's happened, I'm horrible."

"Not from where I am looking," rumbled Lightning's voice behind her.

Rose groaned as she felt her world coming apart at the seams. "I can't believe this!"

The Harpy spoke in a whisper which appeared to blow all around Rose. "Moonstone, I suggest we get Rose dressed and fed. She may feel better once she feels more human."

Rose was about to respond with a cutting reply when a flicker of movement at the edge of the pool made her look up to see the red woman standing there. Rose opened her mouth but did not speak, startled into silence as the tall woman proceeded to strip before her, casting her cloak and robes aside to reveal her dark skin painted with many strange symbols and letters. Letters Rose recognised as magical runes. This woman was a grimoire, her flesh had been drawn on instead of parchment. Once this woman was down to her small clothes she held out her garments and held Rose by the eye.

"Take them, Red Wizard," she said in her deep purr of a voice, her words ringing with power as if her simple words were loaded with the potential to unleash devastation. "Do not despair, you have changed, but change is not always bad even if it seems so at the time. Embrace your power, Rose, and you will save your sister."

Rose reached out and accepted the clothes. She opened her mouth to thank this stranger but before she could there was a flash of sable mane and the tall figure was gone.

"Was that who I thought it was?" the Harpy asked, helping Moonstone lift Rose to her feet.

"I don't know who it was," Rose said, standing weak legged. "She helped me, she gave me..."

"She gave you what?"

"I...I can't remember, a jewel I think."

"We will speak of this later," the Harpy said looking about her, as if fearing being overheard.

Rose was about to reply when Lightning appeared before her. Not the dragon, but the man she had come to know, and love? For a long time she just stared at him, then she reacted. Her hand lashed out, the slap ringing around the mountains. Lightning lifted a hand to his reddening cheek and stared at her with shocked green eyes. "What was that for?"

"For not trusting me! For not telling me you are a dragon," Rose said, her voice almost cracking with the tears springing into her eyes.

"I am sorry if you feel I deceived you, but I did not tell you about my true form because there was nothing to tell."

"Nothing to tell?"

"Please, Rose, we should not discuss such matters here," the Harpy begged, once more glancing about her as if she saw and heard things they did not.

"Not until I have an explanation," Rose snapped, her eyes glaring into Lightning's.

"I did not tell you because I was unable to change. I was trapped in this form."

"Not here," the tall woman snapped, sensing Rose would demand more of Lightning. "Lightning can explain his situation once we are safely in the repository."

"But..."

"Rose, we are in danger here," Moonstone squeaked in her small voice. "We may be seen if we stay here much longer."

Rose wiped at her eyes, and realising she was still naked wrapped the scarlet cloak around her shoulders and padded across the stone after the Harpy.

They approached a stand of trees which had grown so close their upper trunks and branches were entangled in each other so that above their heads it was impossible to tell where one tree ended and the next began. This close knit canopy concealed a secret. In the ground before them there gaped a large round hole, and swung back on its hinges was a heavy trapdoor. As Rose watched, the harpy hopped down into the large, dark hatch. It had looked like a bottomless well to Rose, but had a depth of only a few feet below the level of the ground since the tall woman was still at waist level.

"Follow quickly," she said over her shoulder, and then vanished from sight.

"It's all right, Rose, you don't have to jump," Moonstone said softly at her side, "There are steps, look."

Following the shy girl's finger Rose saw there was indeed a flight of narrow stone steps that wound around the centre of the well, leading into the darkness below.

"Where do they go?"

"Into the hill," Lightning said, tentatively offering his arm to Rose.

Rose stared balefully at it, and spurning it sat down on the first step to pull on the boots the red woman had given her. She would have preferred socks, but even without them the boots felt comfortable enough, being made of soft supple leather. She got shakily to her feet and slowly stepped down the stairs. The top of the well rose around her, and once she had descended something like seven circles of the staircase she came to a landing where the Harpy Stormstrider waited for her. Rose was about to ask her how far this well descended when someone closed the lid of the shaft and she was plunged into darkness. She gasped in surprise but was glad she had not shamed herself by shrieking out when the light went.

"It is all right, Rose," Moonstone's voice whispered somewhere close in the dark. "Your sight will adjust in a moment."

Moonstone was right, and as Rose blinked in the gloom she became aware that far down in the depths of the shaft there were lights. As she realised this, torches flared into life around them. Rose almost screamed, realising the torches were being held in the twisted claw like hands of huge eagle headed monsters towering up around them. She blinked in the sudden light to see the torch bearers were made of stone and were statues, not living creatures.

"Do not be afraid," Stormstrider said, sweeping a feathered hand at them. "The door warders only awaken if the repository is attacked."

Rose looked from her hand to the cruel, hooked beak faces of the statues, and wondered if the woman was joking or if these were sleeping Trolls.

"Do not be afraid, Rose," Moonstone whispered at her shoulder. "Nothing will harm you here."

"Where is here?" Rose asked, following Stormstrider as she stalked down the stone steps into the gloom.

"This is the repository," Stormstrider said, reaching another wider balcony.

Rose reached the balcony and joined the tall woman at the low rail to look down into the darkness below.

"Behold the jewel that is the Repository," Stormstrider said, sweepingher arms wide.

Rose stared into the dim gloom, but for a long time could see nothing. As she turned to say so to the harpy, the entire vast depth of the cavern below brightened. A glow which seemed to shine from the walls themselves climbed towards them, lighting the levels as it did.

Rose could not at first take in what she was looking at, but then her mouth fell open as she realised that below her was a huge cavernous chamber, many storeys high, its walls ringed with large balconies. The whole structure was connected by a series of bridges spanning from a central structure like a huge tree. They climbed past her, to penetrate the roof above them. The cavern and its tree like construct were astounding, but the reason for Rose's astonishment were the row upon row of bookshelves carved into the stone walls and stacked against them, and on every one there was book upon book.

"I did not think there were so many books," she breathed.

"There aren't outside these walls," Lightning said from the shadows behind her. "The Repository is where the cultures were saved."

"Cultures saved?" Rose asked. Though she could not bring herself to look at Lightning, she was willing to learn from him still.

"Look again, Rose, look more closely at the other objects."

Rose turned a little to her left and moving slightly around the encircling balcony she could see more of the walls opposite her. Hung high on the wall was a huge painting displaying a battle, and flanking it a pair of armoured forms, long halberds in their hands.

"More guards?"

"No, they are simply relics of a dead world," Stormstrider said, perching on the balcony's railing, and before Rose's astonished eyes leapt into the air. Her great wings spread wide, catching the updraft that allowed her to sail across the broad space between the balconies.

"Come on, Rose, let's get you fed. You will learn more about this place soon enough."

Rose followed Moonstone along the balcony until they came to one of the many branches of the tree. Rose realised as she reached it that it was also a flight of steps, leading them down to the next level where she found further to her right a small desk, where a Centaur in miniature was bent over a large tome.

"Dirk," Moonstone cried, beholding the bent blond head and white-blond tail that flicked as the Centaur spun towards the small Werewolf.

Rose, hearing the exaltation in Moonstone's voice, looked to see the young girl's dark cheeks glowing red with embarrassment. The Centaur was not much taller than the slight girl, but he bowed with great dignity when he saw her and her companions. When he spoke, his voice was surprisingly deep for such a small being. "Lady Moonstone, I am pleased to see you," he said, dancing forwards, his long blond tail flicking behind him. "Lord Lightning, it is a pleasure to see you again."

"Dirk, as always a pleasure," Lightning said gravely, speaking from his place at Rose's left shoulder.

The Centaur bowed in the invisible Lightning's direction, and looking up into Rose's face appeared to be taken aback.

"Lady Lamia?" he asked hesitantly.

The fact that the Centaur had mistaken her for the snake woman who she had met only days ago told Rose better than a mirror just how much her skin had changed.

"This is Rose Canduss, Dirk," Moonstone said quickly. Her blue eyes swivelled from the Centaur to Rose and back again.

"Who is very tired and in need of refreshment," Lightning added. "Dirk, perhaps you would go ahead and have something prepared. If we are not interrupting your studies."

"It might, but I think I can tear myself away from Satan's fall for a few minutes," the Centaur said trotting past them to make his way with the agility of a mountain goat down the many steps leading to the next level.

"Isn't Satan the name of a devil?" Rose asked, glancing at the desk and the book spread upon it.

"Yes, it is," Moonstone said, approaching the table, "but Dirk is not studying magic texts, but the poetry of Milton."

"Who?"

"It will wait," said Stormstrider's voice from the balcony rail. "Moon, take Rose to my chambers where she can wash and eat. The Elders wish to see her."

Rose opened her mouth to ask the woman who the Elders were,

but before she could the tall woman cartwheeled off the rail and dropped into the shaft.

"Does she want to break her neck?"

"It might seem that way, but she is perfectly safe," Lightning said, and he tentatively laid a hand on Rose's arm. "Come, let us feed you."

"Don't touch me," Rose snapped, jerking away from Lightning's touch as if it was burning.

"As you wish," Lightning said, and Rose thought she saw a tear fall from his eye as he turned away from her.

Rose felt slightly ashamed at her cruel words, but she was still shocked by the realisation he was a dragon, and not the man she had grown to like. Moonstone looked uncomfortable by this exchange, but she was able to offer her hand to Rose. The taller girl gladly accepted and was led to the next level. Here there were many more desks upon which there lay both books and writing materials, and at one of them there worked a grey skinned dwarf who appeared to be copying an illuminated manuscript. He did not glance up from the vellum parchment, but he did murmur something to Moonstone as she passed, to which she smiled.

"What did he say?" Rose asked, as they navigated their way past a display case filled with strange looking fossils and drinking vessels.

"He asked me if I was a tourguide now," Moonstone said shyly, leading Rose to the next flight of steps which was several turns around the circle from the last.

"How many stairs and levels are there?" Rose asked, reaching the third level.

"There are seven levels," Lightning said, following them, though Rose realised she had not heard him make a step. "Four more to go, Rose."

Rose ignored him and looked around her as they moved further into the bowels of the cavern. More inhabitants made their presence known. At a row of desks, what Rose at first took to be a stone statue was bent over a large stone, seemingly examining it through some kind of lens. It was only when the statue reached out for another stone from its pile that she realised it was not a statue, but a Troll. An Elf with a small set of antlers was examining a wire bound human skeleton, and ticking off each of the bones on a diagram.

"What are they doing?" Rose asked, passing the Troll and Elf.

"I am not entirely sure," Moonstone said hesitantly. "But at a guess I would say that Flintskin was cataloguing those fossils and Goldskin is learning the human skeleton."

Rose was about to ask another question when she felt a strange sensation. A thing like a gentle touch brushed her mind. It was like a butterfly fluttering against her skin, except it was her mind, and not her flesh against which this presence danced. Rose stopped in her tracks and raised a hand to her head. The butterfly coalesced into a voice, soft and whispery. "Greetings, Rose. We welcome you to the Repository."

"Thank you," Rose said, feeling daft speaking to a whisper in her mind, but she did not know how else to react. "But who are you?"

"We are the carers," came the whisper. "We look forwards to seeing you."

With that the butterfly flew away and left her.

"Rose, are you all right?" Lightning asked, supporting her on one side with Moonstone on the other.

Rose was too dazed to refuse his help.

"I'm not sure, I think so...that was very strange."

"It was the Elders, wasn't it?" Moonstone asked excitedly.

"I don't know, there was a voice in my mind."

"That's the Elders," Lightning said, nodding sagely.

"What did they say to you?" Moonstone asked eagerly.

"That they were pleased to greet me and looked forward to meeting me."

"Then you should be," Moonstone said breathlessly.

"Why?"

"The Elders rarely speak to anyone except the Harpies or someone like Great Mother or another high druid," Moonstone explained. "I have been here for five years and have not heard them once."

"Steps," Lightning warned, as they came to the next flight.

The sound of her boots on the steps made Rose look down. Whereas the previous steps had been stone or wood these were metal, and appeared to have many branches-arms which reached out to brace the balcony-level above. On the fourth level there were even more members of the Wereding nations. Rose saw several of the mossy gnomes examining several exquisite statues, carved from black stone, their table surrounded by several dwarfs and even a small stone Troll. When Rose glanced across the well it was to see on the other side of the chamber a herd of Centaurs being lectured by a creature that resembled the half horse half human creatures, but it had the slender flanks of a deer rather than a horse, and from its temples there grew a rack of deer antlers.

"That is Skycrown," Lightning said, seeing her staring at the creature expounding his points with a long metal stylus. "And before you ask, yes he is a Heorotaura, a Stag Centaur."

"What is he doing?"

"Well, since his specialty is ancient languages, I would say something in that line."

"That's the Rosetta stone he's pointing at," Moonstone observed as they watched the Deer Centaur use the metal wand to point at a large stone displayed in a glass cabinet.

"A pity it's not the original, and only a memory," Lightning said. "But we are lucky to have a memory at all."

"A memory?" Rose asked, watching the Deer Centaur tap the glass with his stylus.

"The original was lost in the great burning, but this copy was reproduced by the council so that we should have a version to help teach us hieroglyphics."

"So this place is a school, as well as a library?" Rose asked, seeing the Heorotaura make a Centaur repeat what he was saying.

"The Repository teaches what it has gathered," Moonstone said, guiding Rose to yet another flight of steps. "I myself have learnt three languages and many skills since I have been here."

"And do you only teach Weredings here?"

"Mostly," Lightning said, coming behind them down the steps. "But before you accuse us of favouritism, we have taught some of your Scholars."

"But why have I not heard of this or this place."

"Because the Repository is a closely guarded secret, Rose, even some of the Weredings do not know of its location and those who do, do not like to discuss it."

The fourth level they came to appeared to be dedicated to music, bursting with every musical instrument Rose had heard of, and several that she had not. On a free spot a tall figure with the signature silver mane of a Werewolf was conducting a small orchestra and as they descended into the well the air was filled with slow, gentle music that reminded Rose of rain falling softly on her.

"They are very good," she said, pausing on a step to cock her head back in the music's direction.

"They should be," Lightning said, gently nudging Rose in the back to get her moving again. "They have been practicing for the last decade."

"Decade," Rose said, taken aback. "How long are they here for?"

"Bards can have a twenty-five year apprenticeship," Moonstone said, tugging on Rose's hand. "Please, Rose, we have little time."

Rose felt reluctant to leave the music. it stirred memories and thoughts she had half forgotten, but after a moments meditation she let Moonstone lead her down the flight to the next level. This circle was a museum similar to the one at the royal palace. It was filled with the stuffed and preserved husks of animals, both known and unknown to her. The next stairs were flanked by a stag and a rearing black bear.

They descended the last flight of steps, and Rose found herself among towering bookcases surrounding her on every side. Moonstone guided Rose through them, and then through a ring of desks over which there were bent many heads. As they passed one desk a hawk's head rose from examining a book with its golden eye, and opening its mouth it put a question to Lightning in a strange whistling language. Rose wanted to hear his reply, but Moonstone was having none of it and virtually dragged Rose towards one of the cave's great walls. Rose saw the walls were covered by tapestries of bright designs. It looked like the walls were undressed stone, and this huge cavern seemed to have been carved from the hill itself. Moonstone drew Rose to one of the bright tapestries, drawing it aside to reveal a low arch beyond. From within the arch candles flickered, and a familiar deep purr spoke out of its flickering gloom, "What took you so long, too busy sightseeing?"

"Eloo!" Rose gasped and leapt into the gloom to collide with the small woman's body in a mutual hug.

THE CARETAKERS

"Just because you don't see me doing anything does not mean I am idle.
There is much that can be done with the mind alone."

Stormstrider to Healm, the Wereding Chronicles.

Once the two women had embraced for what felt like an eternity, Eloo put Rose away from her, and from the extent of her short arm examined Rose from head to toe.

"It seems the magic has gotten hold of you," Eloo said, her voice attempting to be carefree, but she could not keep a note of fear from creeping in.

"The question is, is it an improvement?" came Kye's hoarse voice from behind Rose.

Rose spun on her heel to snap back a rebuke, but the words caught in her throat when she saw the state he was in. The last time Rose had seen him he had been trading blows with the dark armoured Kain, their blades sheathed in silver and black fire. Kye, it seemed, had come off worse from their confrontation. His left arm was in a sling, and most of his left side covered in burns which looked raw and shiny.

"Kye!" Rose exclaimed, frozen in place by indecision, for she did not know whether to embrace him or weep over him.

The tall, dark Werewolf offered her a grim smile though it did not hide the pain in his eyes. "It is not as bad as it looks."

"Yes it is," Silver Skin snapped, appearing behind her brother. "As soon as you have eaten I want you to take another healing potion, and once I have broken my fast I will see what I can do with my magic."

"But I must go to Grandmere and give her my memories," Kye whispered in protest.

"Not until you have been healed," Silver Skin ordered.

Kye grunted, reached for the medallion which hung about his

neck on a silver chain, closed his eyes, and began to silently mouth words. Rose realised, as she saw the disk that resembled a three-quarter moon begin to glow with a dim light, that Kye was drawing on the divine magic he wielded in his Goddesses name. She gasped as his eyes flew open to blaze yellow, as Eloo struck the disk with the tip of her four foot wand.

"None of that, Kye," she growled, her green cat's eyes flickering with the light of anger. "You are too weak to try spellcasting, and you know it."

"Eloo is quite right," Silver Skin said, putting a restraining hand on Kye's uninjured arm.

The yellow glare in Kye's eyes faded and they returned to adark blue, then were hooded as he cast them down and nodded his agreement of their wisdom.

"Come, Kye, break bread with me," Eloo coaxed, wrapping herself around Kye, making sure not to touch his burnt side.

Kye, with his usual silence, smoothed a jet black lock of hair from his lover's face, and nodding, limped with her assistance to where a long table was groaning under the weight of a king's feast. As Rose watched, Kye and Eloo exchange little gestures of love, like Kye feeding Eloo a morsel. She wondered, not for the first time, what their story was, and how a Werewolf and an Elf had met, let alone fallen in love. Even as she thought this, Lightning cleared his throat, making Rose look at him, and she was possessed with the idea that he had read her thoughts. He tentatively smiled at her and Rose turned away, not in anger, but to hide her own grin from him. For as before, she could not but find his smile infectious.

Rose moved to the table and broke off a hunk of bread to use as a trencher for some hot stew that turned out to be rabbit. Chewing on the food she reflected on her feelings for Lightning. Had she been falling in love with him? Was it just a crush, or had it been love? If it had been love, was it shattered now she knew he was something else, a dragon? Did it matter he was not human, or that he was not what she thought he was? Was the face he wore now a real one, or just a mask, was he a weredragon?

Rose's musings were interrupted as Stormstrider appeared in the archway, her great black wings filling the doorway. "Are you ready?"

"No..." Rose sputtered around a mouthful of sausage.

"She has not had chance to bathe or change," Eloo said, explaining for her.

"Then do so, the Elders will wait, but even their patience is not endless."

"I'm not so sure of that," Kye muttered from Rose's left.

"Rose, step this way," Silver Skin said, leading the girl towards a curtained corner of the chamber.

Silver drew the curtain back to reveal a small alcove with a grid in the floor, below the level of the larger chamber floor. Rose looked around her, spotting a tap high on the wall, at head level.

"I don't understand, where is the sink?"

"It is a shower," Silver Skin explained, handing Rose a towel. "You stand under the tap and let the water fall on you."

Rose removed the cloak and boots, and handed them to Silver Skin, who drew the curtain back. Rose took the soap from the dish and turning the tap on let the water flow over her. It was a sensation Rose found pleasantly soothing. She took a towel from a rail from just outside the shower and dressed in the clothes the red woman had given her. They fit like a glove, as if they had been made for her, but still possessed the hint of scent about them, the stranger's perfume perhaps.

"Are you ready now?" Stormstrider asked, stalking back and forth.

"As I'll ever be," Rose said, realising she had no idea what she was doing.

"Come, then," Stormstrider said, beckoning.

Rose followed her tall form back into the main chamber, walking past the huge base of the tree structure and through the bookcase maze, and into a side chamber where Stormstrider made Rose stand at her side. As Rose looked around her, she realised she was in the middle of a horseshoe of seated figures who surrounded her. As she looked at each of the twelve figures, a strange thing happened, for Rose at once knew their names, and who they were. Although the fact that one was a Centaur and one a Werewolf was obvious to her, how could she know their names. She had never met them before, and yet she was left with the impression that she had. Was this some subtle magic? The first to speak(or was it think, for the voice appeared in Rose's mind without traveling through her ears) was the voice which had greeted her before. This gentle butterfly of a voice belonged to the fairy who sat before her. A tiny woman, little more than a child, her fragile form was made even more so by the gossamer dragonfly like wings that protruded from her back, fluttering against the great stone seat that dwarfed her.

"Once again, greetings Rose, I welcome you on behalf of the collective." This winged child, though her body was a woman's, was the Elf Queeloo, the mistress of history.

Rose bowed to her, and after clearing a dry mouth replied, "I thank you, Lady Queeloo."

"You are wondering how you know me?"

"I am, for I have not been introduced to you before."

A new voice entered her thoughts. This one was deep as a lake and felt heavy as a stone in the lake. It came from the seven foot tall figure that Rose would have thought was a statue rather than a living being if she did not know better, for it did not seem to breathe.

"Apart from the scales, she could be her."

Rose would have asked the Troll, Slate, what he meant, but Queeloo interrupted.

"One question at a time. You wanted to know how you know us, it is because the Red Queen gave you some of her memories. So you do know us, in a way."

"The Red Queen? The woman who gave me these clothes?"

"Yes, she gave them to you as well as other things," came a voice like a creaking door, and Rose realised this voice was that of Acorn, the gnome. He looked like he had melded with the stone throne that held him. His long mossy hair seemed to have grown up to twine

60

itself into cracks in the stone, binding him.

Rose was about to ask Acorn what other things when she was distracted by the sight of Kye kneeling before the enthroned Werewolf known as Rose Skin who appeared to be asleep, for her eyes were closed. Kye knelt before her and laid his head in her lap, and despite the fact that her eyes were closed the woman, whose hair was a solid mane of silver, lifted one of her long nailed hands and placed it on his head as if in benediction. As she lifted a hand her eyes opened, and Rose blinked as a silver light spilled from them. Rose turned aside from this light to find herself facing the Centaur Thunder Heart who was not in a throne, but more a couch which allowed him to accommodate his jet black lower body. His eyes were jet black also, and they appeared to laugh at her. When she heard his voice in her head it bubbled with mirth, and made Rose think of a brook.

"What the Red Queen has given you is yours to discover for yourself, but..." As Thunder Heart stopped Queeloo took up his words as if she were finishing his thought for him.

"We would like to help you to..." As Queeloo did not finish the thought Acorn took over for her.

"Discover what it is..."

"We wish for you to stay and study..." Slate's voice took over for the gnome.

"Here where we can teach you what you need to know," the voice which took over from Slate was soft and murmured in Rose's mind, like water lapping. This was Rose Skin, the Werewolf who now had both Lea and Lor under a hand and Silver at her side, a hand placed on the enthroned woman's temple.

"Here," Rose asked, slightly dazed, for the feeling of all these voices in her mind was a little overwhelming. "You want me to stay here, for how long?"

"Until you are ready to leave," spoke a new voice in her thoughts. This voice was deep and gravelly and Rose turned to her left to meet the eyes of the pale skinned giant that loomed in his throne. Massive as it was, it seemed to hardly contain his bulk. "You can leave when you want, we do not hold anyone against their will."

"But Lord Grey Peak, I cannot stay," Rose said, though she tried to meet the eyes of all the seated figures as she spoke. "I have to save Robin."

Lightning spoke up from beside her, though Rose had not been aware of him. She had become used to the smell of pipe weed and sulphur which hung about him. "Lords, Rose's sister has fallen foul of Luna and the Crimson Circle. Rose has sworn to try to save her, and I have given my word to help her."

"We are aware of her situation," Rose Skin whispered. "But we believe that she would benefit from a short time to meditate and learn what she has gained."

In Rose's mind's eye, she saw Silver Skin touching her enthroned Elders head, and was engulfed in a flash of insight. Though she did not know how she knew it, Rose suddenly knew Silver Skin and possibly Kye before her had passed their memories and impressions to this woman telepathically.

"You know of my situation," Rose repeated in a shocked whisper. "Then if you know of it how can you ask me to wait here while Robin is..."

"We can ask it," Rose Skin answered after a slight pause, as if she were considering the question. "Because it is necessary."

"I'm sorry," Rose said, her anger rising. "But I have already been delayed. I must get to Robin before, before..."

Rose felt a sob hitching up in her throat, and her anger and frustration seemed to gather like a ball of bile in her chest. She felt a heat growing in the pit of her stomach. She had come to recognise this growing heat. It was her magic gathering itself for a burst of energy and Rose was not sure she could keep it back. As if she sensed the magic coiling to strike within Rose, Queeloo tried to reason with her. "Rose, you can better help your sister if you learn what you have been gifted..."

"You may also learn to control your magic," growled the bestial voice of Blackclaw, the male Fury. The cat like Centaur had not spoken till now, but it was clear he had not only followed the conversation, but also sensed the magic that was boiling up within Rose's bowels. "If you leave here you are as likely to blast your friends with magic as your enemies. Remember what happened with Lightning."

"But that worked out all right," Lightning objected. "Rose, after all, broke my curse."

"Curse?"

"I can as a Fire Drake change my form, but during a spell battle with another Fire Drake I was cursed and trapped in the human form you have come to know."

"And that is why you lied to me?"

"I never lied to you, Rose," Lightning said, seeming to plead with her. "I just didn't tell you what I was."

"And that wasn't a lie," Rose shot back, the ball of fire in her stomach growing.

"I suppose it was," Lightning admitted, lowering his eyes. "But I never meant to hurt you, you must believe me."

Rose could not bring herself to answer him. So she turned her attention, and her anger, on the huge lion like man who was glaring at her with golden eyes.

"I cannot stay here while Robin is in danger! I am sorry, but there it is."

"As you wish," Queeloo said, her wings beating themselves into a blur.

"I can?"

"We have said that you are free to come and go," Thunder Heart said. "But we do ask that you would return to us once you have helped your sister, there is much that we can learn from you."

"And much that we can teach you, too," added Rose Skin, gesturing for Kye to approach.

The fire that had been rising in Rose's stomach suddenly disappeared, and Rose felt drained of strength.

"I thank you for your hospitality," Rose said, feeling a wave of exhaustion flow over her.

"You are welcome," Queeloo said smiling at Rose. "Lightning, please take Rose to the guest rooms and she can rest."

"I need to go to Robin," Rose protested, though weakly.

"You will not help Robin if you can't stand," Lightning objected, slipping an arm around Rose's shoulders.

Rose might have protested or shrugged him off, but she was too tired to murmur some protest before the darkness took her.

"Did you do this?" Lightning asked, looking from the unconscious Rose to Thunder Heart.

"No," the Centaur said in Lightning's mind. "She has been through much, and she just tried to draw on her magic that I think was the last straw. Put her to bed and she will be fine in the morning."

"And what will be happening in the morning?"

"You will take Rose to Firethorn," Rose Skin said, giving Kye a scrap of parchment.

"Then she will not stay here?"

When Rose Skin replied, her voice was in harmony with the rest of the council as they spoke as not individuals, but as a single mind. "We have said that Rose may come and go as she wills, did you not believe us?"

"No, of course," Lightning whispered, feeling the huge weight of the collective mind settle on his own. "I was just checking, Rose will ask me in the morning."

"Then go and put her to bed and rest yourself, Lightning, you too will feel better in the morning," Silver Skin said, supporting Rose on the other side. "Come, to bed with both of you."

It was only once Lightning and Rose had left the chamber that Rose Skin spoke to Kye, who was receiving a treatment of salve from Eloo.

"And he is in love with her?"

"Yes," Kye grunted and then added, "And she with him."

"The revelation of his true nature has not broken that love?" Thunder Heart asked.

"It has angered her," Eloo added, stepping back to inspect her handiwork.

"That is fleeting," Kye grunted.

"And she wants to save her sister's corrupted soul?" Slate asked.

"Yes," Silver Skin said grimly. "Though she has no idea what that might cost her."

"She would be better staying and learning," Acorn said.

"She will rush to her doom, if she continues down this path," Blackclaw growled.

"I will not let that happen," Kye said, his yellow eyes meeting and contending with the Fury's golden ones.

"And what of the war?" Thunder Heart asked.

"The war, if there is one," Lea said quietly, "will not stop us."

"I wish we better understood the Pilgrim's prophecies," Rose Skin said. "I feel that we are missing an important piece of this puzzle, and somehow these two girls are at the heart of it."

"Do the prophecies give no more clues?" Silver Skin asked, returning with several mugs of mulled wine.

"We have re-examined the texts," Slate grated. "But even the Pilgrim did not know what most of the prophecies meant."

"In other words, we are hunting in the dark," Lor put in.

"It is often so when it comes to prophecies," Kye whispered. "The lady allows us a glimpse of the future so that we may prepare for it, but even she cannot tell us what may happen when the smallest decision may change the future."

None disputed Kye. The council, with all its accumulated knowledge, did not argue. Amongst them, only Kye, an Ovate in the Druid order, knew what it was to receive a prophecy.

"So where do we go from here?" Eloo asked, toasting Silver.

"We go south and try to save a soul," Silver said, meeting Rose Skin's glowing silver eyes.

"Yes, but in doing so you mustn't lose Rose's soul," Rose Skin replied. "Kye, are you aware that you might have to pluck this little Rose?"

Kye did not reply in words, but he drew his short sword from its sheath and saluted her with it.

"Kye, you couldn't!" Eloo asked, appearing shocked.

"Eloo, if Rose turns evil or mad she could unleash an unknown amount of magic on our world," Silver explained while watching her brother.

Kye did not answer Eloo, but lowered the sword and would not meet her eyes.

"Then we will have to make sure it doesn't come to that," Eloo said, glaring at Kye.

For his part he nodded, and chinked Eloo's cup with his own in assent and perhaps apology.

ON THE WINGS OF LIGHTNING

"To ride a dragon is to be a god!"
The Red Wizard, the Wereding Chronicles.

When Rose woke it was to find herself in a closet of a cell which hardly had room for the bench bed. She felt refreshed and renewed as she rose and bathed, but as she did she caught her reflection in the basin's mirror. It still shocked her to see the transformation which had changed her appearance, but now she studied her reflection more closely. Her mane of red hair was unchanged, and it formed a frame for Rose to look at her changed face. The right side of her face was the same as it had been for years, but the left side was a mask of red, glittering scales, which were not as sensitive as her right side. She took a drop of water and touched it to each cheek. The left one hardly felt the touch of the water. Her eyes were different now too. They were mismatched, for the right was green as it had always been, but her left had become a glaring ruby. She was still getting used to the idea that her magic had changed her. She was not used to this reflection, and what would Robin say when she saw her? Would she recognise her? It also made Rose think of a darker idea; what else would happen to her? How much more would the magic change her? Would she be even human by the end of this process? Was she still normal, and human now? She shook her head, realising that she did not know the answers to the questions because she did not understand the question, let alone the answer.

A tentative knock came at the door.

"Come," Rose said, turning to the door to find Moonstone peeking around the edge.

Rose grinned at the shy girl, and instead of inviting her in she strode to the door and reaching, pulled Moonstone around it and embraced her in a huge hug. She became aware as she hugged the girl of a low growling, and around the door there poked a grey dog's head.

"Quiet, Smoke," Moonstone whispered, shyly hugging Rose back. "The Lady Rose is only hugging me."

The dog (which Rose realised was a wolf) stopped growling and whined as it shrank around the door. Padding to Moonstone, it lay at her feet, its ears back and tail tucked between its legs.

"Please don't take offence at Smoke, he means no harm."

Rose looked down at the wolf cub, who could not be very old, and saw that he was well named. He was a grey the colour of fire smoke, his very eyes seeming grey.

"Your familiar?" Rose asked, finally releasing the small girl.

"No, Smoke is my companion only," Moonstone said reaching down to stroke the wolf cub's head. "We are not bonded."

"Bonded?"

"A true familiar is magically bonded to its master," cut in a new voice from outside the room, and the white-blond head of the Centaur Dirk cocked around the door frame. "I hope Lady Canduss slept well?"

"Yes, I did, thank you."

Rose looked from the blond Centaur to Moonstone's blushing face.

"So what happens next?"

"First, you break your fast," Moonstone squeaked, trying to hide her blushing face from the Centaur. "Then the Elders would speak with you one last time."

"Why?" Rose asked, her stomach which had till that moment been grumbling, clenching as she imagined them trying to compel her to stay.

"I have no idea," the Centaur said, and his head withdrew.

"Come, Rose, the breakfast is going cold."

Rose sighed and followed the small girl to a long hall that was below the level of the main chamber. Rose's cell was on the same level as most of the living quarters for both the scholars and the hundred or so beings that served them. Here several servants were serving bowls of porridge and other food at long tables to Dirk, a larger Centaur and several others. Rose looked for her companions, but saw none of the Werewolves, although Eloo and Lightning were seated at a nearby table, so Moonstone, Rose and Dirk joined them.

"Where are the rest of our party?" Rose asked, accepting a bowl of steaming porridge from Dirk.

"Kye and the twins were out before moonset scouting our route to the south," Eloo said, wrapping her oatcake around a rasher of bacon.

"Then we are leaving today?" Rose asked, spooning honey into her porridge.

"Once you have met with the council," Lightning put in. "They wish to see you before we go to Firethorn, as we had originally intended."

"Then we are going there today?"

As Rose asked this, she wondered how she would feel about travelling with Lightning, now she knew what he really was. She examined him stealthily as she ate her porridge. His long narrow face with its beak of a nose and those huge green eyes were the face he wore now, but as Rose looked at him her mind cast over it the shadow of the dragon she had seen, and yet that shadow would not hold and she found herself looking at his open honest face. The face might not be his true one, but at the same time it was not a mask of deception. Rose had learned enough of him to know that his heart was on his sleeve. That thought was eclipsed by the realisation that the hand raising the oatcake to his lips was wounded. The ring he had worn on that hand was gone, but in its place Lightning wore a band of burnt flesh, the emblem of the ring burnt as a brand into his skin.

"What happened to your hand?"

Lightning looked down at his hand and shrugged.

"What happened?" Rose pressed, a suspicion growing in her breast. "Did I do that?"

"When you were struck by the Troll's spell your magic burnt away all magic in its path and my ring was consumed in your spell fire."

Rose looked down at the table, ashamed and hurt that she had brought him pain.

"I am sorry," she muttered.

She looked up sharply when she heard Lightning laugh.

"Do not be alarmed, Rose. You may have given me a scar, but you have set me free."

"Free?" Rose asked in confusion.

"I was trapped in this form, but now thanks to you I can take on my true form."

"Your true form," Rose echoed, shivering as she remembered the giant red creature which Lightning claimed to be his real form. That form was powerful, but she had not felt afraid of it.

As she looked at Lightning she wondered if she could accept him in that other form or should she accept this face and run with that. Her thoughts were interrupted by Stormstrider appearing behind him, her dark blue eyes locking with her own. Rose found herself staring into those dark pools and she dropped her gaze to her hands to find them clenched into fists.

"Are you fed and watered?" the Harpy asked in a whisper.

"I suppose so," Rose said, forcing her hands to relax.

"Then come, the Elders await us."

Rose found the figures seated as before, and for a long time they seemed just statues, graven figures with no spirit within them, but gradually they appeared to come awake, as if they had only just become aware of Rose's presence.

"Did you sleep well?" the butterfly voice of Queeloo brushed Rose's mind.

"Yes, thank you," Rose said, looking into the tiny fairy's eyes.

"And now you wish to leave us," thought-spoke the deep voice of the giant to Rose's left.

"Yes, I do," Rose said, but did not look in his direction. "I believe that there are many miles between here and Firethorn's lair. Then I must go even further to find Robin."

"And you would be up and doing?" Rose Skin asked, a faint smile touching her lips, perhaps.

"We will not keep you long," Thunder Heart said quietly. "But before you go we have some questions for you."

Rose tried to keep her calm, but she could feel it slipping.

"What kind of questions?" she asked through gritted teeth.

"Do you know what this means?" Queeloo asked, and with a muttered word and a flick of her wrist she made a rune appear to hang in glowing red light between them.

Rose stared at the symbol and realised she did.

"It means close."

"It does, and is part of the binding spell," Rose Skin said. "And what about this one."

Rose Skin made a second rune appear next to the first.

"Stone or rock," Rose said, surprising herself for as far as she knew she had never seen these characters before.

"What do they mean when you combine them with this rune?" Blackclaw asked as he produced a third rune.

"To bind with stone." Rose said, suddenly realising they had just revealed to her a spell for holding any enemy in place. A spell which would freeze them into a statue.

"You have just shown me a spell for holding," she gasped, examining the hanging runes more closely. "But how do I know these runes?"

"We suspect that this knowledge comes from the gift the Red Queen gave you. We believe that it not only allows you to understand the runes, but also stores spells inside your mind so you can learn magic more easily."

"That could make my job easier," Lightning quipped from behind Rose.

"What is happening to me?" Rose moaned, as suddenly many runes seemed to dance behind her eyes.

"You are taking steps into a larger world," Queeloo fluttered.

"With that in mind and since you have gained a new understanding of runes, we give this to you."

Rose realised Rose Skin was holding out the Wand of Wisdom. Rose stared at the four foot long staff, with its many rune inscribed rings. The last time she had touched it the wand had come alive and made her cast a spell, a scrying which had allowed her to see Robin, and had informed Kye and the rest of her friends that she was a new member of the dark spell casting brotherhood the Crimson Circle. So she was wary as she reached out to touch the metal points of the staff. Rose half expected another vision as her fingers closed on the rod, and she was relieved and surprised when nothing happened, and she released a breath she had not realised she was holding in.

"I did not know you had it," she conceded, holding the long staff down at her side.

"Silver Skin presented it to us for study," Queeloo said.

"But we believe that you may be in need of it in the days to come," Rose Skin said, her glowing eyes appearing to cloud, as if she were seeing things beyond everyone's sight.

"Why, what do you know about my future?"

"Know," Thunder Heart said. "What we *know* is nothing, but what we suspect is that you will confront many spellcasters if you try to save your sister, and you will therefore need every help you can get."

Rose looked down, breaking her glare with Rose Skin. Her right cheek darkened and she clutched at the wand as she realised that what the dark Centaur said was probably true. The idea of fighting spell to spell with shadowy spell casters made her legs feel watery. Lightning appearing to sense her fear and whispered in her ear, "Don't fear, Rose, I will be with you."

Rose only realised minutes later that she had not reacted harshly to his familiar and soothing voice.

"I thank you for your help," she said, addressing the half circle of seated figures. "But I must be on my way."

"Ah yes, Firethorn," Acorn rustled. "There we may be able to help you."

"Help me?" Rose asked in confusion. "I thought Firethorn was miles away."

"She does live many leagues from here," Queeloo fluttered. "But we can shift you to her, saving you many hours'trek."

"Magic?"

"Magic," Blackclaw growled. "We can create a door that will join here with a point just outside Firethorn's lair."

Rose's heart gave a lurch and she finally felt they were getting somewhere.

"That sounds like powerful magic," she said.

"Powerful," Rose Skin confirmed. "But we have performed more powerful rites in our time."

"Then thank you."

When the seated figures responded they did not as individuals but spoke as one being. Their individual voices mingled and harmonised, so Blackclaw's low growl did not sound harsh, beside Queeloos. "You are welcome, daughter of Canduss. Go with hope in your heart and wisdom in your mind and return to us as soon as you can."

Rose bowed her head in acknowledgement of them. She did not see or hear them cast a spell, but at the middle of the horseshoe the air seemed to fold in on itself as if a giant's hand was moulding it like clay. Then the disturbance vanished to reveal a view of a windswept mountain side. Rose might have believed it was an illusion, but as she thought this the wind that swept the bent bushes swirled around her, making her scarlet mane and red cloak snap in their invisible hands. This window was barely as tall as Rose, and only several hands wide.

"How do I fit through there?"

"The size of the wormhole is deceptive. You are looking through the wrong end of a telescope," Lightning explained. "You only have to step into it and you will fit."

"If you say so," Rose said, though her voice conveyed that she did not quite believe him.

Rose was about to step through the door when she realised

something, and looking around saw that of the Werewolves only Moonstone was present.

"But what of Kye and Silver Skin and the twins?"

"They and I will follow on foot," Eloo said, placing a kiss on Rose's cheek. "We will meet you at Care Diff or Firethorn's if we can. Now go, and speak with Firethorn."

Rose nodded, and taking a deep breath stepped through the door and felt herself falling as if she had stepped off a cliff. When she landed, it was in a dazed state. Her confusion was not helped by a weight landing on her back, pinning her to the ground. The next thing she knew was Lightning pulling her to her feet.

"You were supposed to move out of the way," he said, brushing her down.

"No one told me," Rose said, shaking her head in an attempt to clear it and to clear her mane from her eyes, for the wind was blowing it around her head. "Does traveling like that always leave you feeling like you've been through a whirlwind?"

"Only the first couple of times," Lightning said, proffering Rose a water skin, "But you soon get used to it."

"I'm not sure about that," Rose said, after taking a long pull of the bottle.

"Better?"

"Better," she agreed. "Is this Firethorn's home?"

Lightning looked about him and shook his head. "No, her lair is over there," he said, pointing to a great hill that resembled a crown, a ring of sharp stones forming the points of the crown.

"This must be as close as the Elders were able to get us. Firethorn's lair is powerfully warded against such magic. We will have to walk from here."

"It looks a long way down," Rose commented, scouting about them for a path down from the tall cliff.

"Well, we could..."

"What?" Rose asked, watching an excited look kindle in Lightning's eyes.

He shrugged and shook his head. "No, it's crazy, you would never agree to it."

"How do I know if I'll agree to it, if I don't know what it is?"

Lightning stared at her, clearly excited and expectant, but seemingly unable to bring himself to speak what was in his mind.

"What I was going to suggest was that if you didn't want to walk, you could always fly."

"Fly?" Rose said, not understanding him. "Can the magic do that?"

"It can," Lightning said, a look of disappointment on his face. "But what I meant was you could ride there."

"Ride? Ride on what…"

Lightning's face lit up with delight, as he saw Rose had finally caught on to what he was trying to suggest.

"Ride? Ride you, you mean?"

"I said you wouldn't like it," Lightning said, disappointment written all over his face as he turned away from Rose.

"Wait," Rose said, grabbing his shoulder. "I didn't say no. It's just…"

Just what? Rose asked herself as she tried to sort out her churning emotions. The first one had been shock. Then surprise, mixed with a little fear, but she realised the overriding emotion which filled her as she considered Lightning's proposal was excitement.

"I would love to ride you," she said in a whisper.

When Lightning spun back to see her, Rose could not but mirror the huge smile lighting up his face.

"Your wish is my command. You had better stand back a little, though."

Rose did as he suggested, and before her eyes Lightning's shape shimmered as though she was seeing him through a wall of smoke, and then Lightning the Fire Mage was gone, and crouching in his place was the great Fire Drake that had carried her from the battle, although her memory of that journey was just a blur.

The creature must have been at least thirty feet from whiskered nose to spiny tail and swung its horned head towards her. Rose looked into the green pool that was its eye and knew, despite the unfamiliar shape, that she was looking into Lightning's eye. So when his voice growled out from between long fangs she recognised it.

"My lady, your steed awaits," he growled mockingly, but still lowered his head so that it nearly touched the ground.

"I can't believe this," Rose muttered, staring at the huge head lowered before her. Lightning's long neck providing a kind of bridge to a hollow between his large blade like frills where he intended her to sit.

Rose took a great breath and stepped onto his back, scrambling none too gracefully up the steps formed by his double row of crest like neck plates, till she reached the hollow where she slid into the gap. Facing forwards, she found this narrow space between the armoured fins was surprisingly comfortable, as comfortable as any saddle for the space was lined with his scales and they feltmore like leather than armour beneath her. The large horn like spines that rose before her and at her back supported her like the horn and seat of a saddle.

"Are you all right up there?"

The sensation of Lightning's voice vibrating below Rose was a strange one and she suddenly realised she was sitting on a creature that contained incredible energies.

"I would prefer stirrups and reins," Rose muttered, wondering what she could hold on to.

Lightning heard her whisper, and it took Rose a moment to realise the vibrations which quivered through the mighty beast beneath her were the dragon's laughter.

"Do not worry, you will not fall," he whispered. "As to holding on, hold onto my frill."

Rose reached forward and found that just in front of the saddle horn was a pair of long spines which she wrapped her hands round and hung onto for dear life, as Lightning leapt forwards. He took a second bone rattlingjump, and as he did his great red wings spread out around him and then rose up around Rose as they beat the air with a thump that if Rose could see it flattened the grass below them. Rose clung on screaming, though in fear or joy even she could not tell. As the great sails of Lightning's wings rose and fell, the wind of their passage pulled at Rose's long hair and cloak and she felt them flying out behind her. Rose had crouched low in the saddle and closed her eyes when Lightning began his jumps, but as she felt the wind flowing over her she opened her eyes to stare past Lightning's neck, to see the valley floor several hundred feet below, flowing past like a river. Lightning did not approach the crown like hill directly but rose above the valley in a series of ascending spirals which allowed them to climb and see the whole hill and the lands surrounding it. As they seemed to climb for the sun, Rose saw several large birds take off from among the spiky rocks. Lightning's sudden appearance startled them to flight.

"Those are large birds," Rose shouted to Lightning for the roar of the wind required her to shout.

"Those aren't birds," Lightning purred, his deep growl allowing him to speak to Rose without having to raise his voice above a low rumble.

Rose looked at the four or five winged creatures swiftly rising to meet them. As she squinted against the bright sunlight, she realised the creatures were dragons. None of them was as large as Lightning, but Rose was still concerned that four Fire Drakes were flying to intercept, and perhaps attack them.

"Are they going to attack?"

"Of course not," Lightning said. "They are my cousins. They are coming to meet us and provide an escort to Firethorn."

Rose was still not sure how she felt about these dragons approaching, but before she could think about it they were about them, their voices hissing in their own tongue. Glancing down at the Wand of Wisdom, which Rose had tucked into her belt, she saw that it had changed and was partly showing her a magic symbol. Before she realised what she was doing, Rose muttered the word she felt in her mind and suddenly the dragon's hissing was transformed into understandable words.

"It has been too long, Lightning," the nearest hovering dragon growled. Its smoky wings hardly moved as it hung beside Lightning's head.

"My studies at the Eyrie have kept me away, Scarlet," Lightning growled back.

"And who is this human that you bear?" growled the largest of the dragons, a creature the size of a great cat, and looked to Rose like a scarlet panther.

"This is Rose Canduss, Flames," Lightning answered, nostrils flaring.

"Is she human?" asked the smallest of the red Fire Drakes. A creature not much more than a bird in size it flew close to stare into Rose's face.

"She is human," Rose replied, surprising them all, as up to now they were not aware that she understood them.

"By the red dragon, she can speak our tongue," hissed the largest dragon. "Lightning, have you been teaching without permission?"

This question must have annoyed Lightning, for he made a deep growling in the back of his throat and twin streams of smoke spouted from his nostrils.

"As it happens, Flames, I have not! However, Rose is a magic user and has apparently learned a spell to translate."

"So it would appear," Rose agreed. "Lightning, perhaps introductions might be in order."

"But of course. Our large friend here is Flames." The panther like dragon flicked his wings so that he bobbed in place, and as Lightning introduced them the other dragons followed his example. "These two are Scarlet and her brother Thornskin, and finally the creature fluttering around you is Dove."

The dragon, probably not larger than a dove, had at that moment stopped fluttering around and landed on Lightning's neck, perching on the saddle horn of his spines. This little dragon cocked its bird like head and considered Rose with a soft brown eye.

"Greeting's, lady," hissed Dove, flicking her forked tongue at Rose.

"Are you the Red Woman that our mother has been waiting for?"

"I don't know about that," Rose replied, considering the tiny creature.

"Where is Firethorn, in her study?"

"No, she will meet you in the audience room," Flames replied over his shoulder, wheeling away to dive towards the great fist of a hill.

"I will guide you," chittered Dove, slithering around on Lightning's neck so that she faced forwards. As Rose watched, the tiny dragon skittered along Lightning's neck to perch between the great dragon's twin horns.

"I think I remember the way," Lightning growled, following the other three dragons towards the hill.

"Mother has changed her trap net," Dove hissed, flaring her wings as Lightning swept towards the hill.

"Then I will land a good way off and we shall walk in," Lightning said, powerfully flexing his wings, and slowing his dive turned it into along sweeping glide that brought them to the valley floor several hundred yards from the foot of the great hill.

"Rose, could you please dismount? I think I will enter in my other form."

Rose gulped, and scrambling out of the saddle dropped from his lowered neck to land in a crouch beside one of his large bird like feet with its long talons. Rose turned to see what he looked like from this angle but was disappointed. When she turned he was no longer the great dragon but his tall human form. Dove perched on his arm like some large hawk, her long claws clutching his forearm.

"Where to from here?" Rose asked, looking about for the other dragons, but they were nowhere in sight.

"The entrance is in that direction," Lightning said, pointing with a new wand of iron Rose had not seen before.

She turned to consider where he had pointed, but she could not see any break in the vertical cliff face.

"I cannot see an entrance?"

"It is well hidden," Lightning said.

"And well guarded," Dove added.

"Guarded?"

"You'll see," Lightning said, and started walking towards the cliff.

Rose shrugged and trotted after him. As they neared the cliff Dove let go of Lightning's arm and flapped before them, circling to face them.

"Stay to the right," she hissed, swooping around before them.

Rose glanced at her feet when Dove said this and felt some instinct detect something. She knelt to inspect the ground more closely and realised the twigs and earth before her were camouflage. Rose was sure, though she did not want to check, that the ground before her had been arranged to hide a deep pit. If Dove had not warned them Lightning and she would have plunged through the mat of branches and leaves to plunge into a pit trap.

"I don't remember any pit traps," Lightning said to her side, confirming Rose's guess.

"It is new," Dove agreed, pointing with one of her wings tipped with cruel claws. "But you can avoid it if you stay on this side."

"Thank you, Dove," said Lightning.

They followed Dove's directions around the pit and continued towards the cliff that still appeared solid to Rose.

"Stay out of the long grass," Dove hissed.

"More pits?" Rose asked, scanning for a gap through the long grass that grew in a thin line before the cliff.

"No," Lightning said, using the long metal wand to hold the grass aside, revealing the dark rusty teeth of a spring mantrap.

"Nasty," Rose said shivering.

"So are the ones who would steal mother's treasure," Dove growled.

Rose shrugged, unable to disagree.

Then they were at the cliff, and Rose could still see no breach in the flat, vertical rock. She drew the Wand of Wisdom from her belt and held it before her. As she stared at the many symbols engraved in the metal she felt her gaze penetrating the metal rings and the core of the wand. On her mind's eye words appeared, and without knowing what she did she muttered the words and her free left hand made a twisting motion. When Rose looked up from the wand the wall before her glistened as if the stone was wet. It had changed, and was no longer a featureless stone wall. Before Rose there now stood a pair of doors which must have been made for giants. The twin wooden doors stood thirty feet high and almost as wide. Looking more closely, she realised the doors were still glinting, and then she realised that what she was seeing was a web of glowing lines which appeared to thread through the wood. She knew these were lines of power, and the door was magically reinforced.

"I have never seen a door that large," Rose gasped.

"The fact that you can see it is more interesting to my way of thinking," Lightning said beside her. "Rose, you have just cast a Mage Eye spell, a magic that should be beyond you."

"I seem to be hearing that a lot," Rose growled under her breath. "So what do we do, knock?"

"No," spoke a new voice, "you must pass me before you may enter."

Rose's attention was drawn to the spot from where this voice came, and despite herself she gasped when she saw the speaker. The speaker was a head in the centre of the doors, like a gargoyle sitting there, but gargoyles were not made of living flesh. The head was that of a Fire Drake. The Fire Drake considered Rose with eyes of fire, and she felt them penetrating her flesh and scouring her soul.

"State your name and purpose," growled the disembodied head.

Rose subconsciously drew herself up to her full height, and glaring into the fiery eyes responded to its challenge. "I am Rose Canduss, and I am here to see the Lady Firethorn!"

The head appeared to consider this, and then its fiery orbs narrowed to slits as they nearly closed. The head did not respond with words, but as Rose was about to demand entrance the huge doors split down the centre.

FIRETHORN

"Dragons may live for centuries or forever, no one knows, but a dragon will see many generations of men and so they are useful holders of others' heirlooms and their secrets."

The book of the Wolf.

The giant's doors swung outwards, to reveal a cavernous entrance hall.

"Shall we?" Lightning asked, gesturing to the dark mouth of a hall.

"I suppose so," Rose answered, taking hold of his outstretched arm and allowing him to lead her into the hall.

As they stepped over the threshold, Rose wondered where the dragon had gone, and she felt something large above her. Glancing up, she found hanging above them not the expected dragon, but the sharp points of a portcullis. Its many spikes looked like the fangs of a great monster's upper jaw. Noticing where her gaze was Lightning pointed to a second archway that led deeper into the complex, where another gate hung poised to drop.

"These are not for us," he said, drawing her along the long hall.

"Then who are they for?"

"Dragons," Dove hissed, fluttering beside them.

"Dragons??"

"Dragons of Firethorn's age do not fear most humans or elves, what they fear are other dragons coming and stealing their homes. So they make sure that there is at least one gift for visitors to spring."

"Some gift," Rose said, eyeing the spikes on the bottom of the gate.

Then they were under the spikes, and through the arch into what Rose guessed was the audience chamber. She was standing on a small wooden platform projecting over a great drop, into what seemed an abyss. Rose looked across this abyss to see a cliff opposite her, which rose to a point just higher than where she stood. She was wondering about the layout of this chamber when something moved in the gloom above her, and a pebble was knocked over the lip of the cliff to fall past Rose and into the seemingly depthless abyss. Then Rose saw something appear at the top of the cliff, and looking up she gasped for the torches seemed to dim as a huge planet orbited into sight above her. It was a red planet, and it was no globe, but the head of a massive dragon. Rose was looking at the head of a feline Fire Drake which filled the world. It appeared to Rose to be several metres long and wide. The dragon lowered its head so it was craning its neck down to cast its huge cat like eyes over the tiny beings below it. Rose felt as if a sun had cast its gaze over her, and even from many feet away from the creature itself she could feel waves of heat radiate off the great fiery beast. It felt like an eternity as Rose stared into the depths of those glowing, green pools. Eventually the dragon spoke in a voice that was a low whisper, but which filled the air and vibrated through the wood and stone beneath her feet.

"So this is the Red Wizard," the dragon purred and Rose was sure that there was a hint of mockery and amusement in the tone.

"I am Rose Canduss," Rose shot back boldly, though she could hear a tremor in her own voice. "But yes, I have been called the Red Wizard by some people, though I am no mage."

Rose, though her consciousness was dominated by the huge dragon, was aware of Lightning chuckling beside her. The next thing Rose felt was the ground beneath her shake, as if a wave had rolled through the stones. Then the chamber was filled with a deep rumbling, and twin streams of smoke jetted from the dragon's nostrils as if her words had awoken a volcano's wrath, but after clinging to the rail that separated her from the abyss, Rose realised that the dragon was not angry, but simply laughing at her.

"Well, Red Wizard, I have been waiting for you to come for many long years."

"Why?" Rose asked, in almost a snarl herself, for she was getting tired of everyone knowing what she did not.

"Because your mother left things here for you if you should ever come to me. I release them to you now."

"You knew my mother?" Rose asked, hearing the catch in her voice. Her mother had died before she was very old, and all Rose had of her were the faintest of memories.

"Yes, I knew Willow Cloudwalker, your mother," growled the great dragon, "and I agreed to keep certain gifts for her daughters if they ever came to me. I give them over to you, and bid you use them well. Lightning, Velvet has them in my study, would you be good enough to deal with this?"

"It is my pleasure," Lightning said softly.

"Then I wish you well, Rose Canduss, daughter of Willow."

With these words the great head was gone, as if the sun had gone behind a cloud. Rose wanted to call her back and pelt her with questions about her mother. Her heart had swelled with the dull pain of grief.

Lightning, who must have interpreted her inner thoughts, spoke softly. "If she wished to impart more she would have. Firethorn tells you what she wants, and no more. It would be pointless to try to question her."

"I wanted to ask her about my mother," Rose whispered, a single tear running down her cheek.

"I know, Rose, I know," Lightning reassured her and reaching a tentative hand out touched, and then stroked her back.

Rose felt fire in her eyes, and she squeezed them tight to prevent them from falling.

"Is she all right?" Rose heard Dove's voice, from a great distance.

"She will be in a minute, Dove, just give her a moment," murmured Lightning, resting his hand comfortingly on her shoulder.

Rose blinked the tears back, and straightening she gathered herself and decided to put her feeling aside.

"Where are these gifts?"

"Firethorn said that Velvet would give them to you in her study,"

Lightning said, removing his hand. "If you will follow me, I can lead you to him."

"Lead on," Rose snapped, her voice a little harsher than she had intended it.

Lightning did not notice, or if he did he took no offence, but nodded and led Rose back into the entrance hall, out of the gate, out of the smoky torch light, and into the clean fresh air.

SWORDS AND SADDLES

"Dragons hoard wealth, but what is wealth changes from dragon to dragon."

The book of the Wolf.

They skirted the hill and coming around to the back found a thatched house.

"This is her study?"

"The outside of it," Lightning confirmed, rapping on the small, wooden door.

Rose half expected to hear Firethorn's voice roarout of the hill, but instead a voice whispered a response, and Lightning opened the door for Rose, standing aside so that she could enter before him. She smiled at him for this small courtesy, and ducking the low door she entered a well-lit house. A fire crackled in a hearth, and the room was dominated by a large desk behind which there stood a tall, thin figure whose antlers brushed the low beams, their many points rattling against the wood as the figure bowed to Rose.

"Rose," Lightning said from behind her, "this is Velvet, Firethorn's butler."

Velvet was one of the Heorotaura, one of the Deer Centaurs. His upperbody was the sculpted form of a young statue, but as the youth moved from behind the desk to replace a book on the large case, he revealed that his lower body was the slender flanks and tail of a deer. Velvet did not speak at first but stood regarding Rose's face for a long time. When he finally did, his voice was a soft husky whisper which reminded Rose of the rustle of leaves.

"I do not need to ask your family name," he rustled. "You are the spitting image of your mother Willow."

"You knew my mother too?" Rose asked eagerly, hoping that here she had found someone who could answer her questions.

The half deer youth shook his spiky head. "Knew her, no, I'm afraid not. I met her only once."

"Oh," sighed Rose in disappointment.

"But I have what she left for you."

As he spoke, he went to a substantial trunk and casting back the lid, withdrew from its depths a large bundle, bound with many thongs, which he placed on the desk, and stood back gesturing to Rose to accept it.

Rose glanced from this gentle youth to Lightning, and back again. "Did my mother really leave this here for me to have?"

"So I have been told by my mistress."

"Open it," Lightning prompted her, giving her an encouraging smile.

With a deep sigh, Rose unbuckled the first belt, and after afew minutes was able to unfurl the large wrapping. When unrolled it revealed several large items, all wrapped in what Rose now saw was a great scarlet cloak, complete with a deep cowl like hood.

"It appears that your mother planned ahead," Lightning commented, seeing what was lying before them.

Rose could not dispute this statement as she took in the items before her. Lying on the desk was a large bow, its string gleaming golden in the light. Beside it there lay a magnificent longsword, its hilt crafted in the likeness of an eagle's head.

"One of the fabled eagle swords, I presume," Lightning asked, as Rose picked the sword up.

Rose could not reply as she reverently drew the long blade from its red, leather wrapped wood scabbard. The pommel gleamed golden in the light, the bird's eyes a pair of amber jewels. They appeared to consider Rose back from their gold mountings.

"There is this as well," Velvet said, once more delving into the chest and lifting out something large.

When he turned back to Rose, he was holding out a large round shield made of some reddish metal. Rose lay the sword back on the table and reached out for the shield that she expected to be heavy, but as she took it she found that it was as light as a feather. She scrutinised the design on the front to see many runes engraved in its surface.

"Is it magical?" she asked in a dreamy voice, gazing at this treasure, a gift from her mother.

"You tell us!"

"What do you mean?"

"You seem to know the mage eye spell," Lightning said. "Use it now."

Rose stared at him for a long moment, then she recalled the words and gestures, and repeated them. As she finished the spell, the shield in her hand flared with light. Rose blinked as the shield glowed with a red flame that flickered across the surface of the shield, and when she looked at the bow a baleful red glow shone from within as if it was a smoked glass lantern. Beside them lay the sword, its hilt giving off a golden glow that contested with the light of the bow.

"They're all magical," she gasped. "Even the cloak."

Indeed, the red cloak flickered with a smoky aura. But the spell revealed to Rose other things, concealed within the folds of the cloak. She reached out and plucked a pair of rings from where they lay hidden. One was a band of gold, with a sapphire set in it and the second was a ring of strange metal Rose did not recognise, but set in it was a diamond. Both rings glowed with bright magical light.

"A ring of air and earth," Lightning said, considering the rings over Rose's shoulder.

"Are they like the ring Takana gave me?"

"In a way," Velvet agreed. "They will fuel any spells of air and earth."

"But you have to learn spells first."

"Put them on, Rose," Lightning encouraged. "They are yours to wear."

Rose slipped the air ring onto her left hand first, and as she did she thought for an instant that she heard the wind whisper words in her ear, but she could not be sure it was not her imagination. As she slid the earth ring onto the other hand, she felt suddenly very heavy as if she had gained weight, but that feeling too was gone within a breath.

"All right?" Lightning asked, his hand on her arm.

"I think so," Rose said, taking several deep steadying breaths.

"There is one other thing to give you," Velvet said. "But this is not from your mother, this is a gift from my lady."

Velvet held up an object that fluttered in his hands, as if it was a living thing. It appeared to jump from his hands to hers. Rose looked down at the cloth object stretched between her hands. It was a mask, made of dark red material as soft as silk and which covered most of the face.

"Am I that changed?" Rose asked in a shocked whisper.

"You are beautiful," Lightning whispered behind her, his voice breaking.

"Please do not misunderstand us," Velvet said in a shocked rustle. "The mask is not meant as an insult, but as an aid."

"Covering my face is an aid?"

"Sometimes it is wise to hide your identity," Velvet whispered, "but the mask is meant to help you in another way."

"What way?"

"Do you like your face as it is?"

This question from Velvet drove Rose back on her heels, and for a long moment she was left speechless as she considered it. It was true she was not happy with the changes wrought on her body, but was she prepared to hide behind a mask to hide them?

"Put the mask on, and you will realise why Firethorn has provided it."

Rose hesitantly raised the mask to her face and lowered the strap that held it against her flesh. As she did she felt a slight tingling on her skin, and surprisingly she felt the tingle even through the scaled side of her face.

"How is this different?"

"Look here, and you will know the answer," Velvet replied, taking a looking glass from the fireplace mantle and handing it to Rose so she could see her masked face in it.

"All I see is a mask," Rose said disappointedly.

"You must concentrate for its magic to work. Think about what you want to see."

Rose scowled, but closing her eyes she concentrated on her reflection as it had been before the magic changed her.

"Rose, open your eyes," Lightning whispered in her ear.

When she looked at the glass again, she gasped for it was not a masked face that she saw before her, but her own unblemished flesh. It was as if the scales had never been. Rose could feel the soft silky material of the mask against her flesh, and when she reached up she could feel the scales beneath the mask, but her left cheek appeared free of scales in the glass.

"The mask conceals scars and blemishes," Velvet explained. "Firethorn perhaps felt that you might want to appear as you were, and the mask has other powers."

"Such as what?" Lightning asked.

Rose, however, wasn't listening to Lightning, for she was too amazed by the face gazing back at her from the mirror. Her wave of delight appeared to wash the face away, and as soon as the familiar reflection had appeared it was gone and the dark mask was in its place.

"No," Rose moaned in despair as the reflection vanished.

"You must concentrate to keep the mask working," Velvet said.

"Then what is the point of the mask?" Rose spat, making to rip it off.

"Like with most things you will grow used to it," Velvet protested in his soft whisper. "Soon it will become second nature, and you will have your face without having to even think about it."

Rose did not feel convinced, lowering the mask to hang about her neck. As she did, she realised that the Deerman was watching her with fear and expectation.

"Please thank your mistress for this gift," Rose said haltingly, realising she had not thanked Velvet or through him the giver of this gift.

"I will convey your thanks to her."

"Thank you," Rose said haltingly. "Please do thank her, and thank you too, Velvet, for helping us."

"Speaking of gifts," Lightning said, holding out the iron wand he had been carrying, "I would pay Firethorn for the Shield scale with this wand of lightning."

"Thank you Lightning, it is a worthy replacement," Velvet said, accepting the metal rod. "And where do you go now?"

"Kye and the rest of our party were to meet us here as soon as they could and then we were to go south."

"Then come, let me feed you while you wait."

"Thank you, but we have imposed on you too much already," Rose replied.

"Not at all, I would feel that I were neglecting my duties if I did not fulfil my role of host."

"Rose, I know you want to be off," Lightning said soothingly, "but we can do nothing until the others arrive. A meal and rest cannot delay that."

Rose turned away, frustrated but defeated. Velvet appeared not to notice and provided them with a meal of freshlybaked bread, goat's cheese and smoked wild boar.

"Boar?"

"The Lady's children catch it in the surrounding woods," Velvet explained, though Rose noticed the Deer Centaur had not himself touched any of the flesh.

As Rose thought about this, she noticed Lightning was eating enough for two, despite his wiry frame, making her wonder about this form, comparing it with the huge dragon he could become. Considering the lithe dragon, a thought exploded inside her head.

"Lightning, you could fly me to Robin," Rose said excitedly.

Lightning nearly choked on his bread, and when he had managed to stop coughing he sat staring at Rose.

"Well, couldn't you?" Rose demanded eagerly.

"Rose, it is hundreds of miles away to Landan," Lightning said hesitantly.

"But you could fly it, couldn't you?"

"In time, perhaps," Lightning conceded. "But it would mean that we leave Kye and the others behind, and we will need their help if the Crimson Circle have their hooks into your sister."

"Oh," Rose said, her hope dying into the silence.

Sensing her disappointment, Velvet suddenly rose from where he had crouched opposite them at the low table at which they had dined. "That has reminded me of one more gift that the lady bade me supply you with."

"No, please, she has been too generous already," Rose protested.

"This gift is as much to Lightning as it is to you. Please come."

Velvet led them back out of the house, to a large paddock where a lean-to shed stood and from inside this Velvet lifted out a great saddle of dark leather.

"A saddle?"

"A saddle made for a dragon," Velvet explained. "You may need it if you ride Lightning into battle."

"Battle?" Rose asked, not sure how she felt about this idea.

"Please try it," Velvet said, gazing past Rose to where Lightning stood.

Rose's attention was drawn from the black saddle to Lightning, as from behind her there was a great flap of wings. When she turned, it was to find the huge red dragon towering up before her.

"My Lady Rose, please watch how I fasten it," Velvet said, moving past her with the saddle. "You will need to know how to do this."

Rose followed him reluctantly, but watched with fascination as Velvet placed the saddle on the hollow at the base of the dragon's neck, where she had sat during their brief flight. She watched as he buckled the large strap of the saddle around the dragon's throat, noticing that the underside of his throat was ridged like bands of armour, a lighter shade of red to the rest of his body. She was suddenly possessed by the desire to touch those scales, but she resisted the desire, believing Lightning would not wish her to do so, at least not with Velvet watching.

"Is that too tight, my lord?" Velvet asked, almost reverently, stepping back to admire his handiwork.

Lightning flexed his jaw and stretched his neck, swinging his head about on the end of his long, serpentine neck. Finally he turned away from them, and with a roar he unleashed a great jet of fire into the air.

"No, Velvet, I hardly feel it."

"My lady Rose, perhaps you would try it," Velvet suggested hesitantly.

For a long time, Rose did not respond. In fact, she had not heard Velvet, for she was stunned by Lightning's display. The jet of fire he had breathed had to be forty feet long, and was hot enough that Rose felt its heat though Lightning's body was between her and the flaming burst.

"He can do that more than once?" she asked, in a shocked whisper.

"He must rest to regain the necessary energies," Velvet said, nodding his antlered head. "But yes, he can produce a flame several times in an hour."

"Rose, are you going to try this saddle or not?" Lightning rumbled at her in his deep purr.

He had turned back to face them and lowered his head so his neck was near the ground.

"If you will permit, my lady?" Velvet said, forming a step with his clasped hands.

"Thank you, Velvet."

Rose stepped into the cupped hands and expected the slender Heorotaura would not be able to lift her weight, but he must have been stronger than he looked. She was smoothly lifted up to the level of the saddle and with little effort she swung a leg over the broad seat.

"How is it?" Velvet asked, peering up at her.

"Comfortable," Rose answered, realising the seat was even more padded than the natural saddle Lightning's scales had formed. "But if we are to fly, how do I stay in it?"

"These straps should keep you secure," Velvet explained, fastening broad straps about her lower legs. "How does that feel?"

"Strange," Rose said, exploring her feelings, "but not uncomfortable."

"They are not too tight?"

"No."

"Then let's see how they feel in the air," Lightning growled, and before Rose could agree or protest, the dragon was leaping forwards and up. His wings pounded up, then down and suddenly the ground was falling away from them. Rose cried out wildly, though whether her cry was of fear or joy she could not at first say. The wind snatched at her cape and hair and flowed into her face. She blinked, and when her vision cleared she craned forwards in the saddle to look past the long backwards swept horns of Lightning's head to seeat the ground. Gasping, she realised they must be several hundred feet above the clenched fist of the dragon's lair.

"Yes!" Rose shouted with glee, as Lightning made a tight turn and wheeled over the hill to face north and swoop higher.

"Yes!" Rose cried again as the joy of the power and emotion flowed over her.

"You like?" Lightning's purr reached Rose despite the loud whistling of the wind.

"I feel like a god!" Rose screamed in exultation.

"Then let's see what the heavens look like."

As Rose realised what he meant, Lightning increased the beats of his huge wings and the ground disappeared. Soon they were among the clouds and Rose was shivering in the damp air.

"Lightning, too high," Rose gasped, finding it hard to breathe.

Rose's senses began to swim and her stomach leapt into her throat as Lightning dropped like a stone fromthe clouds to come to a halt several feet above the paddock.

"I am sorry, Rose, are you all right?" Lightning asked, craning his neck around to look back at Rose.

Rose drew in a long deep breath, and then whispered, "Let's not do that again for a while."

"I am sorry," Lightning said, touching down on the grass. "But it is such a long time since I have really flown that I forgot myself."

"It's fine, Lightning," Rose said, unconsciously reaching out to touch one of his large frills. She realised she had enjoyed most of the flight.

"Well, there's a pretty sight!" said a familiar voice at their side.

"Lor," Rose exclaimed, surprised to hear the Werewolf's deep voice, and looking down from her high seat saw not only the tall Werewolf, but his twin Lea, Eloo, Kye and Silver Skin all looking up at her.

"You made it!" Rose cried, her heart leaping.

"Lightning, are you ready to make another short flight?" Silver Skin asked.

Lightning did not answer her with words but beat his great wings as if showing off just how ready he was.

"What about you, Rose," Kye croaked. "Are you willing to stay up there for a spell longer?"

"All the way tothe south," Rose replied.

"Well, not that far," Eloo said, grinning up at Rose, "but to Care Diff for a start."

"It is a start," Rose muttered, feeling at last that they were getting closer to Robin.

Lightning growled in agreement, and with another bound he was airborne and wheeling to the south. He flew high over the valley's surrounding hills, and they were swooping over the broken ground which led to Care Diff.

* * *

From atop her vast mountain of a hoard, Firethorn watched an image of the vale flickering within the flames of a great fire crackling before her. "The knight is in play, only time will show who wins the game."

AIR DEFENCES

"The land of Silvan is defended by more than word, and wood."
Lightning to the Red Wizard.

Rose enjoyed her ride back to Care Diff. They stayed low to the ground for the most part. The tips of Lightning's wings, which looked as insubstantial as smoke, almost brushed tall outcrops of stone at points. Rose realised Lightning was keeping low to prevent a repeat of earlier.

"Lightning, can't we go higher?"

"If you wish?"

"I don't want to go too high," Rose said, and nearly gasped as Lightning's belly almost scraped a rock. "But if we don't climb I'm afraid you'll smash us on the rocks."

A rumble churned up from deep within Lightning's core, and for a moment Rose thought he was going to roar or spout fire. And indeed, smoke spumed from his nostrils, but when he shook under her she realised he was laughing, not roaring. Once he had recovered he beat his wings more vigorously and the ground dropped away as they climbed, and now Rose could see for miles.

"Better?"

"Yes, Lightning, much," Rose whispered, taking in the miles of land which were revealed to her.

The land that she and Lightning had trailed through when going to the Roaches had been barren and rocky, but she saw now that Lightning had made a path as straight as he could, for while the land that led from the Roaches to the elven city of Care Diff was rocky, the land which surrounded that strip was not. A great lake flashed at her from the east and to the west there marched a seemingly relentless wall of trees as a vast forest formed an almost impenetrable canopy.

"It's not as harsh as I thought."

"You like the North now?"

"I don't know about that, Lightning," Rose shouted, for now he was flying at a great pace, and the roar of the wind and the pounding of his wings made it hard to be heard. "But I must admit it does have a beauty all of its own."

"Care Diff coming up," Lightning remarked.

Rose looked from the canopy rushing past her under Lightning's right wing, and saw in front of them the huge tree of Care Diff, rising like a mountain before them. As they drew closer and the tree grew larger, Rose noticed small flying creatures rising from the branches of the tree.

"That tree is home to a lot of birds."

"Rose, we are still a mile out, those birds are as large as I am."

"What are they, then?"

"Most of them are Gryphons, but unless I am mistaken one of them is Storm Striker."

"Who?"

"The Lady Storm Striker, an Air Drake, and the head of Care Diff's winged guard."

"Care Diff has an airforce?" Rose asked, watching the creatures draw closer and larger as they drew nearer to them with alarming speed.

"The Kingdom is defended by more than spells and woods."

As they approached the city the flying creatures flew to meet them. Rose stared about her as the air above, below, and around them was filled with flying creatures. Several of them were the part cat, part birds they called Gryphons, but there were also the huge raven men and hanging over them all was the massive form Rose guessed was Storm Striker. The dragon reminded Rose of a huge bird more than the cat like Fire Drakes she had seen. The huge creature did not have bat wings, but massive feathered ones that beat the air in white, blue and black hues. Its scales too (for it was as much a snake as a bird), were the hues of the clouds. The dragon's head was more bird like, a large (perhaps a foot tall), crest topping its head. When it opened its jaws to screech in a high voice Rose saw it had a cruelly hooked beak. From between those jaws there leapt a blinding stroke of lightning that smote the air above them.

"Is she going to attack?" Rose asked, suddenly aware that she had left the weapons from her mother back at the mound for Eloo to bring with them, which meant that apart from a dagger, she was unarmed.

"No, she is signalling for us to land."

Lightning gently spiralled down to land in a large field to the north-east of the city's encircling walls. Rose looked about her, expecting some kind of welcoming committee, but there was no one, then a great cloud passed above them and Storm Striker dropped out of the sky to land before them. It was only now, when they were feet apart, that Rose realised this dragon too had a rider. Crouched on the dragon's long neck was a figure that closely resembled the dragon itself. It might have been taken at first glance as a huge bird, save for the fact that it was clearly a human form. Its long feathered upper limbs were arms and not wings. Its chest was protected by a gleaming breastplate, but its head was that of a hawk or other kind of hunting bird.

"Sir Falco," Lightning called out to the hawk-man. "A pleasure to see you again. Greetings, Lady Storm Striker."

"Greetings, Lightning," responded the hawk-man in a whistle of a voice. "Is this the Red Wizard that I have heard so much of?"

"I do wish people would stop calling me that!" Rose grumbled to herself.

"This is the Lady Rose Canduss," Lightning said, tossing his head backwards to nod in Rose's direction. "Rose, may I present Sir Falco, the captain of the wing and lance."

Rose bowed as low as she could over the high horn of her saddle. "A pleasure, my Lord Falco."

The captain returned her courtesy, bowing his head, and as he did his feathered cloak flared behind him. No, not a cloak, Rose saw. Although he was man shaped, a pair of huge feathered wings sprouted from his back like those of the Triplefold God's angels.

"Have we your permission to enter the city?" Lightning asked, fidgeting under the unblinking stare of the Air Drake.

"By all means," Falco said, appearing surprised by the question. "Though I might suggest that you take on a smaller form, the city is not made to accommodate a drake of your size."

"Thank you for your words of wisdom," Lightning said, dipping his head.

Just as Rose thought they had been dismissed Storm Striker finally spoke, in a surprisingly deep voice that sounded more like the purring of a large cat than the screech of a bird or the hiss of a snake.

"Lightning, how is your aunt?"

"Fine when we left her," Lightning replied, his whiskers twitching as if the question puzzled him.

"Has she any word for me?"

"Not that I know, my Lady," Lightning said, his voice showing his confusion.

This reply appeared not to please the larger dragon and with a hiss she turned away. Rose thought they were certainly dismissed, but the dragon appeared to think better of its actions, and turning its long serpentine neck to look over its shoulder said a farewell, if not an apology. "May luck go with you on your journey!"

With those words, the dragon's back legs coiled and the Air Drake sprang into the sky, the spreading of her wings a thunder clap that flattened the grass.

"Is she all right in the head?"

"The Lady Storm Striker? Yes, she is one of the wisest of our kind."

"She seems queer to me."

"Perhaps, but you do not know her."

"I'm not sure I wish to."

This made the great dragon quake with laughter beneath Rose. "Rose, would you be so kind as to dismount so that I can follow the knight's advice."

Lightning dropped his head, and loosening the straps around her legs she athletically stood up on the saddle and skipped across the saddle horn and onto Lightning's neck. She danced down his neck and jumped down to the ground.

"You're getting good at that," Lightning commented. "Now, would you be so kind as to remove the saddle?"

Rose unbuckled the saddle's girth, and as she did so she could not resist stroking his throat.

"Thank you, but could you stand back?"

She did so, the saddle in her arms, gazing up at the dragon before her. Lightning reared up on his hind legs, his wings spread to their full extent as he roared into the sky. Then he appeared to shrink before her, and as Rose blinked he was no longer the huge dragon but the tall, wiry man in his travel stained cloak and boots.

"Here, let me take that," Lightning said and taking the saddle from Rose, tucked it under one arm. With the other hand he took Rose's arm and led her towards the city.

"How long will we have to wait for the others?"

"It depends if Eloo and the other come on foot or if they use magic. Werewolves are swift, but even they cannot run all day and night."

"Thanks for no answer," Rose said sarcastically.

"What do you expect, when I don't know the answer," Lightning shot back.

"What do we do in the meantime?"

"We can either wait at the tower of the Eagle or explore the city. The decision is yours."

Rose stopped in her tracks, considering the options. She did want to see more of this strange city, but if she was honest with herself she was tired after the long day, and at that moment her stomach rumbled its protest.

"I think your stomach has decided the course of action for the moment," Lightning said, grinning. "The Tower of the Eagle, and a hot meal, then we can decide on other actions afterwards."

"Sounds good to me."

FINALLY GOING SOUTH

"Sometimes the destination is the journey."
Bright Eyes to Kye, the Wereding Chronicles.

Rose and Lightning had just finished a meal of bread and mutton stew when Emerald, the housekeeper of the Tower of the Eagle, entered carrying a scroll.

"Lord Lightning," Emerald said, bowing to the tall Fire Drake, "The Lady Takana left this here, if you should return."

"Thank you, Emerald," Lightning said, putting his plate to one side and accepting the scroll. He held it up to the candlelight so he could inspect the wax seal.

"What is it?" Rose asked, cutting a piece of cheese to polish off her meal.

Lightning did not answer for a moment, but breaking the seal flattened the parchment on his knee. As he did, something fell from the roll and tinkled across the floor to rest against Rose's foot. Glancing down, she saw it was a large gold ring.

"What's this?" she asked, retrieving the ring and holding it up to the light, seeing that it was one of the large gold rings members of the Fire School wore. "It looks like a fire ring."

"It is," Lightning said, looking up from the parchment. "To replace the one I lost. She asks me to take better care of this one."

"But how did she know you lost the first one?"

Lightning shrugged, obviously having no more idea than Rose.

"When can we start, Lightning?"

"I would guess first thing, if Kye and the others make good time."

Rose tried to hide her impatience and disappointment, but Lightning did not miss them.

"I know you want to be off, Rose," he said, sympathetically, "but believe me, it will be better waiting for them. I tell you what, while we're waiting why don't we make as much of the time as we can. Why don't we practice a little magic."

"What did you have in mind?"

"Seeing that ring gives me an idea. You now possess an earth ring, and the school of earth is all about strengthening and defending yourself. You might want to learn a few defensive spells so that next time we face Kain at least you can protect yourself against his magic."

"Like you did with that tiny shield?"

"That's the kind of thing I am talking about, yes, though you are not quite ready for that one yet."

"So what would you teach me?"

"Let's start with something simple, shall we," Lightning said, standing and crossing to where a large case of books stood against the wall, removing from the highest shelf a large and musty tome.

"That has spells in it?"

"This is a grimoire, yes," Lightning said, placing the book on the desk and flicking through its pages until he found what he wanted. "Here we are, the glance spell."

When he looked up it was to find Rose staring not at him or the book, but at the bookcase.

"Rose, is something wrong?"

"This was my father's tower, but there are spell books here?"

"Yes, of course..." Lightning trailed off, realising where she was going with this. "You did not know he studied magic."

"I suspected," Rose said, shrugging a shoulder. "But never knew."

"Well, shall we put his work to use?"

Rose shook herself and met Lightning's green eyes. "What must I do?"

Lightning checked the book, and nodding snapped it shut.

"This spell is called glance, because it means that attacks do not actually hit you but glance off your ward."

"It will turnaside arrows?"

"To a point, but it will not protect you entirely, well not at this level. As you become more powerful you will learn spells that will protect you from a giant's strike, but you aren't ready for that yet."

"So what do I do?"

"Just a moment, Rose, I think this might best be done outside, and there are a few things we need first," he said, ringing the bell.

"Yes, my Lady?" Emerald asked, appearing as if out of the air at Rose's side.

"It was Lightning that rang for you."

The tiny woman turned to face Lightning who was now staring into the flames of the fire and turning his new ring over and over in his hands.

"Emerald, I need some sand or something. I know, do you have rock salt?"

"But of course, Lord," Emerald said, looking slightly affronted that he would ask.

"Would you bring a handful and one of the practice swords outside?"

The little woman nodded and was gone.

"You're actually going to batter at me?"

"No, of course not," Lightning said aghast. "But I do need something to prove the spell works. If I can touch you with the blade we know it's not working."

Rose nodded and followed him out to the small flat clearing which lay at the feet of the Tower of the Eagle. No sooner than they had arrived than Emerald appeared at their side, a block of salt in one hand and a blunted longsword in the other.

"Are they what you wanted?"

"I couldn't ask for better," Lightning said, smiling at the tiny statue of a woman.

He took the longsword but held the salt out to Rose.

"A spell component?"

"You need earth, stone or sand to give its hardness to yourself, glass or obsidian would be best but salt should do."

Rose took the block of salt and weighed it in her hand.

"So what do I do?"

As Rose performed the spell the diamond ring on her hand appeared to pulse like a tiny heart on her fingers. She felt the ground quake beneath her, and the block of salt crumbled into nothing in her hand. At first she felt as if nothing had happened, then she noticed a slight glitter in the air around her. As she realised this, Lightning swung the blunted sword at her. Rose gasped and flung up an arm to block it. The sword did connect, but the blade did not actually touch her flesh, instead crashing against the glass bubble now surrounding her. As Lightning tried to force the blade home Rose heard a sound like something scratching against glass, and the blade slid off her arm.

"Did it work?"

Lightning's response was to lift the sword in a two handed grip and make a mighty swing at Rose. Rose was ready this time, however, and leapt to one side. The swing connected with the glittering halo and slid off it.

"It looks like it," was Lightning's comment.

Rose was about to give Lightning a mouthful when from nowhere an arrow flew out of the dark to strike at Rose's left breast. The arrow would have struck her heart and killed her, but as it neared her it was drawn as if by a magnet away from her heart and towards the hand that wore the diamond ring. The arrow fell spent at her feet.

"Rose!" Lightning cried, spinning around to look in the direction of the shot, the blunted sword held defensively in front of him, , his eyes searching the dimming dusk light.

Rose, too, spun in this direction, and stared with amazement when she saw Kye standing there, his great black longbow in hand.

"Kye?"

"She has mastered glance, it seems," was his hoarse response.

"Kye, the arrow could have killed her," Lightning shouted, his green eyes flaring with anger.

"Not that shaft," was Kye's reply.

"You don't know that," Lightning snarled, swelling in size, making Rose wonder if he was beginning to transform into a dragon.

"It was a blunted training arrow," Kye said, his face a stone mask as he faced Lightning's growing anger unmoving.

Then Rose realised that not only was Kye standing before them, but beside him stood Eloo and Silver Skin.

"You're here!"

"Yes," Eloo said, running forwards to jump into Rose's embrace. "We are here!"

"Then we can go south at last?"

"At last, yes," Silver Skin said, embracing Rose too. "Yes, Rose, at last we go to find your sister."

"Come," Eloo cried, as if speaking to the night, "to the road."

THE ROAD SOUTH

"The road is often not straight, but its twists can take you where you need to be rather than where you want to be."

The Prophecies of the Grey Pilgrim.

Rose's party did not set off that very moment as it was full night, but Rose did not need Emerald to wake her, she was up before dawn ready to leave. However, when she stepped out onto the tower's front steps, it was to find she was not the firstup. Kye was there with a handful of small horses laden with provisions. Feeling Rose's eyes on him, Kye removed the long stemmed pipe from his mouth and pointed with it off to the side. Following his pipe, Rose saw the great draconic form of Lightning glowing like a banked fire in the predawn light. To her delight, she saw Lightning was wearing his saddle. She strode to his side and moving to where his head rested on his forepaws, bent close to see if he was still asleep. As she reached out a tentative hand, his great eye cracked open and her face was lit by the green glow of his cat's eye.

"Ah, Rose, you are up before the birds," Lightning purred, and lifting his head, he pressed it against her hand like a cat.

Lightning's scales were hard as stone, but Rose shivered with pleasure at the gentle heat radiating from him, helping to drive out the chill of the morning.

"We are going to fly south?"

"We are, while Kye and the others stay on the ground," Lightning said, nodding in Kye's direction. "But first you should break your fast."

"Can't we do that on the wing?"

"Ah, my little Rose, you are too eager. We could, but it is difficult," Lightning said, stretching his long serpentine neck. "Break your fast, and then we can fly."

Rose made a face, but turning to the Tower of the Eagle went back to her roomwhere she found Eloo and Silver Skin waiting for her with breakfast.

"Rose, we were wondering where you had gotten to," Eloo said, shelling a boiled egg.

"I went to see where everyone was," Rose said, spearing her own egg on the point of her dagger.

"Eager, aren't we?"

"Yes, I am," Rose said, taking a huge bite of her egg.

"Don't eat too quickly," Silver Skin admonished her. "You'll only give yourself a bad stomach."

Rose grunted around an even bigger mouthful of egg.

"Once you're done eating," Eloo said, wrapping an oatcake round her bacon, "you can don your mother's gifts."

"But I am already wearing them," Rose said, holding up her hands before her so that the rings flashed in the candlelight.

"Eloo means the cloak and weapons," Silver Skin clarified, filling her own wrap of an oatcake.

Rose shrugged, but only for a moment, before she swallowed.

"What's so special about that cloak?"

"Apart from it being agift fromyour mother?"

Rose felt a little guilty at Silver's remark, but the tall Werewolf was right.

"Apart from that," Rose admitted.

"You used the mage eye spell, didn't you?"

"Yes, but that only tells me that it has some enchantment on it," Rose said. "Do you know what its properties are?"

"Did you not note the runes on the clasp?" Eloo asked, as rising she went to where the great cloak lay stretched across Rose's bed.

"What rune?"

"This one," Eloo said, holding the cloak up for her inspection.

"Oh, that rune."

The cloak was held together by a large gold shield like brooch, fashioned to resemble a flame like rune.

"It resembles some of the runes on my fire ring, but I don't know what it means."

"It is the protective fire rune," Eloo said, stalking round Rose, the cloak in hand.

"So?"

"So this cloak should provide you with some protection against fire," Eloo said, gently placing the heavy folds over Rose's shoulders and fastening the great brooch at her throat.

Rose shivered as the heaviness of the cloak settled about her, its folds falling about her with a feeling of doom. Rose felt as if Eloo had just fastened a shroud about her. No not that, don't think like that. Rose pushed the thoughts of death aside, but still she felt as if some weight more than the cloak had been placed upon her shoulders.

"Do I have to speak the rune or anything?"

"No," Eloo said, stepping back to admire Rose. "The rune is on the brooch and woven into the cloak, so that the magic is imbued into the cloth itself. Simply wearing it should protect whatever it covers."

"What of the bow and sword?"

Silver Skin, who had been looking closely at runes engraved into the sword's blade, glanced up and frowned as if she was translating and was not pleased with her translation. "This sword talon..."

"It has a name?"

"It does, and as I was saying. Talon has the power of flight."

"It can fly?"

"It can, though it was designed I guess to allow its wielder to fly," Silver Skin said, slamming the blade back into its woodenscabbard.

Silver Skin held out the sheathed sword to Rose, who taking the blade, held it horizontally before her, considering the eagle head. She could not explain why, but she had the feeling the eagle head was considering her with its bejewelled eyes.

"Flight," she murmured. "The words for this sword?"

"You will have to wait for that," Silver Skin said. "Time is pressing."

Rose did not disagree with that, and lifting the sword she looped its strap over one shoulder and let it hang down her back.

"Now the bow," Eloo said, hefting the recurved bow, and approaching Rose with it.

"Does this protect me from fire?"

"No, if the runes are right it gives the property of lightning to its arrows."

Rose took it from Eloo and as she did she felt a startling, but not painful shock of electricity. The jolt made Rose look more closely at the lightning like runes which bracketed and snaked about the bow's grip. "Lightning by name and lightning by nature."

Eloo started at these words. "Why did you say that, Rose?"

"I don't know," Rose said shrugging, but stopping when she glimpsed a look of amazement and resignation on Eloo's cat like face. "What?"

"The bow is called Lightning's Kiss," Eloo said, examining Rose. "And it seems that somehow you knew it."

"A guess," she said, in an attempt to make light of it.

Eloo's soul penetrating stare was thankfully broken by Kye's hoarse whisper from behind Rose. "Are you ready, the day is getting away from us."

"Ready and eager," Rose agreed, and turning found the tall Werewolf considering her almost as closely as his lover.

Kye may have seen something in his close scrutiny, but if he did he kept it to himself. Without another word he turned and led them out of the tower to where Lightning was impatiently flexing his wings.

"Nice cloak," he commented, when Rose stood at his side.

"I have a bow and arrows, is there somewhere I can strap them?"

"The saddle is ready for them," Lightning said, a smile in his cat like purr. "Climb on and you will see."

Lightning lowered his head and neck to Rose's level, and she swung up into the saddle to find (as Lightning had said), that it had two tube like sleeves which comfortably accepted the bow and its quiver.

"Ready back there?" Lightning asked, turning away from the tower and beginning to pace.

"Ready!"

Lightning grunted, and crouching, sprang into the air. His great wings snapped out and down to push them higher. Then before Rose knew where she was, they were airborne, the Tower of the Eagle falling away behind them. Rose screamed in joy as the wind tore at her long hair and snatched at her cloak.

"You enjoy flying as much as me, don't you?" Lightning roared into the wind.

"Yes!" Rose shouted, realising that she did. When the world fell away, and the wind tore at her, all her feelings of fear and confusion were left on the ground behind her and her spirit was lifted to the clouds.

On the ground, Lightning and Rose were watched by Kye, Eloo and Silver Skin.

"A natural dragon rider," Eloo said, grinning from cat like pointed ear to ear.

"Perhaps, but is she ready for this road?"

"Are you Kye, am I?" Silver Skin said, a grim tone to her question.

"Whether we are ready or not, we had better set off or they will be at the Kings before the day is through."

Rose and Lightning flew through the morning, sweeping over the woods and coming to the clearing that the Centaurs of the Silver Guard had led them to by noon. As they soared over the great trees and headed towards the clearing, they were greeted by an unexpected guardian. As Lightning slackened the beat of his great wings and began to fold them for a dive, a bird like scream rang out and a great feathered form almost as large as Lightning swooped up at them from the clearing below. Lightning swerved aside, and spreading his wings hovered in place as they considered what threat may be facing them. Rose saw to her amazed wonder it was one of the cat-bird Gryphons, and seated on its back was one of the statuesque Amazons. Rose stared at the bronzed woman with her waistlength black hair and blinked when she realised the woman was pointing anarrow at her.

"Who are yeh? And what be yeh purpose in the Elf lands?" shouted the woman, in an accent so thick you could have cut it with a knife.

"We are friends, Raven's Wing," Lightning roared back. "I am Lightning, and this is Rose Canduss, an Elf friend."

At that the hawk's head topping the Gryphon opened its hooked beak and screamed. The great feathered wings folded, and the bird dropped below them.

"She believes us?"

"Probably not," Lightning growled back, "but I think that Wind Rider recognised me."

"Wind who?"

"The Gryphon, it is probable that he recognised my scent."

Before Rose could ask another question Lightning was stooping, and the ground was rushing up at them. Rose closed her eyes as she saw the huge stump at the clearings centre rushing up at them, but when she thought that they must mash into it with bone crushing force, there was a great crack. Rose's stomach, which had risen in her throat, suddenly came to a jolting halt. When she reluctantly opened her eyes it was to see Lightning had opened his wings at the last moment and somehow stopped his plunge only feet above the huge stump that acted as a launching point for the Gryphon. Rose gasped with relief as Lightning folded his wings and landed with a clack of claws on the stump. From there he leapt down to the ground, where Lor, Kye's brother, was waiting for them, though he was not alone. Beside him stood one of the tall Amazons. Rose was not sure if the leather clad woman was the same one who had just greeted them.

"Good to see you again, Rose," Lor said, as Rose vaulted from Lightning's neck. "May I present Flight captain Star Strider, lady captain of the Golden Winged."

"Charmed, I'm sure," Rose said, giving the tall woman a short bow.

As Rose completed her bow, she was sure that this woman was not the one astride the hawk Gryphon. That one had black hair, but this one had a honey gold shoulder length mane and wore about her neck a large war horn. She regarded Rose with the blackest eyes Rose had ever seen.

"We are sorry for our greeting, lady," the woman said in a voice as deep as the sea, though at least her accent was not as hard to understand. "We had not heard that Lightning had returned to us and did not know you. If Lor had not brought word to me of you, we may have attacked you."

For a long moment Rose did not know how to react to this, other than to shudder, for she had seen the hawk's beak, and its talons were almost as long as her arm.

"Then I am glad that Lor was swift," Rose eventually squeaked.

The tall woman nodded, and turning to Lor bent to give him a kiss on the cheek.

"I will see you later, my Grey Lord." Without another word, the woman strode away.

Watching her leave Rose saw her stride to the side of the clearing, where at least three Gryphons stood waiting for their riders. Rose would have turned back to Lor, to ask him about his relationship with this god like woman, but she was captivated by the strange beauty of the winged steeds. Rose had thought that all Gryphons had the bodies of lions and the heads and wings of hawks, but she saw now that she had only seen one kind of this strange beast. Under the trees there crouched at least three different beasts. One had the jet body of a panther and the head and wings of a raven. Its brother had the black and yellow stripes of a tiger and the head of an eagle. Finally, the one that crouched alone as if it was apart from the others, had the white pelt of a snow leopard and the mask like face of an owl.

If the steeds were as different from one to another, it was nothing to their riders. Standing to one side of their steeds stood a small crowd of the tall women. One of them was the black maned hawk Gryphon rider, but at her side in black raven feathered cloak and raven winged helmet there stood a woman of the same statue like build and features, but with skin as black as the raven wings atop her helm. As Rose examined the woman, she realised the women were as different and as like their steeds. The white leopard's rider had milk white skin, and a cloak of white feathers. Her scanty leathers were bleached white. The tiger rider wore no cloak, but had a necklace of tiger claws about her swan like neck.

"They are beautiful, aren't they?" Lor said, his voice in Rose's ear.

"Yes, they are," Rose admitted grudgingly.

"As beautiful as one of the cats, and as deadly."

"You seem familiar with this woman?"

"Star Strider," Lor said chuckling, though his voice was sober enough when he continued. "She has a soft spot for me it is true, but I am not her lover, thank the gods."

This made Rose turn and look at him.

"She is an Amazon after the traditions of old," Lor explained, to a blank Rose. "They live in a society in which men are little more than slaves and it is said, though not known, that they keep their husbands locked up most of the year until they grow needful..."

"For company," Lightning finished for Lor, who was struggling for a way to spare Rose's blushes. "Enough of the Amazons, are the rest of our party here yet?"

"Yes, they are waiting for you to join them for dinner with what is left of the Silver Guard," Lor said, nodding to the trees to the south.

"Wind Fist?"

"I'm afraid not," Lor said, beckoning her to follow him. "Most of the silver Guard have gone south."

Rose was turning back to Lightning to ask if he was joining them, only to see him leap onto the stump, and from there into the sky.

"Where is he off to?"

"To find his own meal, I would guess," Lor said, watching the dragon fly back to the north.

"But where..." Rose broke off, realising Lightning would probably hunt something for his meal.

"Most Fire Drakes prefer to hunt and kill deer or something of the like," Lor said, reading her thoughts. "But come, our deer awaits."

As it turned out Lor was quite right, the few Centaurs who waited on them provided a venison stew, fresh black bread and goats cheese and a selection of fruit.

"A fine meal, Sunset," Eloo complimented the Centaur who had been left in charge of the token guard that protected the Green Gates.

"Thank you, my Princess," the red haired Centaur said in his gravelly voice. "I am only sorry that we could not offer you better than our garrison rations."

"Sunset, that is a better meal than I have eaten in weeks," Eloo said, smiling up at the giant.

The great Centaur bowed his head, and turning left the companions to themselves. Lea lit his pipe and was the first one to break the silence. "So, Rose, how do you find travelling by dragon back?"

Rose wiped her mouth on the linen napkin the Centaurs had provided and considered the question.

"It's amazing..."

"I am pleased to hear it," said Lightning's whisper, which came to them as if on the wind. "Because if you are fed and watered, I am ready to move on."

Rose looked about for him but could see him nowhere. "Where is he?"

"He is probably awaiting you at the perch," Eloo said, grinning at Rose. "He has used a spell to speak to you."

Kye leapt to his feet and kicked dirt over the smouldering camp fire. With one hand he lifted Rose to her feet, and with the other Eloo.

"Shall we try the Grey Desert?"

"What about the Orcs?"

"The Shield has swept the ruins clear," Lor claimed. "We won't be bothered, I promise you."

THE RUINS FROM DRAGON BACK

"Only on the wing can you understand the breadth of the world."
Lightning, the Wereding Chronicles.

Eloo was right, Lightning was ready and waiting for her back on the stump. Rose was wondering how she was going to get up to his six foot perch when Eloo sidled up beside her. "You are wondering how to get up to him?"

Rose nodded.

"Use your magic."

"What? How?"

"Concentrate on the air stone. Summon its magic and then say these words," Eloo whispered the magical words into Rose's ear, and then standing back from her showed her how.

As Rose watched, Eloo appeared to become lighter than air and float up to the stump. Closing her eyes, she did as Eloo had instructed and focused her mind on the emerald in the air ring. As she did, she felt a wind blowing around her and as she whispered the words Eloo had taught her, suddenly felt lighter. When she opened her eyes it was to find to her shock that she was floating several feet off the ground.

"How do I control it?"

"Think about your goal, where do you want to be? Concentrate on that goal, and you will be there."

Rose concentrated on Lightning's saddle, and suddenly she was hovering beside him.

"Excellent," he cried with delight and swiftly maneuvered his neck so that the saddle was placed beneath her, allowing a tiring Rose to release her concentration and sink down gratefully.

"That was hard," she said wiping a hand across a dewy brow.

"That is not a powerful spell," Lightning purred to her, "in itself, but it is difficult because it strains the mind. It is a useful spell to train your mind's muscles. Congratulations, you performed like a true mage."

"I hope I don't have to do it for a while," Rose said after sliding her legs into their saddle straps and tightening them so that she was secure.

"Oh no, we are flying for the rest of the day." With that he made a huge bound and they were airborne, climbing in great wheeling sweeps.

When Rose glanced down it was to see a narrow strip of green before her, the trees they had just left. Then as she looked forwards there was a straight line of green which seemed to go on and on as far as the eye could see to east or west.

"That is the hedge?"

"Yes, that is the wall that the green gates break," Lightning said, dropping slightly so that she could see a little clearer. "And beyond it is the grey desert."

Rose was about to ask Lightning a question when he beat his wings twice and they were beyond the hedge, probably ten feet thick. Rose could now see the dead land she had once travelled through. Before her stretched the grey landscape of broken towers and gaping holes which had been buildings. It was different than the last time she had been here, for the grey land now bore marks of war. Some of the buildings had been blasted away and new scorch marks etched the buildings. If Rose could see them from this far up, she realised that they must be on a huge scale.

"There has been battle here!"

Rose was about to ask Lightning more about the battle when she spotted a flicker of movement out of the corner of her eye. Turning her head, she saw they were not alone up here. Gliding thirty feet off Lightning's right wing was the raven-panther Gryphon, her black rider's feathered cloak flowing out behind her like a set of wings.

"Lightning, we have company!"

"Yes, the Golden Winged are giving us an escort through the

desert," Lightning said without turning his head. "Did not Eloo mention it?"

"No, she must have forgotten!"

Looking to her left Rose saw a second Gryphon, the owl-snow leopard creature was on that side. The white woman on its back, seeing Rose's glance, raised a javelin in salute and Rose nodded back.

"What about the others, are they going through on their own?"

"Look down and you will see."

When Rose glanced down, she realised Lightning had dropped lower. Now they were only a tall tree's height above the ruins, and just below Lightning's belly was Kye leading a pair of the small horses, Eloo on one of their backs.

"They're alone."

"Look forwards."

Rose followed Lightning's advice and saw a line of deer forming a thin screen before the small party.

"Deer?"

"Look again."

Rose did, and realised that they were not deer exactly, but rather the deer like Centaurs, the Heorotaura, like Firethorn's servant Velvet.

"They are guiding them through?"

"Yes, though the Amazons assure me that they have driven every Goblin out of the ruins."

"And you believe them?"

A tremor vibrated through the saddle and into Roses lower body. She realised Lightning was chuckling.

"Let's say that I believe that the Amazons believe it."

"Then I should keep an eye out, and my bow ready?"

"If you feel it is necessary," Lightning rumbled back, as he climbed higher so that they could avoid a towering ruin. "But I hope you will not need it."

"My father used to say hope for the best, but prepare for the worst," Rose said, drawing the bow from its sheath.

"Your father sounds like a very wise man."

"He was." Rose's voice cracked and she wiped a tear from her eye, but the next moment she was scanning the nearest ruin for Goblins.

Despite Rose's vigilance, when they landed to camp that night they had not seen so much as a Goblin's whisker. The party did not hide in one of the ruins this time, but camped in a large plaza in the middle of the ruins. When Lightning landed with a clatter of claws on the hard grey surface of the square, Eloo had kindled a large fire and the Deer Centaurs had formed a protective circle, their pointed antlers facing out, like a defensive circle of tiny spears that cast strange shadows on the walls of the ruins that rose around them.

"Is it safe camping out in the open here?"

Rose looked up sharply at a clatter from the top of one of the nearby ruins, but to her relief it was not a horde of Goblins disturbing the rubble but the great panther Gryphon landing above them. Her raven cloaked rider gazed down, not at Rose, but scanning the buildings which stretched around them.

"With the Golden Winged and the Shield watching over us we will be fine," Lightning reassured her.

Rose was not as sure as Lightning, but nevertheless she swung out of the saddle and dropped to the ground as soon as Lightning lowered her. Coming to the fire, she was immediately aware of a stomach rumbling smell coming from the kettle Kye was hanging over the flames.

"What is that smell?"

"Kye has brought some wild boar with him," Eloo said, drool all but dripping from her own mouth. "Say what you will about Kye, but he does know how to cook."

Eloo was right, when Kye handed Rose a bowl of the thick stew it was delicious. The boar was full of flavour, and the sauce tasted faintly of garlic.

"Eloo, I can see why you and Kye are mates," Lightning, now in his human form said, mopping his bowl with some black bread.

For some reason Rose blushed when Lightning said this and had to look away from him, only to catch Eloo's eyes and blush even more when the tiny elf woman gave her a wicked grin and wink. Seeking to change the discussion and prevent anyone from noticing her embarrassment, she turned to Kye and asked the question that was on her mind. "Where are we headed?"

"At first the Birches, and my treehouse."

"And after that?"

"The Kings."

"And where...what are the Kings?"

"Lea." Kye, in the middle of filling his pipe, pointed at his younger brother. "You are the Bard, tell Rose something of the Twins."

"Rose, have you never heard of the Twins?"

"No Lea, I can't say that I have. What are they?"

"You do know that the border of our and your lands are separated, though?"

"Yes, the Watcher's Wall stands as a border between our lands."

"The Sylvan Kingdom does not start on the other side of that wall," Lea said, accepting a wine skin from Lor. "Beyond the wall is a border land, a land like the grey desert left over from the time of burning. It is here that Goblins, Orcs and their like breed. On the other side of this badlands, on the northern side, stands a line of fortresses and watch towers. Our version of your Watch Wall. The Kings, or Twins as they are often called, is one of these fortresses, and is the strongest and the main gateway to the south."

"And our way to Robin?"

"Precisely, if Tristian will let us pass," Silver Skin said, passing the skin to Rose.

Rose found the wine very strong and spiced as if it had been mulled, though it was not hot. She took a long draught from it, and then passing it to Lightning asked her next question. "And who is Tristian, and why might he prevent our path south?"

Lea explained in his deep musical voice, and Rose leaned back on Lightning's strong shoulder and stared into the fire, his words conjuring images from the red flames. Perhaps it was the wine, but as Rose watched the flames appeared to twist and writhe into the faces and places Lea spoke of, as if his words had cast some magic over the flames.

"Tristian Silverbrow, or the White Wolf, is our grandsire, and as far as I know the oldest of our kind..."

"How old?"

As Rose watched the image of a long face with green eyes sink into the flames, she could feel without looking the glance that Lea aimed at Kye. A glance which asked Kye's permission to reveal some secret. Neither did Rose need to see the shake of Kye's shaggy head in denial.

"It is not known, but from what I can tell he is older than the time of Burning. However, his age is not the point, the point is that he is the White Wolf, and Shield of the North."

"Is that something like the Healms and the Warder of the North?"

"Something like and unlike," Lea conceded. "Tristian is the Guardian of the Badlands, and protects us from the Orcs and their like. It is his duty and right to control the gates to the Kings. If he deems it wise, he will deny us passage through his gates."

Rose should get animated and angry atthis, but she was too tired to gather herself. Perhaps she had drunk too much wine.

"He must give us permission..." Rose managed to yawn this out before she fell asleep.

"Only time will tell," Lightning answered her, laying her head on a rolled cloak.

"Aye," Kye said, taking a great gulp of wine. "Only time will tell if the White Wolf will bend to the Rose."

THE MIND OF A WOLF

"The mind of an immortal is an unknowable thing. It is as huge and filled as a palace and as slow and deadly as a glacier."
The Red Wizard for the Wereding Chronicles.

Rose did not sleep long, for when she woke it was still dark and the fire had burnt low. When she turned her head she saw Lightning lying beside her, his head on his arm, though his green eyes flickered open when she turned to look at him as if he had only been waiting for her to look at him.

"You are awake," Lightning asked, sitting up, and looking across her said, "Kye, Rose cannot sleep either."

"Is everyone awake?"

"No, the twins are dead to the world, but it won't hurt to talk. We won't wake them."

"Then perhaps you can tell me about this White Wolf. Is he anything like Flash?"

"Like and unlike, if anything he is probably closest to Kye in looks, and mind. I could not say really, Rose, I have only met him once."

"Will he let us pass south, do you think?"

"I think so, but I am not sure."

She went to ask another question, startled as a figure loomed over her, but when the figure bent near she realised it was Kye.

"Lightning is correct when he says that I am like Tristian. We are similar in thought, but even I could not say what his decision might be. We must simply go to him in the hope that he will permitus passage."

"And if he won't?"

"We will burn that bridge once we have crossed it," Kye whispered as the night brightened behind his head. "But we have not reached that bridge yet, and the sun rises. It is time to rise and meet the day."

$$* * *$$

As Rose and her party were awakening to the dawn, in the south Tristian Silverbrow, the White Wolf, was watching over the desert of the Badlands from the top of his tower, his dark green eyes glinting in the dimness of the night. When he spoke, his whisper was whipped away by the wind, which tugged at his cloak and his mane of snow white hair. "Where are they? I can feel they're out there, but I can't find them."

His whisper was answered by a deep purring voice on the wind. "Sleepless again, my lord?"

"I will not sleep well until I can crush the vermin."

The voice on the wind materialised into a tall woman, wrapped in white robes. The wind made her snow white hair stream out behind her as she moved to his side.

"But you say you cannot find them?"

"I have scryed the Badlands, but much of it is veiled to my sight."

These words drew a deep, animalistic growl from the white woman.

"You mean someone is blocking your sight?"

"I suspect so."

"But who possesses the power to block someone as powerful as you?"

Tristian turned to face his lady, and even she took a step back from the look in his deep green pools.

"I suspect that an old enemy has returned to plague me."

"Who?"

Tristian turned away from her for a moment, as if considering his answer and the land before him at the same time. Then he turned back to her and the look on his face shocked her, for his face was usually a mask.

"I fear that the Wraith King has returned."

The White woman growled like a great jungle cat, but after this shocked response she stepped to her lord and wrapped him in her cloak and embrace. When she spoke, it was in a husky whisper, and into his ear. "Are you sure?"

"No, but he at least would have the power."

"You have defeated him before, you will do so again."

"With you at my side, I feel that I can do anything."

"So come back to bed, and rest."

Tristian stepped back from her and held her at arm's length, staring into her dark black eyes. A smile flickered at his lips.

"I am not sure that I will sleep now."

"Then return to our bed, and I will relax you."

"Relaxation is not what you have in mind."

With a swirl of cloak and hair she spun out of his arms, her back to him. She looked back at him, over her shoulder, her grin mischievous.

"If my lord is displeased with me, he should punish me…"

Her words pulled a deep growl from Tristian. "But first he must catch me."

THE BIRCHES

"A Werewolf might be all but immortal, but they should not forget to appreciate a single moment of their life."

The Book of the Wolf.

The rest of their journey through the ruins was harmless enough, although as Lightning swept over the trees on the other side of the desert they were met by a harmony of ghostly cries as a number of invisible wolves greeted them.

"Are they greeting us?"

"More likely they are greeting Kye, after all they are his brothers."

"I wonder what they are saying to him?"

"Welcome, brother I would guess. You can ask him in a moment, Rose. We will be at his treehouse in a few more wing beats."

"Where will we land, the clearing isn't that large and you can't mean to land on the tree itself!"

"Don't worry, we will land at the stone gate."

"The arch?"

Rose shivered, remembering the stone door and the shadow of the memories of the fight with the wolf like man, Kain.

"Is that a problem?"

"No!"

"Because, if it is we can find somewhere else."

"No, it's fine."

Lightning did not press the point, but as the bear hill and its stone structure appeared he raised the issue once more. "Are you sure about this?"

"Lightning, please land and we can leave this place."

"As you wish."

As they came into land, Rose saw out of the corner of her eye a flicker of movement. Imagining Kain waiting with his black blade she drew her sword and turned in that direction, but found to her relief and surprise it was not the wolf helmed assassin, but an actual wolf standing at the edge of the trees. As Rose watched, the grey wolf sat back on its haunches and let loose the long mournful cry which has haunted man since the beginning of time. Rose shivered, for even after all this time of being around the Werewolves and their kin she still had not gotten used to the cry. She realised the wolf was somehow connected to Kye.

"Black Tail is letting the rest of the pack know we have arrived," Lightning reassured Rose, feeling her shiver.

Lightning was proved right. By the time she had dismounted a small pack of wolves had appeared out of the trees to form a circle around them. They kept their distance and appeared to be waiting for something. Rose was worrying they were about to attack when Kye appeared at the largest wolf's shoulder, his blue eyes fixed on Rose as if the wolves did not exist. The illusion vanished as the great grey with the white stripe down its back lay at Kye's feet and the rest of the wolves flowed to Kye. He hunched down and the wolves crowded round him. Once before Rose had thought wolves were attacking Kye and then it had been Lea and Lor in wolf form, and as then she realised she was wrong. The wolves were not biting Kye but licking him. Kye flung back his head and unleashed a long howl of his own which the wolves followed, and then they were running into the trees, leaving Kye watching after them.

"Is he their father, their brother, or their master?"

"Probably all and none of them. These things are never simple."

Rose thought that her and Lightning's last words had not been overheard by Kye, but Kye's hearing was better than she had suspected. He answered her as he strode up the hill to them. "Root and branch may bind, but they are not as strong as the links between wolf and werewolf."

"Or as tangled, it would appear," Lightning said.

"Was it you the wolves were greeting when they howled at us?"

Kye inclined his head in answer. "Fang and his pack are not my pets, but our bonds are strong. He is pleased to know I have returned to them, if only for a brief time."

"But how can they know that you will not stay?"

"Because, Rose, I have told them."

"And they are happy with that?"

"Wolves do not think like humans, but Fang understands that a threat has come to our woods and he will patrol as far as he can."

"You asked him to do this?"

They and Lightning (now in man form), were moving through the trees by now and Rose was paying more attention to where she put her feet than to Kye, so she did not see the grimace that crossed his face.

"As I have said, Fang is not a pet. He does not obey me. He does what he wants, *when* he wants."

"But he will help us?"

"In his own way. We may come across him again as we move south, that is all I can say."

"And when will that be?"

Kye stopped at that and turned to face Rose. "Rose, we will not move till tomorrow."

"But..."

"Rose, we cannot travel through the Birches at night."

"But we did before, what's changed?"

"These parts of the Birches belong to the clan, but as we move south we enter land claimed by other Werewolf clans. It would not be safe to try moving through them at night."

"So another night is wasted!"

"That depends on what you consider waste?"

"Say what?"

"Eloo is baking bread, and there is a stew on the fire. Lea will give us a recital; does that sound like a waste of time?"

"Well, no...but I'm not getting any closer to Robin!"

"Rose, you have travelled from the Repository to the Birches in a few days. It usually takes weeks."

Rose opened her mouth to object, but realising she had lost the argument she shrugged and followed Kye in resigned silence. When they reached the tree house it was to find exactly the scene Kye had described. The bread was delicious, and the venison stew even better. Perhaps the best part of the evening was Lea's performance, consisting of a story set before the time of Burning, of a powerful wizard, who, persecuted by his own people, battled against demons to protect his world. Although this wizard (Bain), defeated his enemy, it was uncertain if he survived the battle. Long after everyone had gone to sleep, Rose was still left wondering if the story was simply Lea's imagination or if she had been told a piece of history, forgotten or unknown by the rest of the world. It was a question she had not answered by the time Silver Skin woke them to a glorious morning, free of clouds.

"Good flying weather," Lightning said, wolfing down his breakfast.

Rose smiled at him, knowing he was saying this for her benefit.

"We will leave the Birches and travel south into the Long wood."

"Kye, last night you said the land south of here was ruled by other Werewolf clans," Rose asked.

Kye nodded, not having swallowed his breakfast. "Directly to our south lie the White Head clan and to the west the Grey Backs."

"But we can pass through there, right?"

"We believe so."

"You *believe* so! What does that mean?"

"It means, Rose, that I sent ravens asking their captains if we may, but there are many hawks between here and Tall Tree and Fountain Head. They may not have arrived."

"And if they haven't, or they don't allow us to pass?"

"Then we will be hunted by a pack of Werewolves," was Kye's emotionless reply.

"Don't look so grim, Rose," Lea said, grinning largely. "You and Lightning will be in the sky and won't have to face them."

"That isn't fair..."

"Enough," Kye snapped. "The day is growing old. Let us be on our way."

As the others gathered the small horses they were using to carry their supplies, Rose and Lightning returned to the small hill. Rose watched as Lightning shifted from the form of a man into the huge scarlet scaled shape of a dragon. He stripped off his cloak, tunic and boots and stood for a moment naked before her. Then stretching his arms over his head, he growled deep in his chest. As she watched, his form swelled and his red hair spread down his face, becoming scales rolling down his body. Rose found the experience had taken her breath away. She had to calm herself and she tried to do so by reaching out and stroking one of the great horns growing out of the back of Lightning's cat like head. The horns were a paler red (more rose than fire), than the rest of his body. Rose had hoped that this gesture would calm her, but for some reason she found her breathing had not calmed. Lightning did not help when he half closed his glowing, green eyes and made a deep purring noise that vibrated through her hand, up her arm, to her heart. It was only once Rose had removed her hand that her breathing steadied. It was made more difficult as she had to place the saddle on Lightning's neck.

When she cinched the strap she wondered what it felt like to him to have such a collar.

"Not too tight?"

"No, Rose, it's fine. Are you ready?"

Rose stepped back and Lightning lay his head on the ground so that all Rose had to do was place one leg in the sheath and swing her leg and body across him, as if he were a horse. Most horses did not carry you on their necks, Rose thought as she cinched the leg straps tight.

"Comfortable?"

"As I'll ever be."

"Then let's go."

Lightning began to run around the hill top, and at the second circuit he unfurled his wings with a great snap, and at the same time made a huge bound that carried him into the air. His wings beat strongly, and before Rose knew where she was they were high above the bare hill and a sea of trees spread out before them.

"Is that the Long Forest?"

"Not yet, that is the Birches."

"Where does one end and the other begin?"

"There is a clearly defined line of totems that mark out the borders."

"Will we be able to see them from up here?"

"Yes, they are quite clear even from up here."

Rose stared at the canopy, looking for the markers. For a long time she saw nothing other than endless trees, but all at once the trees ended and a great break that spread from east to west appeared between the trees they had just flown over, and a second wall. Lightning swooped lower so they could see the ground more clearly. The break was not featureless, standing at what might have been regular intervals were tall poles of wood, stone or even in one case metal, adorned with feathers, skulls and even a huge animal pelt.

"So these mark the end of the Birches?"

"Yes, which is why Kye is being careful."

Rose had not noticed Kye, but as she looked around she saw that Fang and another wolf were sniffing around two of the poles, and a moment later Kye and the lead horse appeared out of the trees.

"We're not alone."

TALL TREES

"Werewolves may live in different clans, but they are often related nonetheless."

The Book of the Wolf.

L ightning's comment alerted Rose to a pair of figures now emerging from the southern trees.

"Other Werewolves?"

"Members of the White Head clan, I would guess."

The name White Head was appropriate since both of the tall figures had long white-blond hair blowing around them.

"They are armed."

"They're Werewolves," responded Lightning.

As Rose watched, the two parties of Werewolves stopped on either side of the line of poles and appeared to talk. Then Kye passed between two of the poles and embraced one of the figures.

"Looks like Kye's making friends."

"He is greeting a fellow Werewolf, I think that means we can continue."

Lightning's words were proved right moments later when Silver Skin waved at them and used her staff to point to the trees.

"Silver agrees with you."

They flew on for about another ten minutes over the trees until a large lake appeared below them. In the centre of this lake was a large flat rock of an island.

"That looks as good a place as anywhere."

"For what?"

"For a landing."

Rose wanted to ask Lightning why they must land, but her voice along with her stomach leapt into her throat as Lightning dropped like astone, to come to an abrupt stop just a few feet from the flat rock.

"L. please don't do that again!"

"Sorry. Sometimes I forget about yourinnards."

"Well I can't."

Lightning landed with a clack of claw on stone.

"Why are we stopping here?"

"Because I can't fly all day on an empty stomach. I need to hunt, Rose, and you need to meet the Werewolves that are waiting for us. You can do it while I hunt for a little time."

Rose bit back her protests of time wasted, but her own stomach was grumbling and she knew she could not deny him. When Lightning lowered his head she dismounted to find Eloo waiting for her already.

"The White Head clan are waiting for us at Tall Tree, Rose, but they may not be expecting someone like you. Perhaps you want to use your mask."

Rose had almost forgotten the mask, hanging round her neck. She pulled the mask up to her face and found its touch soft, like a second skin. She concentrated on how she remembered her face and looked to Eloo to gauge her reaction.

"Very good, just how you looked when you first came to us."

"But it isn't how I look, is it?"

Her tone of despair and pain touched Eloo, and she placed a tiny, if strong hand on the taller girl's arm.

"It is what is beneath the skin that matters, Rose, not the wrapping."

Rose opened her mouth to snap back some sharp tongued rebuke, but Eloo interrupted her. "But come, Starsheen and her pack mates are waiting for us."

Eloo led Rose to the edge of the water and stepped onto it. Rose thought at first Eloo was using some kind of magic, but looking more closely saw she was stepping onto rocks just below the surface of the water. She followed her, watching where she put her feet, and found that the stones allowed her to hardly touch the water.

"Starsheen, that name seems familiar."

"You saw her at the Moot."

"The Werewolf that gave Kye directions?"

"Well no, but yes, she was that scout."

"So she has come south?"

"Along with the rest of her pack there, yes, but here she is."

Rose looked up from the water to glance over Eloo's shoulder the approaching shorewhere a tall figure dressed in green and brown waited for them. Eloo skipped onto the bank and past the tall blonde girl to where Kye was leaning against a tree. Rose found herself facing the girl across a foot of water. The Werewolf girl was Rose's own height, and her green eyes met the girl's grey ones and saw a look of, what? The girl extended a hand to help Rose onto the bank. When she spoke, it was in a husky whisper, making Rose think of the rustling of leaves.

"Lady Canduss, I am Starsheen, may I welcome you to Tall Tree?"

Rose released the calloused paw and gave the girl a slight bow. "I thank you, Starsheen, for your hospitality."

Rose's courtly curtesy embarrassed the girl and she cast down her grey eyes, not knowing how to respond.

"Rose, for shame, you have embarrassed Starsheen." Eloo giggled.

The girl flinched and mumbled something.

"Starsheen, perhaps you would lead us to your father?"

The girl got a hold of herself at Kye's suggestion, and with a nod led them through a wood of huge trees to where their trunks drew back to form a large clearing. The sky could not be seen for at the centre of this clearing was a giant tree which towered above its neighbours.

"So that's why you call it Tall Tree?"

"Yes, my lady, and it is from here that My Lord Father White Mane rules."

"And these are all his people?"

The people Rose was referring to were a collection of the different Weredings she had come across at their capital, Care Diff. Centaurs galloped around the outskirts of the clearing, while a large group of huge rocky Trolls drilled with six foot long shafted axes. To one side there was a large group of the white maned Werewolves, practicing archery. Starsheen led them to this group of archers and stood with eyes downcast beside the tallest, a Werewolf with a mane so blond it was almost white. He may have been aware of them, but he concentrated on his shot, drawing the string back to his ear before loosing the arrow.

Only once the shaft thumped into the target did he turn his very pale grey eyes on Starsheen. When he spoke, it was in a deep growl which rumbled out of his chest. "Daughter, who have you brought to see me?"

"Friends and family from the north, Father."

The great Werewolf handed his long bow to another of the archers as he strode round them inspecting each with his pale, almost colourless grey eyes.

"Kye, it has been an age, hasn't it?"

"Uncle," Kye grunted, dropping to one knee in honour.

"Get up, nephew, I'm not the White Wolf. Ah, Princess Eloo, always a pleasure."

"As always you are most gracious, Lord White Mane."

When he came to Rose he stopped, and looked long and hard at her face.

"And what do we have here?"

"Father, this is the Lady Canduss."

"Ah, the young lady we have been hearing about."

Rose bowed gratefully, as she dipped below his grey eyes.

"Please, Lady, be welcome in my house. We are soon to go south, but you are welcome to our house until you wish to leave."

"You are going to war?"

"Yes, I have summoned my people to march to the Twins as I have been requested."

"I too wish to go south."

"To the Twins?"

"And beyond."

"If Tristian will allow it," Eloo added.

"Then it appears that your road and ours goes together, but come, where are my manners, you must be hungry, come dine."

He strode to the base of the tree where a trestle was set up. As they arrived at it a Heorotaura and a group of dwarfs began to serve them.

"Lady Canduss, do you take wine," the grey eyed lord asked, taking from the Deer Centaur a stone jug and pouring for them a blood red wine.

"I enjoy wine."

As she accepted a glass she remembered Kye's mulled wine, and how powerful that had been. So as she raised the glass she sniffed at its contents, but the flowery scent was pleasant not overpowering. So she gasped when the fiery liquid hit the back of her throat, almost choking her in its potency.

"You're not supposed to choke on it," Eloo said, slapping her on the back.

"I didn't expect it to be so strong."

This made White Mane laugh and, pouring her water, he passed it to her.

"Mix it with this and it might go down better."

"Thank you, Lord."

"I would have thought that being with Kye would have taught you to be used to our wine."

"I didn't think it would be as strong as the mulled wine."

White Mane laughed again at that, a deep belly laugh that rang like a great bell inside his chest. "I hope this has not spoiled your appetite."

Rose was about to say that it had, but as she formed the words Starsheen uncovered a bowl and a mouth-watering smell reached her and changed her mind.

"What is that?"

"Mushrooms," Starsheen said, plucking one out and offering it to her father.

"Mushrooms?"

"Cooked in butter and garlic. You want one?"

Rose had two of the heavenly mushrooms, followed by bread made with olives, and then lamb baked with mint and other herbs.

"Why do you want to go south, Lady Canduss?"

"You have heard of me, lord, you say, have you not heard of my quest?"

"We do not always hear the news out here, my Lady."

"I have very good reason to know that my sister, Robin, is in danger. I must reach her if I am to save her."

This made White Mane look up from his bowl and study her very closely.

"If that is the case, then we must speed you on your way."

"Are you ready to march?"

"Kye, you should know better, we are always ready to march."

With these words, White Mane turned to the tall Deer Centaur and took from him a long, curved horn mounted with gold. Putting it to his lips he gave a long, low blow. It was not loud, but still cut through the air, vibrating through the air and earth at the same time and filling the world with its note. This horn was the signal to mobilise it appeared, for at its tone the whole clearing and wood rustled with movement. Rose and her party were swept upin a swift movement of many bodies. The woods before them threwback the beating of hooves of Centaur and Heorotaura, and from behind them there came the heavy pounding of booted Dwarfs and from the bowels of the earth the pounding of stone Troll feet. Rose, however, felt as if she was moving in a bubble of silence. It was as though she were in the eye of a storm, the hooves and boots the rumble of thunder, but about her Werewolves moved with hardly a whisper as they slipped between trees. Rose wondered if Lightning would know what had happened, but somehow he had heard and was waiting in a large clearing that lay across their path. The remains of a great stag was spread bloodily before him, and with a word to the White maned Werewolf Rose was back in the saddle and in the air.

THE KINGS

"Many people live within the shadow of fortress, never thinking that they may see the war."

White Mane from the Wereding Chronicles.

Rose and Lightning flew for the rest of the day, but eventually the sun sank in the west. The dragon swooped down through thinning trees to find that the White Head column had stopped in its march to make camp. They had pitched tents or thrown up lean-tos and the camp felt very large to Rose.

"I didn't realise that the clan was so large."

"It has swollen along the way," Kye said, helping her down from Lightning's neck.

"More of the clan?"

"Yes, but we have also been joined by other groups of the Silver Shield."

Kye pointed to where a group of Centaurs were speaking with White Mane.

"Wind Fist?" Rose asked, hoping they had found the Centaur she met back at the Green Gates.

"Unfortunately, no," Eloo replied, passing Rose a water skin. "These are a different company, but I figure that he will be at the Kings already, and we will catch up with him there."

"How much further is it, Kye?"

"We should be there tomorrow or the next day."

"But until then, you shall rest in the company of Werewolves," Lea said, passing Kye a wine skin giving off a smell so potent Rose suspected it would kill her if she drank it.

Rose did not rest at first, instead Starsheen walked her around the camp, showing her the force going south. The Centaurs were not commanded by Wind Fist, but a black skinned and haired Centaur

136

called Woundwort. He was a dark contrast to his company, who were all white skinned and haired. Several of them were also women she noticed, a pleasant surprise. Until now she had not seen a female among the horse men. There were a few of the cat women, the Furies, who had the bodies of women atop the live bodies of great cats. There were only afew of these cat Centaurs, as they told Rose, their sisters were out of camp scouting the small army's route. They ended back at the tall, green and brown tent of White Mane, guarded by seven feet jet statues. These were a pair of Trolls who blocked their way with axes on six foot long shafts.

"Halt," one of the Trolls commanded in a voice sounding like gravel rattling together.

Rose thought they were about to be turned away when the tent flap was flung open and the blond head of White Mane looked out.

"It's all right Cile, let them pass."

The crossed axes parted, and Rose and Starsheen passed into the large tent to find that the tall blond Werewolf was not alone. With him was a tall figure whose arms were covered in feathers, her form familiar.

"Takana!" Rose exclaimed, thinking it was the fire sorceress, but when the tall woman turned to face her Rose saw she was mistaken.

This tall woman was a Harpy, but she was not Takana. Nor was she Storm Strider, the Harpy she had met only a day ago. This harpy's wings were colourless, or rather they were a rainbow of colours, for the shades of her feathers appeared to change as they caught the light. One moment they were Takana's fire red, the next they were Storm Striker's raven black. The next they were blue, almost black, and then they were red and black with white tips. Her waist long hair, however, did not change colour from a snowy white.

"Greetings, Lady Canduss," the Harpy greeted her, in a voice that came to Rose like a tinkle of rain as it trickled into her ears.

"I am sorry, I thought you were Takana."

"No apology is necessary, you are not the first and will probably not be the last to mistake me for one of my sisters."

"Rose, Lady Canduss, this is Wave Walker Snow Cloud," White Mane introduced her. "She has come from the Twins to gather help for the Kings."

"Are they under attack?"

"Not yet, not when I left them two days ago, but if we are right Tristian will need all the help he can get."

"That bad?"

"We are not sure, but if what he figures is right, Tristian will be facing an army of Darklings."

"Then will he let me pass to the south?"

"The South?"

"The Lady Canduss wishes to pass through the Kings, the barrens and to the lands in the south."

At hearing this the tall woman frowned, her blue eyes darkening as if a clear sky had blackened with rain clouds.

"I will not speak for the White Wolf, but even if he did grant you permission you might be wading your way through a Darkling hoard."

"But I must reach Robin!"

"Robin?"

"Her sister, my lady," White Mane explained to the Harpy, passing her a steaming cup. "She believes that she is in some kind of danger."

"I don't believe, I know."

The harpy Snow Cloud took a long draft from the cup and stalked up and down for a few minutes. Her wings changed from blue through to grey and eventually black.

"I will not speak for Tristian, only the White Witch may say she knows his mind better than he."

"Then let's ask him?"

Eloo, who had just entered the tent, smiled at Rose, and leaping up to the tall harpy's level kissed her on the cheek before dropping down to stand before her.

"It's not such a bad idea, Rose. My Lady, you could mind speak to the White Wolf. You are powerful enough."

"Eloo, my dear, it is a joy to see you too, but if it comes to that, White Mane or even your beloved Kye could mind speak to him. After all, they are his blood."

"The blood bond only allows us to communicate with those who are near, as you very well know, Snow Cloud," White Mane growled.

"But you could do it, couldn't you?"

"I wish I could, Eloo, but something, some dark power, is blocking any kind of scrying or communications with the Twins."

"That might explain why I have not been able to reach him," Silver Skin said, joining the group.

"So can you do it or not?"

"Not from here," the harpy admitted, after a long pause.

Rose turned in anger from them and was about to leave the group, when the harpy's next words reached her. "But if this is so important to you, I will try to do it in the river."

"In the river?"

"I am a Wave Walker, my craft is with water magic. There is only a small stream here, it is probably not enough to help me, but tomorrow we will meet the great Sabrina that feeds the Twins. There I will try to contact them for you."

"Then I thank you."

"There is no need to thank me, Lady Canduss, it will repay the debt I owe your house."

These words acted like an invisible chain linking Rose to the harpy, and it jerked her round to face the tall, feathered woman.

"Your debt to my house?"

Snow Cloud made a deep, and gracious bow, which swept her long mane near to the ground.

"Your father saved my life once, Lady. I owe your house this and more."

"He saved your life, when and how?"

"It is a long story, my lady, perhaps you would prefer to hear it over meat and drink, if White Mane will oblige."

"With pleasure," the blond Werewolf agreed. "I too, wish to hear this story."

Over goat stew and black bread the tall harpy told Rose how her father had found her shot down by an enemy's arrow, and had staunched the wound.

"However, the shaft was poisoned," the winged woman said, tearing a loaf apart. "And I might have died still, if he had not realised I was a being of water and lay me in a pool of natural water."

"I'm sorry, but how did that save you?"

"You must excuse Rose," Eloo explained to Snow Cloud. "She has not been raised in our ways."

"So I realised. We are fixed in one element. We need to be returned to that element if we can renew our beings and heal wounds to ourselves."

"So Lightning needs to feel fire to heal?"

"Yes, that is the way of it."

This left Rose with a lot to think about, and the rest of the party left her to her thoughts as they turned to other things. It was only when Rose realised she was half asleep on Lightning's shoulder that she recognised just how tired she was.

"You should get to bed," Lightning said, when Rose moved away from him.

"If the Lady Canduss would follow me, I would lead her to her tent."

"Tent, I have a tent, Starsheen?"

The slender Werewolf rose, and offering Rose a hand led her from White Mane's tent to where a small mushroom like tent had been erected.

"Bedding and your gear are within, and if you require anything else please let me know. I will see what we can do."

"Thank you, Starsheen, I am very grateful."

Starsheen bowed and was gone. Rose entered the tent to find a low camp bed set out for her, and a lamp hung from the central tent pole. As Rose disrobed, she found to her surprise she was still wearing the mask which she had forgotten about. Crossing to where a jug and basin lay beside her bed, she knelt and stared at her reflection in the water, to see looking back at her, her own, unblemished face.

"Did I really keep it up all this time?"

Rose peeled the mask off, dropped it beside her cloak and stared at her true face. The face staring back at her looked as if it were wearing a second mask, albeit a half mask. The left side of her face glowed blood red, the scales glittering in the dim light, her eye glowing like a baleful star back at her.

"I wonder will Robin even recognise me."

"Beauty comes from within, my Lady," Lightning said from behind her.

Rose had not heard him enter and she leapt to her feet.

"Don't do that to me, Lightning!"

"I am sorry, I only came to see if you needed anything?"

Rose looked at his long face and found herself thinking how her bed would be warmer with him lying beside her. She began to reach out to touch his cheek and caught herself, snatching her hand back.

"No, I'm fine, thank you."

"I will be nearby so if you need anything in the night please let me know."

Rose nearly cried out loud as Lightning's naked human form flashed before her mind's eye.

"Good night!" she managed to croak.

"Goodnight."

Rose stood there staring at the swinging tent flap where Lightning had been, but she wasn't seeing it. Her eyes were seeing the image of Lightning before her in just his skin and she tried to get over this image. She couldn't be thinking what she was thinking, but the image of Lightning naked before her moved to her and placed a fiery kiss on her mouth. Rose saw herself melting into that kiss, and then wrap her arms around Lightning...

"No!" she snarled, and shaking her head smashed the fantasy. "What is wrong with me, he is a dragon for God's sakes."

From somewhere within her own mind, a tiny voice whispered in response.

"Maybe, but he looks very good as a human doesn't he?"

"Who are you?"

"Your lusts."

"Then get lost."

Rose tried to close her mind to the images of Lightning. Turning to her bed, she flung herself down and tried to go to sleep, but no matter what she did her mind's eye kept returning to images of Lightning and her inner clinch. Eventually, Rose decided she had to do something to get her mind off these distracting thoughts. Getting up, she slung her cloak about her and stepped to the tent's entrance, pulling the flap back to look out on what lay outside. She gasped, taken aback by what she saw. Across her doorway lay the great glittering, red form of Lightning's dragon shape. She started back, hoping he hadn't noticed her, but she had not escaped his awareness.

"My lady, is something wrong?"

"No, I just can't sleep."

"Then please come join me, and we can be sleepless together."

Rose nodded, and leaving the tent moved up beside his head which lay on his long tail, curled about him.

"Why can't you sleep?"

Rose couldn't bring herself to answer him, so she changed the subject.

"It's cold tonight," she said, drawing her cloak closer about her.

"Please, my lady, sit against me, I will warm you."

"Against you..."

Rose shivered at the idea, though she couldn't say why. After all, she rode him all the time. Perhaps it was those thoughts which were still at the back of her mind, but this was Lightning as a dragon. She did as he suggested, and rested her back against his flank. Through her cloak, she could feel a wave of heat flow from him.

"You are hot."

"It is my nature, my lady, Fire Drakes generate heat."

Rose grunted, as she closed her eyes and began to nod, her half sleep interrupted as one of Lightning's great wings flicked down to half cover her in its warm darkness. Rose now felt as though she was in a warm tent, and closing her eyes was asleep.

When Rose woke it was to find to her shock the dragon gone and Lightning's human form naked beside her. The great red cloak was wrapped about them both, Rose's thin shift the only thing separating them. Rose started and leapt up, waking Lightning who stared up at her with shocked eyes.

"My lady, what is wrong?"

"You were a dragon."

Lightning gazed down at the hand he held out to her and looked shocked when he saw that it was flesh and not scales.

"I am sorry, my lady, I must have changed in the night."

"But what happened?"

Lightning's eyes widened, realising what she was asking. "My Lady, we slept, that's all."

"That's all?"

"My lady, I would never hurt you. I would never take advantage of you."

Rose did not speak. she could not, but she stared into his large green eyes looking for the truth she wanted to see.

"The problem, Lightning," she eventually said, "is I'm not sure if I'm disappointed that we didn't make love."

Lightning looked astonished at this, but after a moment he broke the tension between them by bursting into laughter.

"It's not a laughing matter," Rose snapped, before she broke up in laughter as she too realised they could only laugh or cry.

"Here, cover up before I change my mind," Rose said, tossing him his own cloak which had been flungaside the night before.

Lightning wrapped the cloak around him and followed Rose with his eyes as she went back into her tent to get washed and dressed. When she came back out, it was to find Lightning in human form, dressed, and talking to Eloo who was dancing around him, her cape and hair flicking like wings.

"What's up with her?" Rose asked, watching Eloo dash away.

"Taking my suggestion to Kye, I hope," Lightning answered her, and handed her a steaming cup.

"And what suggestion was that?"

"That we should not wait for White Mane and his party, but move on before them so that we can reach the Twins quicker."

"Really?"

"I am chafing under this slow pace, and if I know Kye he is staying with the Column because, technically, White Mane is his CO, but he would much rather be scouting than bringing up the rear."

"Thank you, Lightning," Rose said, and found herself hugging him in a tight embrace.

Lightning looked embarrassed and delighted at the same time. Rose broke the embrace when she realised her breasts were pressing tightly against Lightning's chest. Both of them did not know how to react, and both blushed, not knowing what to say or where to look. They were grateful when Eloo dashed up with Kye in tow.

"Kye thinks it's a great idea," Eloo cried, before she reached them.

"So we can move at our own speed?"

Kye nodded, and handed Lightning the bread and cheese he was holding.

"As soon as we have broken our fast you can saddle up and fly all the way to the Kings if your wings will take it."

"I might even take that challenge, Kye."

"Enough words," Eloo said, snatching some bread out of Lightning's hand. "Food and then we move."

Rose was soon in the saddle, and on the wing. As they moved south the land began to change. The trees were still thick, but the land began to rise into gentle hills.

"How far are these Kings?"

"If I am not mistaken, they should be just over the next few ridges. Maybe another half an hour."

As they cleared the next ridge they came across a broad river that cut through the ridges and led them south.

"What river is this?"

"The Sabrina, and there is the town of Port Culis," Lightning explained as they swooped over a group of low buildings clustering the river bank on both sides. "And before us is the fortress of the Kings."

Rose gaped as the twin towers of the fort swept below them. Lightning flew over the battlements crossing a broad valley. Its fortifications spanned and blocked the valley and turned the hills into a wall which protected the North from the dead lands to the south.

Lightning flew a little way out into this desert, and then turning to face north again, descended in many circles to land before the fort's closed gates. Rose looked up at the walls and the two great towers that stood before her. The fort guarding the north was called the Kings or the Twins because it was built by no-one knew who to resemble two crowned and helmeted men. The towers were their heads, and the battlements their shoulders. These busts were the same and different; one appeared to have been built out of white marble whereas its brother was of black basalt or some similar stone, but both towered up high into the air and Rose shuddered as she felt them glaring down at her as if at any moment they would reach out and swot her.

"The gates aren't opening."

"No, Tristian has probably sealed them, but I thought you would like to see them from this angle."

"It is an impressive sight, but I think I would rather avoid being shot at."

Rose was referring to the many figures who had crowded the battlements at their appearance, and several of them appeared to be aiming bows at them. Lightning snorted, and with a great flex of his back legs launched himself into the air and was winging his way higher. They swooped back over the fortress and dropped down to the town of Port Culis where Lightning landed on the bank just beyond the town. When Rose leapt down from the saddle it was to find a delegation waiting to meet them. Rose was half expecting Kye and Silver Skin to be waiting for them, but they were nowhere in sight, though the group of Centaurs that formed a small honour guard were led by a familiar face.

"Wind Fist," Rose cried in pleasure when she saw the tall pale Centaur with his horse plumed helmet.

"Lady Canduss," the Centaur greeted her, his scimitar raised in salute. "It is a pleasure to see you again."

"Perhaps you would introduce us, Fist," said a tall figure clad in white who stood surrounded by the Centaurs.

"Sorry, Lady StaffSword," Wind Fist said, half turning to the white figure. "This is the Lady Rose Canduss. Rose, this is the Lady StaffSword."

"Also known as the White Witch," Lightning growled from behind them.

"Lightning, is that you?" the White Witch asked, offering Rose a paw.

"It is."

The two women broke their grasp, and standing back from one another considered each other. Rose thought at first she was looking at Eloo, or Eloo with more fur, but looking more closely she saw a woman dressed in white robes, a long mane of snow white hair flowing in the wind. This woman regarded Rose with a pair of dark, green eyes out of a face which could only be described as feline. White fur covered her face, and long whiskers trembled on her top lip. Long, mobile ears flicked from under the snowy mane and yet despite or because of all these features the White Witch was beautiful. Her robes hardly concealed her hour glass figure beneath them.

"You are the White Wolf's mate?"

The cat woman raised a pale eyebrow at this, but replied in a mild enough voice. "I and Tristian are lovers, but why do you ask?"

"I have been told that I need to get his permission to go south of this place."

"That is true, for the gates are closed, but who told you this and why do you need to go south when we are at war?"

"Are we at war?" Lightning now in his human shape asked, stepping to Rose's side and givingthe White Which a bow.

"Lightning, you are a dragon again," the Witch replied, nodding in reply to his bow. "No, we are not at open war yet, but the blow will fall any day now."

"So will Tristian give his permission or not?"

The white woman stared at Rose with her green eyes and cocked her head as if considering, and then shrugged.

"Why don't you ask him?"

"Where is he?"

"At the Kings awaiting you no doubt," cut in a familiar voice, behind them.

Rose turned to find Takana, the tall bird woman standing behind them, a large grin on her dark, almost red face.

"After such a flashy entrance I should think that the Kings themselves stirred in their sleep."

"Ah, Takana, it is good to see you!"

"And you too, Rose."

"Lady Takana, it is a pleasure to see you again."

"And you are a dragon once more. How nice."

"Tristian," Rose said, trying to bring the conversation back to the subject of her heart. "I need to see him!"

THE WHITE WOLF'S JUDGEMENT

"The White Wolf is one of the oldest living beings. He has seen thousands of years, and with such experience he may have obtained wisdom, but that does not make him a god."

Lightning, from the Wereding Chronicles.

The White Witch led them through the large village of Port Culiswhere Rose was watched by people who bore many strange features. A tall girl with white blonde hair watched her pass, with one green eye and another yellow. Another grinned at her with teeth that must have been three inches long.

"Lightning, what are they?"

"Most of them are Wolfbloods."

"Werewolves?"

"No, the descendants of Werewolves. Many are not true Werewolves. They cannot change, but they carry the mark of the beast still."

Rose, gazing about her, realised many of these Wolfbloods must have a common family for most of them had snow white hair, or blond hair that was almost white.

"They remind me of White Mane."

"That is hardly surprising, as White Mane's father is their sire too."

"The White Wolf?"

"Tristian is more than a thousand years old, he has had a lot of children," the White Witch said without turning to face them.

Rose might have asked her more about the Wolfbloods, but a white blur flashed to stand at the cat-woman's side. It was a Fury, the cat Centaur having the body of a snow leopard. Its long, braided hair was snow white with black rosettes.

"My Lady, you did not tell me you were leaving the fortress," growled the cat woman, her considerable bosom rising under its bleached white leather armour.

"Winter, I am with the Centaurs and in no danger," the White Witch said, smiling at the cat-woman.

The white haired Winter growled at this, and cast her green eyes over Rose and Lightning.

"Who are these?"

"The Lady Canduss and Lightning, may I introduce Winter Mountainsstrider, my personal shadow."

Rose extended a hand, hesitantly. "Pleased to meet you."

The Fury stared at the hand as if she were wondering whether to cut it off with the longsword strapped across her back.

"Why are you here?"

"Please, Winter, show some manners. The Lady Canduss is our guest."

"I am here to see the White Wolf," Rose said. "And I mean no harm to anyone here."

Winter growled at this, but turning on the spot led the party to the back of the Twins. They entered the fortress through a small, iron bound wooden door. It was so low the tall Fury and her even taller mistress had to duck through it. When Rose straightened on the other side of the door, it was to feel a draught on the back of her neck. Looking up she saw in the ceiling above her a grated opening, and realised she was looking at a murder hole. They passed through a pair of iron gates which could be closed to hold an attacker against the door, so they could not escape the murder hole. As they worked through the fortress, Rose saw more murder holes and gates. This was not just a home, but a strong fortress which could be easily defended. Eventually they climbed many stairs to arrive in a small chamber at the top of one of the towers, which formed the head of the Kings. There, in a wooden chair carved to resemble the Kings, wrapped in white furs and with a long sword sheathed in a white scabbard across his lap, sat Tristian Silverbrow, the White Wolf. When he looked up from the blade in his lap and into Rose's face, she saw his eyes were deep green pools that drew you into those bottomless depths. When he spoke, it was in a soft whisper that still filled the little room with its power.

"So, at last the vision has a form, or are you another vision? Am I awake?"

As he asked this, he drew in a deep breath through his large nostrils. His lips peeled back from his long teeth when he smelt her.

"No, you are real enough. I smell your sweat and leather, even a hint of sulphur."

"I am Rose Canduss," Rose said, in a voice little more than a whisper. "We have never met, and yet you know me?"

"I have seen your face many nights in my dreams and meditations."

For a long time they stared at each other, each trying to consume the other's features. Rose saw this was indeed Kye's grandfather. His long jaw and deep eyes reminded her of that other Werewolf. This one's eyes were green, where Kye's were blue. This face was Kye and not Kye. This Werewolf's face was a mask like Kye's, but behind the eyes Rose could sense the ageless mind she could imagine holding the memories and experiences of ages untold. His eyes were bottomless pools, and in them swam the immeasurable grief of lives lived beyond her own mortal existence. For a moment Rose felt dwarfed, as if her needs and wants were petty in this giant's perception.

"Who are you?" he whispered, and broke their eye connection to look past Rose to where Lightning loitered behind her. "So, Lightning, you return to us whole and healed?"

"Yes, thank you, Lord Tristian."

"You say you have seen me in visions?"

Those green pools moved back to Rose's face, and his mouth twisted in a grim smile. "Yes, though your face looked slightly different than it does now."

Rose realised that somehow he knew this was not her true face, and he must know about the mask. With a sigh of reluctance she reached up and pulled the mask down, revealing the scaled ruin that was her face. The White Wolf scanned her face, his eyes drinking in the dark scales which now decorated the left side and once he had scanned it he smiled widely.

"Yes, that is the face I have seen in my dreams."

"What face?"

The White Wolf did not answer, but looking to the White Witch spoke to her. "Kye?"

"He and the rest of their party are nearly to the Port."

"Then we will wait until they join us to unwrap this riddle," he said, looking to Rose. "I think that my grandchildren should be here to hear the explanation and I hate repeating myself. Until they arrive, however, you might as well make yourselves comfortable. My dear Aleena, perhaps you could have some food sent up?"

Rose watched, frustrated, as the White Wolf put his sword aside, and standing walked to a small door which he stepped through. Rose felt her temper flaring, and before Lightning or anyone else could stop her she followed him through the door, gasping with surprise to find herself on a narrow balcony on the outside of the tower, hundreds of feet above the barren land below. She felt her hair and cape snatched at by a strong wind and she had to raise a hand to keep her hair out of her eyes.

"Welcome to my eyrie, my Lady," the Werewolf Lord's voice whispered in her ear, and Rose turned to find the white clad man at her elbow, his green orbs looking past her to the view beyond her.

"It's impressive," Rose shouted in order to make herself heard over the wind.

"This is where I come on long sleepless nights to watch my domain," the White Wolf continued, as if he had not heard her. "Look south, my lady, and tell me what you see."

Rose turned from the Werewolf and did as he suggested. The grey landscape stretched out before her, as featureless as the grey desert.

"So?"

"Look up." The White Wolf's whisper cut through the roar of the wind.

Rose did so, and saw what he meant. High in the sky and nearly above them was a strange cloud, or perhaps it was smoke. It was black, and following it back to the ground she saw the smoke, or whatever it was, was venting from a large crack in the dead ground.

"What is it?"

"I do not know, but I suspect that it is the fumes of our enemy's war machines."

"What do you mean to do with me?"

"Cry chaos and let loose the dogs of war," whispered the White Wolf.

"What will you do with me?"

"Do you know the works of Shakespeare?"

"Who?"

"It appears not." The White Wolf turned and re-entered the tower.

When Rose followed him, it was to find the small room was now crowded by the rest of her party. Kye was in the act of embracing a tall elderly woman, with shoulder long grey hair.

"Rosemary, it has been too long!"

"It has, Father," gravelled the old woman, who was apparently Kye's daughter although she looked like she should be his grandmother, not his daughter.

Rose wanted to ask Lightning about this, but the White Wolf's voice cut through the room and drew her attention back to him.

"For more than thirty years I have had a vision of Lady Canduss, with her scaled face."

"Thirty years!" Rose whispered. "But I wasn't born then."

"Was it always the same dream?"

"Yes, Silver, it was always a vision of her standing on the wind above my domain..."

"On the wind?"

"Yes, you were in mid-air, your hair and cloak, the one you are wearing now, flying out behind you and your Eagle sword in your hand."

"What was I doing?"

"You pointed to the ground where the earth was black with Goblins and Orcs."

"What does it mean?" Rose asked.

"The vision, or the fact that Tristian has had had this dream so long?" the White Witch asked, placing a glass into Tristian's hand.

"Both," Rose said, watching the Werewolf nock the drink back in one go.

"The warning itself is clear," Tristian continued. "It warns me to keep my guard up, but why I have had the vision of you and why for so long is not clear to me."

"Kye, you are an Ovate, can you shed any light?"

"No more than Tristian can, Lea, and he has been dwelling on it for the last thirty years."

"A fresh perspective can shed a great deal of light," Lea argued, picking up a large book from where it lay on a small table and replacing it almost at once.

"Lea, please be careful with my copy of Shakespeare. It is a rare copy," Tristian said, his green eyes not moving from Kye's face. Somehow, he knew what the young Werewolf had been doing. "Well, Kye, anything?"

Kye did not answer at first. He turned away from the company, and looking out one of the slit like windows in the room's wall, he finally spoke haltingly as though he himself was not sure of his own ideas. "The fact that Tristian has had this vision for so long suggests that Rose's coming here may not be by chance. Though why the Lady has not mentioned her before is troubling."

"You speak as if I have no control over my actions," Rose snarled. "I am in control."

"Who of us can truly make that claim," the White Wolf said, his voice smothering her anger with a wave of serenity.

"You all speak as if I am just some god's pawn in some divine chess game," Rose spat, her anger spiking again, and she realised as she heard her voice rising that the fires within her were building force too as if her anger was stoking that fire.

"Girl, we are just pawns in the Gods' chess game," Tristian admonished her. Though his voice was calm enough, his eyessnapped back to her and pierced her to her soul.

"Rose, calm down," Lightning said from behind her, as if he too could sense her rising anger and inner fires.

"I am not a pawn!" Rose snarled between clenched teeth, trying to control her anger. "I want to go south and find Robin and help her. I have no part in any war or your gods."

"I would think, after you heard of my vision, you would believe differently," White Wolf said, and his own eyes sparkled with icy fire in their depths. "But you are your own being. You are free to do as you wish, but if you would hear my counsel I would say that you are very involved in what is about to unfold before us."

"You're wrong!"

"Am I?"

"Will you let me go south or not?"

"Child, you have not been listening," the White Witch answered for Tristian. "My lord has just said you are free to do what you will."

"Then I will go south. Lightning, Kye, are you still with me?"

Kye, who had been staring out the window, now turned to meet Rose's gaze. "I swore to help you, Rose. I do not break my word."

"You, Kye, are a member of the Silver Shield," Tristian said, his face and eyes unreadable. "You have given oaths to land and people to serve in their defence."

"I do not forget my duty, Grandfather," Kye shot back, his features equally inscrutable. "I still keep those oaths by helping Rose."

"Do you, I wonder," Tristian said, his gaze pinning Kye to the spot. "I could order you to stay and man my garrison."

Kye's mask cracked slightly, a grin touched his lips, and he bowed to Tristian.

"You could, my lord. That is your right as both my elder and gate keeper, but I pray you do not for I would not like to break my word."

Tristian regarded him sternly, and just when Rose thought he would forbid Kye from helping her his statue like mask broke and his wide mouth curled into a great grin. Rising from his carved throne, he returned Kye's bow.

"So be it, you go south if it is possible."

"If it is possible?"

Rose's emotional leap of joy was halted by those words.

"Yes, girl, if it is possible. I give you my permission and blessing, but unless you have forgotten I cannot speak for the Darklings. They may attack in the next hour, and if they do then I fear that neither you nor I can make a way south. If that happens, you may have to fight to survive."

Rose took a long pause to digest this idea and nodded slowly as his words made sense.

"If that happens," she said slowly, choosing her words carefully. "I will take up arms in your peoples' defence."

The White Wolf raised a snowy eyebrow as he took in these words.

"Will you? That is kind and gracious, but perhaps a little rash. Are you sure of these words, for you may come to regret them."

Rose's pause was only for a moment. "I mean what I say. If the Darklings come I will help, for in helping you I help myself, if only to survive."

Lightning gasped at this, and Tristian chuckled.

"So be it! You may set out tomorrow, but for tonight I hope you will accept whatever meagre hospitality my hall can offer."

Rose felt as if she had finished running a marathon, and she was all at once drained of strength. "I could do with a nap."

"Excellent. Aleena, would you please see to our guests' comfort?"

"It is already done."

"Good, then go and refresh yourself."

The company was leaving when Tristian called Kye back. "Kye, a word, if you would?"

Kye shrugged at Eloo and gestured for her to go on ahead. Grandfather and grandson were now alone with eachother. Kye stood before his elder, looking down at the floor, not meeting Tristian's eye. Then he went down on one knee before the seated Werewolf.

"Grandfather, I hope I have not angered you in this matter?"

"Please, Kye, make easy, I am not Manticore. Please sit."

Kye sat cross-legged at his grandsire's feet, looking up into a smiling face.

"You were always your own master, Kye. You are a little wild for good judgement, but in that regard you are like me when I was your age. No, you have not angered me. It is not about this matter south, but I would use you while I can. You may go south with my blessing, but since you are here, I would be grateful if you would turn an eye to my archers and light fighters. There is not a Werewolf in the garrison with your experience and knowledge of the bow."

"I thought that Apollo was in charge of the garrison."

"He is, and he is good, but he has not your skill with the bow. Please, Kye, look them over as a favour to a grandfather."

"Then I will do so willingly, my lord," Kye said and rising to his knees, offered his cheek.

Tristian bowed forwards, kissed Kye on the cheek, and then raised him to his feet and embraced him warmly.

"Truly, Kye, it has been too long since I saw you. How are your mother and father?"

"Tristian, the girl Rose is more important than you or I can know. I prayed for guidance at the Lake of Tears, and she showed me visions, one of them with her face changed as it is now, but this was before I had seen her so."

"What else did you see?"

"A vision similar to your own, but I saw more. Rose was facing a figure similar to her, but it was as black as night."

"Did the Lady tell you what it meant?"

"No, my lord, I know no more than you."

"Well, let us pray that we obtain understanding, before the visions come true."

"Armen."

THE STUDY OF THE BOW AND THE BLADE

*"It is not enough to fire an arrow, at your enemy. You cannot hide
behind a wall and shoot, you must be aware of the shifting lines of
battle. What may be a safe shooting nest one moment, may be encircled
in the next. You must be aware of the flowing nature of a battle."*

Kye to the garrison of the Kings, the Wereding Chronicles.

Kye watched as several of the Twins garrison fired arrows at
the targets of their training ground.

"The blond is better than the rest," Lea commented from
beside his brother.

"The Wolfblood is good," Kye grunted, watching a girl with white
blonde hair shoot her shortbow at the target. "Though she is more a
hunter than a fighter."

"The longbow isn't the only weapon."

"It is known as the warbow."

"You are prejudiced, Kye."

"Perhaps, but I doubt she has seen any combat."

"She wears scimitars," Lea pointed out.

"But does she know how to use them?"

"I have an idea that you are going to find out," Lea commented,
watching the girl's body move gracefully as she plucked an arrow
from a quiver on her back.

Kye only grunted, and taking his long bow he walked off towards
the targets. Lea, seeing where he was going, waved a red flag twice
signalling that shooting should stop and the archers should collect
their arrows. As the handful of archers moved towards the targets
three arrows fell amongst them. The startled archers leapt in all
directions to avoid the arrows.

"Are you mad?" shouted the blonde archer woman, looking up to
see Kye step from behind the buts, his bow in hand.

His blue eyes met her mismatched yellow and green ones. "In battle you must always be aware of enemies; you cannot be complacent and think you are safe, because you may be crushed beneath the hooves of cavalry."

"I don't remember that one in the Art of War, Kye," spoke a deep voice from the back of the grassy square. The girl and the rest of the archers, realising who this new speaker was, spun to face him and stood to attention. Lea, from his observation point, realised the speaker was their commanding officer. Looking over their heads he saw a tall man clad in a mirror bright breastplate. His long brown hair flowed out behind him. Hair sprouted from between a small pair of deer like antlers which marked this man as a son of Hunter, the Elven king.

"I speak from personal experience, Apollo, not a tactical manual," Kye replied drily, his tone neither respectful nor scornful, but merely stating the truth.

Apollo snorted, and turned to the girl with the blonde hair and the mismatched eyes. "Dancing Falcon, what do you think of Captain Silverbrow's advice?"

"Dancing Falcon," Lea murmured to himself, rolling the name around his mouth, as if he was tasting it.

The girl looked from Apollo to Kye and shrugged.

"It has some merit," she admitted in a husky whisper. "But I would prefer to have heard it without the arrows."

This made Kye's lips quirk in what might have been a smile, but when he spoke his voice was grave. "The arrow proved a better lesson than any of my words."

The girl nodded, and shouldering her bow reached for the hilts of her scimitars. "Are there other lessons the captain wishes to teach me?"

Kye raised an eyebrow, and handing his bow to Lea walked to a nearby table and picked up a pair of wooden scimitars.

"Your name is Dancer, can you do so with the blade?"

Dancing Falcon smiled broadly and retrieved a pair of wooden swords from the table. Walking to the middle of the practice yard, she assumed a ready stance. She held her swords low, their points aimed at the ground, inviting an attack. Kye ignored her at first, looking to Apollo. "You permit?"

Apollo shrugged.

"Go easy on him, girl, his grandfather may not forgive me if we hand him back in pieces."

The girl grinned, but Kye ignored the banter and walking to face the girl saluted her. As she returned the salute, his swords were stabbing at her stomach. The Falcon girl recovered well, her raised sword hand sweeping down to block Kye's left sword. Her left hand, which had not moved, tried to sweep his righthand sword aside. However, despite her recovery, she was still not quick enough. Even as she reacted Kye had retracted and stabbed again. His swords came in over her own swords to stab high. The girl lifted her hands, her curved swords hooking Kye's blades and locking them in place. So she thought, until Kye's foot swept her legs out from under her. From her back she looked up into his face and his swords raised high above her.

"Your feet are just as important as your hands. You have to be aware of your footing at all times."

Dancing Falcon snarled and launched a kick at his groin, but Kye had danced back, his blades weaving a defensive pattern before him. The girl took the opportunity to shoulder roll up onto her feet, but before she could do anything more Kye was coming at her, his curved blades slashing at her head and stomach. She raised her right hand to block Kye's high slash and tried to sweep his other sword aside. As she swept the lower blade aside, she dropped the other blade to try to make an advantage of the opening, but both her swords were swept to one side by Kye's single blade. He had retracted and disengaged it as the girl swept at it and as she realised it his other sword came to rest against her neck.

"If this was a real sword you would be dead now."

The girl's response was to spit in his face. Kye stepped back and raised an eyebrow. "Brave, but spit will not save you in battle."

"What is the lesson here, that you are better?"

"I am better, but there is always someone better. Pray you meet them in the practice yard and not the battlefield. The aim of this lesson, however, is that you should stay as far away from anopponent as possible."

The girl appeared confused at that.

"You are telling me not to fight?"

"I am telling you that if you wish to survive, you would be better using hit and run tactics. Shoot at your enemy, and retreat before he can reach you with a sword."

Apollo's voice broke in on them from behind Kye. "And when you cannot retreat?"

Kye turned to find him standing there, a wooden long sword in hand. Kye lifted a blade to touch the long sword. "You must stand and fight, or die."

THE VOICE OF WAR

"War speaks with a deadly voice that warns of the lives suddenly snuffed out like so many candles. War is not a horseman you would wish to summon."

The White Wolf, the Wereding Chronicles.

Tristian sat in his throne room, his head resting against the throne's headrest, his eyes closed. The White Witch stood in front of him, standing a few feet away, watching his chest rise and fall. As she watched a deep animalistic growl boiled up from deep within his chest and when his eyes flew open they burned with a bright yellow light.

"What is it?"

He did not answer at once, collecting his wits and realising where he was.

"The war has begun," he whispered, as in the oppositetower a bell began to ring.

"The beacon bell," the White Witch cried, hearing the bell.

In her room lower in the tower complex Rose woke to hear a bell ringing a constant tolling.

"What is it?"

"The beacon bell," Lightning said from her side. "It only rings when one of the warning beacons have been sighted."

"Meaning?"

"That we are at war!"

Rose opened her mouth to speak when a knock came at her door and from beyond the door.

"Lady Canduss, Lord Tristian would like to speak to you."

"I'll be ready in a moment," Rose answered, reaching for her clothes.

Moments later she was before the white clad Werewolf. His green eyes met her own, and conveyed regret.

"Lady Canduss, perhaps you have noticed the bell is ringing."

"Yes, it woke me." As she said this, the ringing stopped, its sudden silence almost as unnerving as its ringing hadbeen.

"It is an alarm, to warn us if one of the beacon fires is lit. It means that someone has attacked one of the beacon towers."

"You're telling me that I'm not going south after all."

A sad smile twitched his broad mouth. "I'm afraid not," the White Wolf whispered.

"What do you want me to do?"

Tristian's words were interrupted by Kye's voice from the doorway. "The dwarfs have been attacked."

"Grandson, do you never sleep?"

"He would if I wasn't insatiable," Eloo answered for the tall Werewolf.

"Report," Tristian commanded.

"The reports are not yet in, Apollo has taken the cavalry to investigate," Kye said, moving to stand beside Rose.

"Kye, Tristian has just told me we won't be going south," Rose said in a neutral voice.

Kye turned to look at her, and although Rose tried to keep her face impassive her pain must have shown, because the next thing she knew Kye was wrapping her in a great embrace. His hoarse voice whispered in her ear, "I will keep my promise, but first we must win this war. Do you understand that?"

Rose blinked away tears she didn't know she had been holding back, and squeezed the iron hard body embracing her.

Tristian cleared his throat. "When you're quite finished, Kye, perhaps you would enquire what Apollo is about?"

"As you command, my lord," Kye said, giving Rose a last squeeze, and releasing her to spin with a swirl of cloak out of the room.

Rose turned to see where he had gone but he had vanished, leaving Eloo standing behind her.

"Rose, we will save your sister," the little woman said, and before

Rose could react the tiny woman had leapt up into her arms to kiss her on the lips, before dropping back to the ground, and then she too was gone.

"They like you," Tristian said, and Rose thought she detected a hint of mirth in his voice. "Kye, in particular, rarely shows so much emotion to people outside the clan."

"You didn't answer my question?"

"Which was?"

"Where do you want me? How can I be most useful?"

The White Wolf did not answer for a long time but gave her one of those soul searching looks. "I am not sure of an answer. I suspect that you will find your own place to stand."

From behind Rose's left shoulder, Lightning cleared his throat. "If I might be so bold, I would suggest that I and Rose provide air support to whatever force you put out."

Tristian looked past Rose to gaze at Lightning. "That seems a very good idea. If Rose agrees, of course."

"Of course," Lightning agreed, knowing already she would as they had already debated this contingent.

"I do agree, but it occurs to me that I might need more magic before I go into battle with Orcs. If there is time?"

"There will be time," Silver Skin said from the door and strode into the room. Her sleeves were rolled up to the elbow, her hands stained with blood, as was her robe.

"Silver, you're hurt," Rose cried in fear and shock.

"What? Oh, it is nothing, Rose. This is not my blood."

"There cannot be fighting here in the Kings yet. I would know," Tristian declared, his head cocked on one side as if listening to something they could not hear.

"No, not here, my lord. I went with Apollo to see what help I could bring."

"You saw battle?"

"I saw casualties," Silver spat, striding to a bowl of water and beginning to scrub her hands.

"How bad is it?"

"Get Apollo to tell you, I do not think I can."

Tristian might have pursued the point, but at this moment Apollo bowed through the door, his antlers too high to fit. "My Lord Gate Keeper, I have come to report."

Rose had not yet met Apollo, and she blinked as his breastplate glowed even in the dim light of the chamber. Once Rose had adjusted to this glow she gawped at this tall man, crowned with antlers. She was reminded of Hunter and realised that here before her was his son. She might have asked this of him, but the White Wolf's voice drove that thought from her mind.

"Is the wall safe?" Tristian's voice rang with iron control, but Rose noticed that his eyes had changed from green to a glowing yellow.

"For now, my Lord," Apollo answered in his deep voice, which filled the small room. "But how long I cannot say."

"Report," commanded Tristian.

"The mine of the Dwarfs was attacked from below by a horde of Goblins."

"Was?"

"Yes, my lord. The dwarfs flooded the lower halls, and then dropped the tunnel entrances."

"Then the threat is over?"

"This one." Kye spoke from behind Apollo.

"The Goblins were driven back?"

"The Goblins were ground to dust," Apollo said with glee.

"But at a dreadful cost," Silver barked from the bowl where she still scrubbed, though to Rose's eye the blood was gone.

"How many?"

"The numbers are not yet in," Apollo said, his voice softer and tinged with regret. "But many dwarfs lost their lives this night in the defence of our flank."

"I saw a hundred in the makeshift infirmary," Silver put in. "And I heard that many were dead or missing."

"They will be honoured," Apollo said grandly.

"They might prefer to be alive and whole," snapped Silver, who was clearly upset and drained emotionally.

"They fell in battle, they would want it this way!"

"They would like to live?"

"Silver, enough," Tristian snapped, his soft voice a steely whisper. "Their deaths are regrettable, I feel your pain, but this is now war. Many more will die before long. Can you live with that or should I send you to Care Diff?"

Silver turned her back on her grandfather and her shoulders rose and fell as she took a long, deep breath. When she spoke her voice was weary, but calm. "No, Gate Keeper, that will not be necessary."

"Why don't they attack now?" Rose asked.

"It is a good question," Tristian said, a faint smile touching his lips. "Goblins and Orcs prefer the dark. They should attack now, and might."

"So why aren't they?"

"Because they are not ready yet," Apollo suggested.

"We shall see," whispered the White Wolf.

"Your orders," Kye said, from beside his sister.

Tristian did not respond for a long moment, his head laid back against the head rest. His eyes were vacant, as though Tristian's mind or spirit had left his body and gone out into the battle ground. When he did speak, his voice was distant as though he were not quite with them, but viewing the ground with spectral eyes. "We do not yet know the nature of the force that will come against us, but with the mines closed the only way at us is across the ford and the Bridge of Tears."

"Agreed," Apollo said.

"Kye, I want you commanding the archers on this side of the gorge. You are to hold our west flank, but until I know better I can only give you a token force. You will have to hold it as long as you can."

"Understood." Kye's quiet voice was calm, but somehow Rose sensed in that one word he was saying many things.

"Well then, Rose," Lightning said as cheerfully as he could, "It looks like we know where we are in the battle!"

"Where?"

"Keeping Kye's ass out of the fire."

Rose turned to see how Kye reacted to this but he had disappeared, as had Eloo.

"Come on, Rose, it looks like I have some teaching to do before the sun rises."

DRAWING LINES

"The lines of battle are not just drawn on maps, they are drawn in blood, sweat, and tears."
Law to the Red Wizard, the Wereding Chronicles.

Kye surveyed his battle ground under a crescent moon, his faintly glowing eyes taking in the thin strip of grass that lay between his first line of battle and the edge of a narrow gorge between him and the opposite edge of the land. The gorge had been cut by the river that fell in falls below him and was spanned by the Bridge of Tears. A span of rope bridge, the Bridge of Tears was so narrow it could be crossed by only one man at a time. It was across this bridge the enemy would come. Kye would not fight the enemy on the bridge, he decided, but from the line of defence, a long, thin line of pits and stakes which would shield his archers from any cavalry the enemy might have while their long bows cut them to ribbons.

"Not a bad defensive position," Lea said from behind Kye's left shoulder.

Detecting something more than what Lea was saying, Kye turned his yellow eyes on his shorter, younger brother. "And yet you disapprove of it?"

Lea looked surprised, as if Kye had plucked the thought out of his mind. "You know, Kye, I am beginning to understand why people think you can read their minds."

Kye did not respond, but focused his penetrating gaze on his brother.

"All right, you needn't brow beat me. You're right, I suppose." Lea turned his gaze away from Kye and looked once more at the gorge and its defences. "It's just that we are taking too much of a defensive position, and fortresses make for poor battle tactics."

"Tristian knows what he's doing."

"I suppose so."

"How would you handle our command, if you were in charge?"

Lea looked taken aback, but collecting himself looked over the ground before him.

"I would do all this, but..."

"But what?"

"I would use you and the rest of our scouts to find out what is really going on out there. We need to know what the enemy is doing..."

Lea broke off, watching a grin touch his brother's face.

"What?"

"Your brother is smiling," came Tristian's whisper from behind Lea, "because he knows that I have already sent those scouts into the field."

"I am sorry, Grandfather," Lea said, turning and bowing to his elder.

Tristian did not acknowledge Lea's apology, other than to lay a hand on his bowed head. Instead, his green eyes met Kye's, and held them.

"You at least approve of our dispositions, do you not?"

"Yes, my lord," Kye said, giving an inclination of his own head.

"Do you require anything else?"

Kye turned to look up the gentle hill which rose to a ridge crest, before frowning at the fence of woodland. His yellow eyes took in the lines of low earthen and stone walls forming the second line of defence (the fall back positions) and behind them a squad of the statue like Trolls standing by to protect the archers against foot soldiers, their long axes glinting in the dim light. He counted the many cooking fires springing up beyond the walls and in the fringes of the wood, and knew that many of them would be surrounded by the men and women who would comprise his fighting force. When his eyes met Tristian's again, a faint but grim smile was on his lips. "I could do with five more companies of archers, but as I am not going to get them I will make do with what I have."

"If wishes were fishes," Tristian said smiling.

"Will I have any cavalry support?"

"Even as we speak Wind Fist and his Centaurs are moving through the wood."

"Then I think there is nothing more, apart from a sheath of arrows."

"Speaking of bows and arrows, I have gifts for you."

As if from thin air, Tristian plucked a great long bow which he held out to Kye. The younger Werewolf took the shaft and regarded it. It was jet black, as if it had been carved from the night, rather than wood. Just below where the archer's hand would hold the bow there was a small badge of silver, carved to resemble a wolf's head.

"My black bow," Kye murmured, staring at the ebony bow as if he was seeing an old friend, or lover.

"You left it in my armoury the last time you were here," Tristian explained, smiling as he looked at the enchanted Kye.

"I thought it would serve the nations better here than in my hands."

"And so it will, but only in your hands does it sing best."

"I have missed her," Kye admitted in a wistful voice. "Thank you, Grandfather."

"You left this here as well."

Tristian took from a belt pouch a platinum ring, a large moonstone set in its claws.

"The ring of rank," Kye whispered.

"You left it here, but it belongs on your hand. It will strengthen you and I need a strong commander. Here, take it, Kye, and wield it with my blessing."

Kye made a low bow which he held until Tristian touched the nape of his neck.

"You will make me proud, I have no doubt," and with that the White Wolf was gone.

"Whenever I meet him I feel as if I'm in the presence of a..." Lea broke off, not able to find the words to describe his emotions.

Kye chuckled, a sound Lea did not often hear from his brother. He looked to Kye to see if he was being mocked.

"The White Wolf is the oldest of us. He has been in the presence of the Goddess. He is the greatest of us, but it is not always easy to experience his presence."

Lea nodded in agreement with Kye's words, their weight all the more powerful for the fact that Kye had taken the time to speak them and break his usual silence. Lea wanted to ask Kye to tell him more about their grandfather who Lea did not know well, but at that moment Eloo bounded out of the dark and leapt up into Kye's arms.

"Have you finished being commander of archers for a while?"

"Eloo, we are at war," Kye said drily.

"You can leave off warmongering long enough to pleasure an elf."

"Eloo, I have duties."

"Which will wait," Eloo said sternly, leading a protesting Kye off towards the camp fires, and the all concealing dark.

"I'll see you in a little while," Lea called after Kye's retreating back.

"Do you have no one to lead you into the woods?"

Lea turned to the voice whispering to him out of the gloom. He saw a glint of white-blonde hair and realised it was the blonde archer Wolfblood.

"Dancing Falcon," he gasped, suddenly breathless.

"My friends call me Dancer," the girl said, moving closer, allowing Lea to see she was now swathed in a huge bear skin cloak which should have hidden her curves, but which only served to emphasise them.

"I was not aware you were with us," Lea stammered.

His fluster was being made worse by her mismatched eyes gazing boldly into his own.

"You did not answer my question," she breathed into his face, swaying before him.

"Question," Lea asked, gasping, his acute sense of smell picking up the wave of pheromones pouring off this girl, who was, he realised, in heat.

"Do you have a lover to stave off the horrors of the morrow?"

the girl asked, holding out a hand and giving Lea one of those come hither looks which only a woman in need can give the man she wants.

"Not till now," Lea replied, grasping the girl's long callused hand in his.

"Then come, the dawn comes quickly."

* * *

Kye gazed down at Eloo's sleep smoothed face, and wished he had more time. He did not want to leave their makeshift bed of cloaks and leaves, but he must do his round of the lines and ensure that their pickets were keeping sharp and awake. Staring at Eloo's face, Kye was drawn back in time to their first meeting in a glade very much like this one. For a long moment he dwelled in the past, and then like a dog ridding itself of water he shook himself and returned to the present. His eyes slid lower to her bare breast, rising and falling steadily. His lust was rekindled but he must do his duty, so with regret he covered her with his cloak, turned away and moved into the trees. Kye knew that others like he and Eloo had moved into the trees to chase the threat of war away, but he was slightly surprised to find Lea in the next bower. His younger brother lay on a huge bearskin, beside a girl with long, white blonde hair. Lea did not stir as he approached but the girl opened her green and yellow eyes, and stared up at Kye's glowing ones.

"Dancing Falcon," Kye breathed, recognising the girl.

The girl did not reply or move, not wanting to disturb a sated Lea, but she gave Kye a wary smile. She made no move to cover her slender nakedness but gave Kye a stare which appeared to tell him to "move on." He was her commander, but he had no business here. Kye gave her a grim smile, and turning, strode away.

Dancer watched him go and sighed with relief, a movement which made her breast brush against Lea's arm, and his hand closed on her breast drawing a gasp of pleasure from her lips.

Kye did not look back to the trees, but strode past the large bonfire the Trolls had lit and among the dying camp fires, to stop at the first line of pits and stakes. He stared out into the night, and into the gorge before him. The night appeared still enough. The falls whispered in his ear, but apart from a rustle of grass there was no movement before him. Kye cocked his head, attempting to establish if the rustle was one of his guards, a wild animal, or an enemy. The rustle came again, and Kye's eyes snapped to it to see a short figure moving across the line of sight. Kye drew in a deep breath and smelt leather, fire smoke and pipe weed. He smiled and relaxed, recognising the dwarf he had placed on sentry duty several hours earlier. Kye jumped over the line of pits and strode up to where the dwarf was trying to light hispipe.

"How goes it, Stoneskin?"

Stoneskin the dwarf must not have heard Kye approaching for he nearly dropped his pipe as he came to attention. "My lord."

"At ease," Kye said, face a stone mask though his voice was gentle enough. "Any sign of the enemy?"

"No, my captain," said the dwarf in his gravelly voice. "If there was, I'd 'ave blown me horn."

"As you say," Kye said, looking into the night. "Shouldn't you have been relieved yet?"

"I've another hour or so before Hammerstriker replaces me."

"Very good," Kye said, though he never looked at the dwarf as he spoke. "Have you eaten yet?"

"N't yet."

"I will have some food sent out to you."

"Thank yeh."

Kye nodded, and glided away to find the second sentry he had posted at the head of the bridge. As he approached the bridge a yip of a wolf came out of the dark, and a second later a grey form bounded out to leap at Kye. At first Kye thought he was being attacked and reached for his short sword, but as the large grey form leapt around him and licked his hand he recognised the wolf.

"Fang," Kye exclaimed in surprise and delight. "Where did you come from?"

"He turned up half an hour ago as far as I can tell," Lor said from the bridge.

"Yes, yes, I'm pleased to see you too," Kye said to the wolf as it whined at his feet, and reaching down he scratched the wolf behind his ears. "Lor, anything to report?"

"Apart from Fang turning up, nothing has moved for hours."

"Stay alert, and sound the alarm at the first sign."

"And then fall back to the first line, I know."

"Good, I don't want to lose you to needless heroics."

"I thought you didn't care!" Lor said.

"It won't be long till you are released, stay focused till then, and then you can rest."

"As if I could sleep."

"Fang, come," Kye said, and he and the wolf moved back to the pit line.

Once he was back among the camp fires he found the gnome in charge of their supplies stirring a pot on a tripod over a fire.

"Soup for the guards," said the gnome Picklefingers in her high squeaky voice.

"You never told me you were a mind reader," Kye grunted.

"It's my job to know when the troops need feeding," returned the gnome.

"Then carry on, by all means."

Kye moved to one of the camp fires, to find Silver Skin boiling her own pot.

"Silver, I did not know you were out here with us?"

"Hello, Fang," Silver Skin said, extending a hand for the wolf to lick. "It occurs to me that you may need your big sister to watch over you so that you do not get into any trouble."

"In case you haven't noticed, I am a big boy now," Kye said, squatting beside her, and sniffing at the pot. "Venison?"

"You maybe a big boy, but you can still get into trouble," said a new voice out of the dark, and Lor materialised out of the gloom to crouch opposite them.

"Your watch isn't over yet, what are you doing here?"

Lor threw up his hands in surrender. "Calm down, Kye! I have been relieved by Father and Mother."

"Flash and Great Mother are here?" Kye asked in surprise.

"They are at the bridge head and are asking to see you," Lor said, accepting a bowl of Silver's soup.

Without another word, Kye rose to his feet and all but ran to his end of the bridge where the giant forms of his mother and father waited for him.

CATCHING HOLD OF THE LIGHTNING

"Wielding magic can be like catching hold of a lightning bolt. So much power will probably kill you, but you must try to hold on, and when you do you feel like a god."
The White Witch to the Red Wizard, the Wereding Chronicles.

After leaving the White Wolf in his throne room Lightning took Rose into the bowels of the keep where they entered a room constructed of a material Rose did not recognise. The material appeared to be a black metal, but it was so dark it was like standing in a void. A light in the ceiling lit once they entered, but it failed to illuminate the room fully. Rose approached one of the walls, expecting to see her reflection in the mirror smooth metal but was surprised to see nothing.

"What is this stuff?"

"It is called voidium," Lightning said from behind her. Rose could no more see him in the metal than she could see herself.

"Why can't I see myself in it?"

"Because of the nature of this material. It is known as void metal. It absorbs all known energies."

"Including magic?"

"Including magic. This room is where the White Witch and her apprentices practice in the knowledge that their spells will not bring the rest of the keep down about their ears."

Rose looked about her, realising the room was a long narrow one. At the opposite side of the long chamber was a painted target like a bullseye.

"What are we going to be learning?"

"First, I want you to learn a few protective spells so that I know you will be safe out there."

The disappointment must have shown on her face.

"Ah, I know you want to learn how to blow Orcs away with fireballs," Lightning said, hands on hips. "We may get to that, but to my way of thinking you are trying to run before you can walk. After all, you have cast what, the lighting spell and a shield spell."

Rose tried not to let her disappointment show but her face must have fallen and Lightning's look of annoyance was gone at once. When he spoke, his voice was no longer aggravated but patient and understanding. "Sorry, Rose, but what I say is true. I know you want to blow all the Orcs away so that you can get to Robin, but you have to be careful with magic. If you hurry and cut corners the magic is likely to make you pay for it."

"Very well, where do we start?"

"Although I hope that you don't come into direct combat, I do think that we should protect you. You need some extra armour."

"Magical armour?"

"Yes."

"But you already taught me the Glance spell. Won't that protect me?"

"Yes, but as you saw, Kye's arrow still sought you out. This spell should prevent arrows from coming anywhere near you."

"What do I do?"

"Concentrate on your earth ring and summon up its magic, and then take this and imagine a wall of stone about you."

"No words?"

"I was coming to that, the word is Stalag Malik."

Lightning handed her a small piece of rock, and then took several steps back from her. Rose concentrated on the diamond ring, feeling the great pool of power swirling at its heart. She willed some to come to her command and at the same time envisioned the wall of stone around her while muttering the words. At first, nothing happened, and Rose almost broke the mental image when Lightning tossed a small stone at her. The stone hit her on the arm with bruising force and fell to the floor.

"That hurt," she exclaimed, her image of the wall faltering.

"Concentrate harder," Lightning hissed, retrieving the pebble and cocking his arm again.

Rose snarled as she gritted her teeth and willed the wall to appear. The result was not quite what she expected. A wall of stone did not appear, but instead a shimmering field of brownish light appeared a few inches away from Rose's skin, and when Lightning snapped the stone at her it was blocked by the field.

"Excellent," Lightning cried.

Rose grinned, but in doing so lost concentration. The field flickered and might have died, but Rose felt another pulse of the ring. Glancing down she saw the stone was glowing with the same light as the field.

"What is happening, Lightning?"

"The ring is powering your spell, quickly end the spell or it might drain your ring."

"How?"

"Reversio," Lightning said, with a snap of his fingers, and when Rose mimicked him the spell shut off, and she felt as though she had run a race.

"Are you all right?"

Rose nodded.

"You have to concentrate on the spell to keep it running until you get used to the feel of the spell, and then once your mind knows what it is doing it will subconsciously run the spell until the energy you invested in it expires. Do you understand?"

"I think so."

"Do you feel like you can try it again?"

"Let's see?"

Lightning stood further back, and when Rose conjured the field again it was further from her skin. She did not have to concentrate on it for the stone flew off to one side when it impacted with the field and Rose did not even have to think about the spell. The field did not draw more energy from the ring but instead Rose felt something being drawn from inside herself, and as she watched the field expanded and Lightning was pushed back. Rose, surprised, tried to turn the field off, but although she felt the tug of internal magic stop the field continued and lasted for at least another minute before winking out, leaving Rose winded and drained of strength.

"Can we rest a minute," Rose asked, and she could hear the fatigue in her voice.

Lightning led her to where a chair and table stood against one wall, and she sank into the seat, grateful when he handed her a glass of water.

"Thank you."

Lightning looked at her with concern in his green eyes. "Do you feel up to continuing?"

"I guess."

"I am glad to hear it, because I think that you are ready to learn an offensive spell."

Rose felt a burst of adrenalin shoot through her and leapt to her feet.

"Not so fast!"

"What spell?"

In reply, Lightning handed her a lump of coal.

"Fireblast," he replied as he walked behind her and turned her to face the target.

"Hold the coal in your hands and focus on it."

Rose felt the roughrock and focused her mind on its black substance.

"Draw from your fire ring and imagine a flame."

"But Lightning, I don't have one. The Troll women took it from me."

"Oh, of course, I forgot," Lightning said, and slid something cold onto her hand.

Looking down, Rose saw a ruby ring, a fire ring, and felt its magic flickering in her mind.

"It is yours," Lightning told her, "the one that Takana gave you."

"But it was lost!"

"Kye found it at the battle site and gave it to me, but I forgot it until now."

"Better late than never."

Rose concentrated on the ruby like stone of her fire ring and felt heat rise to embrace her.

"Good, now speak the words Insendium scawl, and imagine that flame reaching out to the target."

As Lightning said the words Rose muttered them and felt the coal crumble to dust in her hand. From the hand that wore the fire ring there leapt a bird shaped gout of fire that screamed out to blacken the target.

"Is that what is supposed to happen?" she gasped through dry and cracked lips.

"Yes, that is what is supposed to happen," Lightning replied, in a voice which implied he was as surprised as Rose. "Though I didn't think you would master it on your first try. It appears that you are even more powerful than I imagined."

"I don't feel powerful," Rose said as the room spun around her.

"Yes, you do look a little drained. Here, come sit down and rest."

"The bird, Lightning, is that normal?"

"No, the shape of a bird is not normal, but it is proof to me that you are naturally a great wizard."

"How do you figure that?"

"Those of us spellcasters who have mastered this spell, or any spell for that matter, can change certain aspects to make them their signature spells. My blast, for instance, is shaped to resemble a dragon, but yours, it seems, you have shaped to resemble a bird, probably because of your coat of arms."

"I want to try it again."

"Oh no you don't," Lightning said, pressing his hand on her shoulder to keep her in the chair. "You have strained yourself for too long already. I don't want you to go into battle exhausted."

"But how am I supposed to fight with just one spell?"

"The fireblast spell is only a short range spell, and I have taught it to you so that you have something to use if you have to, but for long range you do have your bow."

"My bow, I had forgotten about it."

"Well I haven't, here, give it a try," Lightning said, picking it up from the floor next to his chair and handing it and its quiver to Rose.

Rose took the bow and felt a slight tingle as she gripped it as though she was receiving a tiny electrical shock. She notched the arrow, and taking aim, drew the bow back to her ear. As she did she heard a slight crackle, and felt a charge in the air around her. When she let fly, the arrow hissed through the air and struck the target with a spray of sparks as though the arrow's metal head had been charged with power.

"Impressive," Lightning had hardly said when Rose's second arrow hit with a concussive blast which blew a fist sized hole in the target.

"Let's hope it does the same to Orcs," Rose said, grinning from ear to ear.

"Indeed, let's hope. Now come, young lady, it is nearly morning, and even if you don't, I need my beauty sleep."

Before Rose could stop herself, the words slipped out. "I don't think you need it, you're beautiful enough."

Lightning stood there for a long moment, staring open mouthed, but then he swept Rose into a huge embrace and she found her lips locked with his.

THE PASSING OF A MANTLE

"The passing of leadership is never an easy transition, especially when death is present."

From Kye's journals.

Kye rushed through the night to attend his parents at the Bridge of Tears, a mixture of fear and love roiling inside him. When he was only a foot from them he dropped to one knee and bowed low before them. "Father, Mother I am pleased and surprised to see you here."

Flash chuckled, a sound like rocks grating together, and reaching out touched his son's bowed head. "Rise, Kye, you have no need for formalities here."

Kye raised his head and looked up at his father but did not rise from his knee until Great Mother smiled at him.

"Have you new orders for me?"

"At ease, Kye," Flash growled. "I and your mother are here not as clan Elders. Nor as your commanders. The bridge is yours to command, but we have come to contribute to your defence."

"You intend to hold the bridge?"

"Now that's why I love you," Grate Mother murmured. "Yes, Kye, your father and I will defend the bridge as well as we can, but we may be bypassed, so do not depend on us."

"I must depend on myself."

"I could not have put it better myself."

"You did put it, it is the first lesson you taught me, Father."

"I also taught you not to live without hope. With that in mind, receive your due."

As he spoke Flash removed from around his shoulders the long sword he carried in a wood and metal scabbard. He held it out to Kye, who stood staring at his father with uncomprehending eyes.

"Take it, son."

Kye reached out, his movement slow and dreamlike as he accepted the sword and held it up before him.

"The Silver Death!" Kye breathed, staring down at the sword's pommel which was similar to his short sword. A silver wolf's head with yellow stones for eyes, a moonstone clasped between its fangs. "Why would you present this to me?"

"I would have thought the answer was obvious," growled a voice in Kye's mind. The sword was like his Wolf's Fang, intelligent, and like that sword communicating telepathically with him. "I am yours now, Flash is giving you to me."

Kye ignored the sword's voice and repeated his question. "Why are you giving this to me?"

"Take it, Kye, and use it well," Flash said, and made to turn away.

Kye saw a flicker in his father's eyes and grabbed Flash's massive shoulder to stop his turn. "You are giving this sword to me because you do not want it to fall into the hands of our enemies. You do not expect to survive this fight!"

"Let go, Kye," rumbled Flash though he did not move or try to break Kye's grip on him.

"You've seen the black unicorn!"

Flash tried to hide his reaction, but Kye, who spent his life shielding his own feelings, recognised the smallest flicker of emotion in Flash's eyes.

"You have seen him, when, where?"

For a long time, Flash stared at the opposite end of the bridge though Kye doubted he actually saw it for his sight was turned inwards.

"As I passed through the woods to come here, he was waiting for me in a glade."

"Are you sure? It could have been another unicorn," Kye said desperately. Panic flickered in his voice.

Flash shrugged, but not to loose Kye's grip, so much as to deny his words.

"Kye, when you see the Lady's harbinger you will know him from an ordinary unicorn," Flash said, voice devoid of emotion.

Kye could feel tears pricking his eyes. "But you may not die tomorrow. The Black Unicorn is sent as a portent, not a herald of death always."

Now Flash did turn back to Kye, and his great arms enfolded Kye in a hug that made Kye feel he was a child again, and he could hold the floodgate of tears back no longer.

"Do not grieve for me now or in the future, Kye," Flash whispered into his son's hair. "I have lived a full life and will continue to live after my death through you, my children, who are strong, and you perhaps the strongest. Explain this to your siblings when you must and tell them that I love you all."

Without another word Flash released Kye and turning, walked out onto the bridge. He stood for a long time looking into the night, and then as Kye watched his form shimmered. At first Kye thought it was because of his tears, but quickly understood this was a mistake as his father's form dropped forwards onto allfours and was no longer a man, but the huge jet black wolf that flung back its head to howl a warning to any who would come to challenge his guard.

"Remember his words in the day to come," Great Mother murmured, as she too embraced her son. "And know that I too love you, and your brothers and sisters."

"Have you seen the EclipseStallion too?"

"Remember our words," Great Mother whispered, turning away.

She had taken only afew strides before Kye's whisper stopped her in her tracks. "Have you passed your burden to Silver Skin? Does she know what is to come?"

Great Mother turned slowly and regarded Kye gravely. "Most of the order, not evenmost Ovates, know of the pearl. How is it that you do?"

"Do not worry, Mother. No one has broken your secret. I was taught to watch and listen and judge."

"The role of a druid, and yet you are not a druid, Kye. To answer your question, yes, Silver Skin now carries the bulk of my knowledge and memories which she will pass on to her sisters in the druid order, when time permits."

"Then she knows, and did not tell me."

"Only because she was sworn to silence, do not blame her in your grief, Kye."

A grim smile touched Kye's lips. "I do not blame, but I do grieve."

"Despite your father's words?"

"I may act like it, but I am not made of stone."

"No, you are made of water, Kye. Never forget it."

With these last words, Great Mother joined her mate on the bridge, but she did not change. Kye could hear her voice murmuring, and her form was outlined by the glow of her pendant. He knew she was casting spells.

"So this is how it feels to say goodbye. I will never see you again," Kye muttered to himself.

He used his long hair to wipe his eyes and was just considering whether to seek Silver Skin out and seek her counsel, when from out of the darkness Eloo bounded, her body thankfully not naked, but clad in her form fitting leathers although they did, he granted, leave little to the imagination, so form fitting were they.

"Where did you go? I am not finished with you yet!" Eloo purred, her large, red tongue licking her lips. Her tail flicked about her with suppressed excitement.

"I have duties, as I explained to you."

"The sun hasn't come up yet. You're mine till dawn."

Kye shook his head in exasperation, and noticed a long hair hanging down into his face.

"Before you practice any of your wicked arts on me I want you to cut this hair."

"Cut it, but why?"

"Do you want someone using it to cut my throat?"

"Don't tempt me," she said jokingly, but then went serious. "Does that mean you submit?"

"Till just before moonset."

"You are a killjoy."

Kye did not answer but turned back to the bridge, but both his parents had gone still and silent and Kye turned away before he could start crying. He let Eloo draw him away so he could forget for a while in her arms.

CHESS AND WAR

"Some say that war is like chess, but they haven't played with death like I have."

Tristian, the Wereding Chronicles.

The Wraith King listened to his lieutenants arguing around him, their voices like wasps buzzing in his ears.

"Why did you order the attack on the dwarfs?" snarled Sable, the priestess of the Eclipsegod, from behind her jet black mask.

Her question was addressed to the general of the Orcs, a giant, grey skinned monster, who due to an old wound was known as Cyclops.

"Because we are at war, woman," rumbled the giant. His top lip curled back from his dog like muzzle to reveal long, yellow fangs.

"The plan was to wait till noon tomorrow," put in Kain, Sable's partner, and dark assassin.

"Plans have to be altered in the field," Cyclops shot back, his single yellow orb boring into the eyes looking back at him from behind Kain's wolf crafted helm.

"You lost a divisionof Goblins and alerted the White Wolf to our attack," objected Sable.

"So," Cyclops growled, his ham sized hands tightening their grip on his long handled battle axe. "It's difficult to keep so many Orcs and Goblins in one place at any time. They get restless, but give them dwarfs to attack and they will move mountains to get to their flesh and blood."

The Wraith King had heard enough, and as Sable was drawing breath to berate the Orc captain more his cold whisper cut through the air, freezing them all in place. "Enough. Cyclops, you have acted too soon."

Cyclops blanched, but straightened his back as if to defy his master, but the Wraith King cut him off. "However, it does not matter, Tristian would have sniffed that force out before we were ready."

"My lord," Cyclops said, bowing, unable to keep the smugness out of his voice. Smugness which turned to pain, as the spectre that was his master raised a gauntletedhand and whispered a word of power.

Cyclops did not fall, nor cry out, but he quivered in place. His teeth gritted against the numbing cold which embraced him.

"That does not mean that you have not displeased me."

"Yes, my lord," whispered Cyclops when he was released from the spell's soul chilling touch.

Sable turned from the huge Orc to face the Wraith King's masked face. "But the plan..."

"I am aware of your timetable, Sable," the armoured giant cut her off. "The bulk of the attack will not take place until the appointed time but Tristian will be aware of our forces by now. He will have mounted a defence. We shall engage those forces to make him think that he is fighting a winnable fight, and when the time is right we shall close the trap."

"But most of my Orcs and Goblins are not protected from the sun," Cyclops dared to ask, even though he quailed as the Wraith King looked on him with red eyes.

"Which is why we shall send the Trolls and our human mercenariesto engage such forces as Tristian has risked," Kain said.

"Who said you are general, assassin," Cyclops snarled at Kain.

"I did, Cyclops," the Wraith King reminded him, but then turned his attention to a new presence.

As they had been arguing a tall figure wrapped in a great cloak had slipped into the dark chamber. Her hood now thrown back she was revealed as a woman with ashen white skin, ruby red lips, and glowing red eyes.

"Lady Shere, what have you learned?"

The lady bowed her head to the Wraith King, and when she spoke it was in a hissing voice almost as cold as his own. "I and my sisters have flown over the Kings and its surroundings."

"And what have your vampires found?"

"The dwarfs appear to have doubled the guards at their watch towers, and a light force has been sent to guard the Bridge of Tears."

"What kind of force?" Cyclops asked, considering the edge of his axe blade.

"A light screenof archers and infantry supported by a company of Centaurs."

"Then we shall proceed as planned," whispered the Wraith King.

"There is a new complication," cut in the Lady Vampire.

"There often is," the Wraith King said drily.

"This complication is in the form of a Fire Drake and rider."

"A Fire Drake?" Kain asked sharply. "Was the rider a tall, red haired woman?"

"Yes."

"We know that pair," Sable hissed. "They will be trouble."

"Do not concern yourselves with the dragon," the Wraith King hissed.

"Easy for you to say," growled Cyclops. "It won't be your ass he'll be frying."

"He will be taken care of," the Wraith King hissed, and the temperature of the chamber dropped several degrees as he locked gazes with Cyclops.

"We are agreed then," Sable said. "We attack the bridge at dawn."

"That is the plan."

"And if the plan goes wrong?"

"Then, Cyclops, we will see just what your forces are made of," The Wraith King said, and with a swirl of cloak he was gone.

THE FIRST BLOW

"The first blow can come at any time but is usually heralded by a long pause as the two side manoeuvre. It is, however, the calm before the storm."

Kye's journal.

These events were how the dawn found Kye waiting for the mist to clear, an arrow on the string.

"Clear," he growled to himself.

"It is not natural," Eloo purred from beside him.

"Great Mother's work?" Lea asked from Kye's other side.

"She says not," Silver Skin said from behind them. When Kye glanced over his shoulder it was to see she had her eyes closed, and he knew that she was in silent communication with their mother.

"Then we need to get rid of it," Lea said.

"Eloo?"

Eloo did not reply, but when Kye glanced at her she was spinning on the spot. Her cape flew out as she whirled, her voice rising in a chant. As she whirled a wind gathered about her spinning form, and minutes later blew out from her, flowing across the gorge, sweeping away the fog to reveal several dark figures half way along the bridge. Their dark forms squealed as the light of the sun fell on them.

"Goblins," Lea cried out, and his bow creaked as he drew it.

"Wait," Kye ordered, watching the great black form of his father charge towards them.

"Kye," Lea asked.

"Notch," Kye whispered, and moments later Lea repeated the command to the Werewolf next to him, and other officers relayed the order.

"Draw," Kye said, his own black bow creaking.

The order to "loose", however, did not come for as they watched

Flash crashed into the forms. The crowd of rat like Goblins broke and ran back to the other bank.

Kye stood his archers down and was about to go and speak to Flash when from nowhere there appeared twenty or so crossbowmen who fired their bolts at Flash. Flash, however, had been magically protected against projectiles and the bolts deflected off an invisible screen. Not even one scratched him.

"Get them," Kye barked, ignoring the usual set of commands issued to archers as his bow sang.

The rest of the archers, like him, had been taken by surprise by this appearance, but like the trained soldiers they were they had not completely relaxed. Most of them reacted in time to drop a cloud of arrows among the crossbowmen who for some reason had not brought with them their protective shields, and even before they had a chance to reload their crossbows Kye and the rest of his archers had sent a second and third arrow their way. Only a handful of the men managed to turn and run away, leaving more than a third of them dead or dying on the opposite bank.

"Where did they come from?" Lea asked, drawing another arrow from the ground where a line stood point down in the soil.

"I don't know, but if I were to guess, I would say they were concealed by magic," Eloo said, drawing a lens in a silver frame from her pouch and muttering an incantation before putting it to her eye. "I cannot see anyone, invisible or not."

"This was a probe, nothing more," Kye said, notching another arrow. "We have beaten them back for now, but they will return, and soon."

"I still don't understand," Eloo said sharing Kye's water skin. "Orcs and Goblins hate the sun. Why are they attacking during the day?"

"The Goblins came while the fog protected them from the dawn, but those bowmen were not Orc or Goblin if I read it aright."

"Mercenaries?"

"Or half Orcs, they do not share their parents' hatred of the light."

Kye might have said more, but a voice piped his name from behind. Turning, Kye saw a familiar, if small form pelting towards him her long black hair and tail flowing out behind her.

"Fire Feet," Eloo squealed with pleasure, leaping to embrace the tiny Centaur.

"Eloo, put her down," Kye said drily, though he was smiling. "No doubt she has news for us."

"Commander," Fire Feet said, once Eloo had put her down. "I have brought a report from the White Wolf."

"Then give it."

"No direct attack has yet come against the Kings, but our scouts report that several hundred Trolls are advancing on your positions."

"And the Kings?"

"An equal number of Trolls are moving directly for the fords."

"Then Tristian cannot send us more troops?"

"I fear not, my lord."

"Return to him and tell him we shall hold as long as we can."

The tiny Centaur saluted him and turned to go, but turned back when Kye called her name. "Tell him the three hundred will hold the hot gates."

"My lord?" Fire Feet asked, clearly confused.

"Tell him, he will understand it."

Fire Feet saluted and was gone.

"You do know that the three hundred at Thermopylae were all killed, don't you?" Silver Skin asked, pulling a rolled parchment from a scroll tube.

"They still held," Kye said, squinting through his telescope.

"Anything?" Lea asked, accepting the spyglass.

"No, but that doesn't mean they aren't out there."

"We will hear them before we see them," Lor said, for he had left his post on the end of the line opposite to them.

"Trolls," Kye said, sharing an oatcake with his brother.

"Our arrows may not penetrate their hides," Lor said, but low so that only Kye could hear.

"Trolls are stone, they are susceptible to heat, cold, and sonic vibrations, we will have to en-spell our arrows."

"I can help there," Lea said, touching his sickle moon medallion.

"As can I," added Silver, looking up from her scroll.

"Even I can give them a surprise or two," put in Eloo.

"Then let us prepare. Lor, you should return to your post."

"What about the second line," Lea asked, looking back to where Dancing Falcon and many more waited at the line of posts which had been put up to tell them where the second line of defence was. "Should we bring them forward yet?"

"No, leave them where they are. The plan and our lives may depend on their hanging back."

"If you're sure?"

"No, Lea, I am not sure," Kye said in a whisper as his brother moved away to check that the second line were ready for the first line retreat. "Nothing is certain in war, especially the generals."

Lor was quite correct. The beating sound of pounding feet and of weapons striking on shields reached them an hour later. As Kye scanned the opposite ridge a plume of dust rose to mark the enemy's advance.

"How many?" Lea asked, clutching his medallion in one hand and a tuning fork in the other.

"I cannot tell yet, but from the sound and dust I would guess at least a hundred strong."

"How long?" Eloo asked, standing ready to cast magic, a bead rattle in her hands.

"Half an hour to ten minutes, I cannot say."

Kye was only half right. The main force was almost half an hour away, but a single giant Troll had sprinted ahead and was pounding across the bridge towards Flash before anyone could react. Flash howled, and rising on his hind legs stood almost ten feet tall to block the Troll. The seven foot stone statue of Troll did stop, but only to roar its own rage back at Flash and then come on, swinging a great war hammer at the wolf.

"Kye, do we shoot?" Lea asked, watching the two giants come together with a crash that shook the whole bridge.

"No, they are too close, we will hit Flash too," Kye said in a hoarse voice that revealed his frustration.

"What do we do?"

Kye glanced again at the dust cloud, measuring, and then came to a decision. "Eloo, stay here. If they come in sight get Lor to order the attack. Lea, come with me."

A DRAGON EYE VIEW

"The best way to get a real view is on the wing."
Lightning to the Red Wizard, the Wereding Chronicles.

Dawn found Lightning shaking Rose's shoulder. She opened her eyes, almost blinded by the candle he held.

"Is it time already?" She yawned, accepting his cup of tea.

"Dawn is just breaking," Lightning said presenting her with a tray of cheese and fresh baked bread.

"Has the fighting begun?"

"A few exchanges of arrows and some probes, but the armies have not even appeared, let alone come to blows."

"What are we up to?"

"Get that down you, and then we will get on the wing."

Rose gulped down her tea and took a mouthful of food but found that her stomach contracted, and she pushed the trencher away, unable to eat any more.

"You should eat. You will need your strength today," Lightning said, though he too was only picking at his food.

"My stomach is full of butterflies."

This made Lightning grin, grimly. "I've got worms myself."

"Let's get to it then."

They left Rose's sleeping cell and wound their way through the maze of the fortress bowels. They had to make waywhen a Troll carrying arrows as long as spears came up the stairs before them. Eventually they passed out the small door at the back of the castle, was now manned, or rather dwarfed, and as they passed through the metal gate that guarded the back of the entrance Rose was aware of a movement above them. Looking up she saw a pair of eyes staringback at them through the grating of the murder hole.

"There were no guards yesterday," Rose commented as the dwarf closed and barred the small door behind them.

"We were not at war yesterday," Lightning said, leading her through the deserted village.

"Lightning, aren't we heading the wrong way?"

"For fighting, yes, but I like to take off from an open area."

Once they reached the outskirts of the village they moved to a broad, open space by the river.

"Stand back, while I slip into something more comfortable."

Rose did as he asked and watched as his shape shimmered and swelled into the flaming form of the dragon which blazed in the steadily growing light.

"If my lady is ready," rumbled Lightning, dipping his head low to the ground, "perhaps you would like to mount."

Rose approached him and strapped the saddle about his neck. "How does that feel?"

"Fine," he replied, after taking several deep breaths.

"Not too tight, is it?"

"No, it's just right."

"Then you're ready?"

Lightning flared his wings and snapped his tail from side to side. "Mount, and we'll be away."

Rose hooked a foot into a stirrup and flung her other leg across the saddle to slide it into the strap which would bind her to it.

"Ready?" Lightning vibrated beneath her.

Rose opened her mouth to reply, but hesitated. After all, she was about to go into combat, she was about to fight in a war that was not necessarily her concern. Was she ready?

"Rose," Lightning asked, perhaps sensing her hesitance, "are you all right?"

"Yes, yes, let's go!"

"Are you sure?"

"Let's fly."

"Sure?"

"Fly," Rose insisted.

Lightning did not ask again but began to pound across the ground. His wings began to beat the air. He reached his pace and made a great bound into the air, his wings rising and falling, and they were rising to meet the sun. Rose felt all doubts fall away with the ground and she screamed with joy as the wind snapped her cloak out behind her.

* * *

In his tower room Tristianlooked at the image that surrounded him through his mage magic. Tristian had before him an illusion of the land that spread out before the Kings. As he watched, the tiny form of Lightning appeared over the valley.

"A dragon may turn the tide in our favour," the White Witch said.

"It may, it may not," Tristian said, watching a dark stain spread across the map.

"Is that?"

"I am afraid so," Tristian said grimly, watching the map turning dark.

"But it is still day, they can't be Orcs, can they?"

"I do not know about that, but they are the enemy."

"The western wing appears to be advancing more quickly," Apollo said from the other side of the room.

"Yes, Kye will engage the enemy first."

"Should I reinforce him?"

Tristian did not answer Apolloat first as he stared at the map. "No, Kye will stand as he can. We will need every blade here, it appears. Apollo, man the ballista, we will need to support the first brigade."

"We are going to meet them?"

"Yes, but only as far as the fords."

"My lord?"

"We shall contest the crossings, no more," Tristian said coldly.

"But my lord..."

"That is all, Apollo," the White Wolf broke in. "We do not have the men to meet them in the field, but I will not let them drive us out. We stand here, stand, not you Apollo."

"As you command, my lord," Apollo said stiffly, and left the room.

Tristian watched as the dark stain spread towards him. "I hope Lightning does tip the balance, because if he doesn't we may not win."

* * *

Rose looked down to see the Kings below her, and the land of the barrens stretching out. As she watched, a dark shadow rolled across the scene and cut off her sight.

"Lightning, what is that?"

"Not a cloud," Lightning growled back.

Rose looked again and saw that he might be right. It looked more like black smoke.

"I can't see for it."

"Hang on, and we'll take a closer look."

Rose continued to stare at the bank of dark fog, or whatever it was, as Lightning folded his wings and stooped towards it. When they were just a few feet above it Lightning spread his wings, bringing them to ahalt with a jerk. Rose grunted at the jolt, but ignoring it stared at the dark cloud. It looked like a black curtain, so dark and thick was it.

"What is it?"

"It might have been smoke once," Lightning said, extending a claw to probe the curtain.

His claw stirred the black substance but Rose could not tell if it penetrated the material or not.

"Is it solid?"

"No, my claw goes through it."

"Then we can get through it?"

"Yes, but Rose, I am not sure if we should."

Rose eyed the black smoke and watched an unfelt wind move it as though it were cloth.

"Is it poisonous?"

"Just a moment," Lightning said, and rose a little above the cloud. From there he proceeded to cast a spell.

"What are you doing?"

"The spell should tell me the nature of the cloud," Lightning said, after completing the casting, and breathing a cloud of green light into the black cloud.

"And the spell tells you?"

"That the cloud is smoke, but a spell of darkness has been used to thicken it."

"That doesn't tell me if it is safe to pass through?"

"It is not healthy," Lightning growled. "Cover your mouth with your cloak and hold your breath, and we will go through it and see what is hiding below, shall we?"

Rose did not really want to go through but realised they would have to. She pulled her cloak before her face and took a long breath. As she did, she felt Lightning taking a deep breath beneath her, and with that they plunged into the cloud. For a stifling moment they were engulfed by the cloud and Rose thought she would never see or breathe again. Then they were through the ice cold cloud and into breathable air. Rose coughed as she got her breath back.

"Okay?" Lightning asked, streams of smoke flying from his snout.

"Yes, but what's it for?"

"Look down and you will get your answer."

Rose did, and gasped as she saw the barren and empty land that lay before the Kings was no longer empty. Below them there stretched from horizon to horizon a horde of dark bodies.

"Is that the army?"

"That is more Orcs and Goblins than I have ever seen," Lightning said.

"We are supposed to attack that?" Rose asked, feeling a hand of fear grip her heart.

THE BRIDGE OF TEARS

"There is a bridge that links us to the world of the dead, but when we cross it we do not always know it."

Kye to Lea, the Wereding Chronicles.

Kye rushed to the bridge, Lea's panting telling him his brother was running at his side. When they reached it they could not see exactly what was happening as Great Mother's broad back blocked their view. Kye moved to the east to see past her, but even then he could hardly see what was happening, though his keen hearing picked up Flash's high whimper of pain, a sound he thought he would never hear. Then Great Mother's voice was in his mind. "Cover your ears."

Kye had just shoved his fingers in his ears when Flash gave an ululating howl that filled the world with stone splitting screams. Kye, once he had shaken off the disorientating shock of the cry, realised either Great Mother or Flash had enchanted Flash's voice so that his cry acted as a wave of vibrations designed to split the Troll's stony hide. When Kye had recovered enough to look at the bridge everything was still, the battle ended.

"Great Mother, are Father and you safe?" Kye asked through his mental link.

"Flash has received broken ribs from the Troll's war hammer, but he is healing."

"And the Troll?"

"He went into the river, bleeding sand or whatever runs in their veins."

"I hope you and Father have a few more spells like that because here come the rest of the Trolls," Lea broke in. When Kye looked at him he pointed across the river gorge to where the dusk cloud had materialised into a wall of stone giants.

"Kye, get back to your position, I canhold here," Flash's voice growled in his mind.

Kye was not so sure, but turning he beckoned to Lea and sprinted back to the lines. Silver Skin was chanting over the arrows which stood point down in the ground before the line of archers.

"Vibration spell?" Kye asked, drawing an arrow from the earth. As he held it he could feel a vibration quiver through the shaft, reminding him of a struck tuning fork.

"It will not last long. How long have we got?"

Kye glanced up from the bow, across the gorge to see a cloud of statues swirling around the bridge head as they seemed to be deciding what to do. Kye gauged the range and decided that they were close enough.

"Fire high," he said to Lea, drawing his bow.

"Notch," he heard Lea command to the nearest archers.

"Draw," Kye whispered, and when the command to loose was given, a flock of arrows swooped up into the sky to fall glittering amongst the Trolls.

Normally the Trolls should not have been bothered by the arrows, even though they were bodkin points designed to penetrate armour, but Silver's spell appeared to have some effect. There was a grinding of stone on stone that Kye realised were cries of pain and surprise. The Trolls drew back from the bridge as they tried to get out of range, not before a third volley fell on them, and when they did draw back they left at least three outof ten of their number on the ground.

"Are they dead?"

"I cannot tell from here," Kye said. "But they are down, that has to mean something."

"It has pushed them back," Lea said, fingering his medallion.

"Not for long, they will be back," Kye said, reaching for his telescope.

"And next time they will probably be warded against vibration spells," Silver warned.

"We may have a bigger problem," Eloo said, staring not at the Trolls but the sky above them. "Silver, what do you make of that cloud?"

Silver raised her gaze from the gorge to consider the black cloud bank turning the sky dark.

"It doesn't look good."

"It is not natural," Eloo stated flatly.

Kye wetted a finger and tested the wind.

"It is moving against the wind."

"It is coming on quickly," Lea observed.

"It is the work of the enemy!"

"We shall soon see," Kye said, and he placed another arrow on the string.

Silence fell over the camp as they watched and waited. Sooner than they would have believed possible the cloud filled the sky and spread its dark veil across the vale.

"Impressive," Kye muttered.

"Eloo, can you do what you did with the fog?" Lea asked.

"I could try," Eloo said, "but I doubt I could move that. It is too large, too powerful."

"It will hide Orcs and Goblins from their fear of the sun," Silver said, cupping her silver pendant.

Kye was about to reply when there was a disturbance on the bridge. A high pitched squealing filled the air and for a long moment the camp held its breath, a collective sigh released when Flash's great howl answered it.

"Goblins," Silver confirmed moments later.

"Problem?" Kye asked.

"Not anymore."

"Flash is keeping them back," Eloo said gleefully.

Her grin failed when she saw Kye's grim face.

"What is it?"

But before Kye could reply something fell out of the black clouds to land on the bridge.

"By the Lady, what is that?" Lea asked spotting a huge creature that made the bridge creak with its weight.

"Kain has come," Kye snarled through gritted teeth.

* * *

Rose watched as the tide of bodies swept towards a broad ford of the river Sabrina that stretched before the gates of the Kings and defined the line between the desert and the lands north. As she watched, she saw a flash from the direction of the Kings.

"Lightning, what is happening at the Kings?"

Lightning banked so that they were side on to the enemy and the Kings which gave them a better view of what was happening on both sides of the ford.

"It looks like Apollo is responding," Lightning observed.

Lightning was correct, Rose saw. As they watched, a dark column streamed out from the Kings to form a thin line on the other side of the ford.

"I can't see who's down there. Lightning, are your senses better than mine?"

"They are, but wait a moment."

Rose heard Lightning mutter a spell and suddenly her world expanded. She gasped, as her hearing picked up snarls and growls from the dark tide's side, and the creak of harness from the Kings side. Her nostrils picked up the tang of dust, kicked up by hundreds of marching feet and mixed with the musky stench of sweat that stank of fear blended with the musk of wild cats. Her sight, too, improved incredibly. She could now see figures below her, still very small, but she could pick out every detail of their armour and weapons.

"Lightning, what have you done?"

"Linked your senses to mine," Lightning said.

"This is how you see the world?" she asked, startled and delighted at the extent of his perceptions.

"Yes, but watch while you can. The spell will not last forever."

Rose watched as the Kings' force was led out by the large Apollo, mounted on a huge and magnificent looking stag. At his shoulder stood the tall and gleaming form of the White Witch. Her long white hair flew out behind her, and mixed with the mane of her Fury bodyguard, Winter. Behind them stood a column of Trolls, bearing huge shields and spears, their flanks bracketed by wings of cavalry, Centaurs on one flank and Furies on the other. At the back came a screen of archers.

"They are hopelessly outnumbered," Rose cried.

"Perhaps."

"Can we help them?"

"I would, Rose, but we have stayed too long. Kye may need us in the west."

"I had forgotten," Rose whispered.

"Then let us see what is happening with him."

Rose agreed, but she could not tear her eyes away from the tiny figures below them. As she watched, the first blow was struck. Arrows and spears reached out from the dark tide's side, but most fell short. The White Witch raised her staff above her head and her voice filled the world. A great wind sprang up from nowhere to drive back anymore darts. The wind, unfortunately, buffeted Lightning, and they lurched to one side.

"Lightning let's get out of here."

"Yes, we do seem to be in the way, don't we."

Lightning, with considerable effort, turned and flew to the west.

* * *

The creature on the bridge was clearly much larger than Flash.

"That's Kain?" Lea asked, struggling to see what was happening.

"He has gained a steed from somewhere," Silver Skin said, her voice distant, and it was clear she was mindlinked with Great Mother. "He is riding a Panther bat Gryphon."

"Flash is in trouble," Lea gasped.

"Can we help?" Eloo asked.

"Great Mother orders us to stay," Silver said, her voice taut with pain and doubt.

"Why?"

"The Black Horn," Kye whispered.

Eloo opened her mouth to ask him what he meant, but her voice was drowned out by Flash's cry of pain. All of the Silverbrow Werewolves clutched their heads and fell to their knees.

"Flash," Kye cried.

Although Eloo was not as tightly bound, she too felt the backlash of Flash's mind as it died in a burst of pain.

"He is gone," Lea whispered.

∗ ∗ ∗

In his tower room a tear ran down Tristian's dark cheek. "Another of my children goes before me."

∗ ∗ ∗

Eloo looked up at the bridge but it was now engulfed in a cloud of darkness.

"Great Mother is alone against him," Lor shouted from his end of the line.

But not even Lor's powerful voice could speak over the sudden roar which filled the gorge. The roar was not Great Mother or even Kain or his dreadful mount, but the voice of the Sabrina which had, for some unknown reason, stopped its flow as if dammed, and then once it gathered its waters had let them cascade forth in a tidal wave of roaring force that instead of falling over the falls rose up above the bridge in a wave that stood as tall as a giant, before crashing down on the bridge. Kain, his mount, and Great Mother were swept away.

WASHING AWAY THE DARK TIDE

"Water is cleansing, but it can be unpredictable."

Bright Eyes to Kye, the Wereding Chronicles.

At the fords of the Sabrina, Apollo watched as the dark tide of the enemy swept towards him. He looked up at the roiling cloud of darkness and understood it was the only thing keeping the Orcsfrom running in terror of the sun.

"My Lady, can you use your storm powers to remove that cloud?"

"I can try, but first I think I might need other spells. They approach."

Apollo grunted and turning his head to his standardbearer, a Herotaura, ordered, "Tell the archers to fire as soon as they are in range."

"Yes, my Lord," said the Stag Centaur, and lifting a bugle to his lips called several notes.

As he gave this order, the dark tide launched their own cloud of arrows, spears and sling stones, many of which fell short as they were not in range. One javelin fell at Apollo's feet. Gazing down at it he gave a grim smile, and raising his right hand to his lips he kissed the gold ringwhich sat there. His lips touched the ruby.

"Horned God, fill me with your fires," he implored, before growling the words to a spell that warded him against most physical attacks.

For her part, the White Witch raised her twisted rune capped staff above her head and shouted a word of power. From nowhere, a powerful wind sprang up and blew towards the enemy. Its power turned back or knocked out of the air all the projectiles flung their way.

"Thank you, my lady," Apollo said, and spoke a word of his own, making his large spiked mace glow with the light of the sun. "Can you make a wind that will push their owners back too?"

"Given time, perhaps," Aleena said, lowering her staff to the ground and igniting the metal cap with her own light. "But I am not sure I have the time."

Apollo was about to reply when a shadow passed over them and dozens of long bow arrows fell among the enemy. The wave screamed and swirled as the first lines fell dead and dying under the rain of death, but it was not enough to stop the horde. The archers pored five volleys into the tide, and although the Orcs who led the charge were climbing over the bodies of their fellows three deep, they kept coming.

"They must not get over the ford," Apollo said, and turned to his second to give the order for the Trolls to advance, when someone tugged at his leg. He spun on the person ready to give them a mouthful but when he turned found no one. He was taken aback 'till a voice at his feet piped up at him.

"My Lord, we must not enter the water yet." The voice belonged to a Gnome.

"Holly, I am about to counter attack," Apollo growled at the small Gnome, the army's Druid.

"I have been sent a warning by Lady Great Mother. The river will keep them back for now, we must not enter the waters."

Apollo was about to argue with the tiny druid when his herald Thorn's exclamation turned his attention. "My lord, the river, it is gone."

Apollo, looking up, saw that the Deer Centaur was right. The broad but shallow river which covered several yards was suddenly gone leaving only drying mud, as if the ground had swallowed it.

"This is some design of the enemy," Winter growled in the sudden silence.

"No, it is the Lady's work," cried the Gnome Druidess.

Apollo wanted to order his Trolls forward to engage the horde, but hesitated. The Goblins and larger Orcs squelched into the mud and some stopped to fire crossbows and heave spears. The White

206

Witch intoned a magic couplet and a glowing wall appeared between her forces and the Orcs, protecting them from the projectiles. The Orcs, seeing, howled with defiance and poured towards them.

"Brace yourself," Apollo said, watching the horde spilling towards him.

His next words were drowned out by a roar as the river suddenly came rushing back in a great surge, its power magnified to many times more than before. Its waters rose in a tidal wave that stood several feet high and had so much power behind its white crest that the Orcs and Goblins before it were swept off their feet and flung like rag dolls before its raging fury, their bodies just more flotsam on its fast flowing rage. Apollo looked up from the swollen waters to the opposite bank where the dark tide had come to a stop, shocked, perhaps, by this turn of events. For a brief moment the enemy's momentum had stopped, and Apollo decided to take advantage of it.

"Phalanx advance," he cried, and calling upon his faith in the Horned God, he lifted his mace above and cried the words to a spell. The Orcline was suddenly torn aside by the power of his calling. From above poured the light of a sun, not the real sun, but the summoned power of his god. The Orcs and Goblins screamed and cowered back, covering their eyes. Into this confused horde there crashed a phalanx of Trolls followed by two wings of cavalry. The horde was driven back from the river and into the desert. Apollo would have chased them, but into his mind the cold voice of Tristian intruded. "Apollo, do not pursue, you must not over extend your line."

Apollo snarled with frustration but reined in his great stag. Raising his voice, he shouted to Thorn who had stayed at his shoulder, "Sound the withdrawal."

Although Apollo did not like giving up the ground he had gained, he understood the tactical wisdom of the withdrawal. As the Orcs regained the shadows of the clouds they lost their fear of the light and were turning back to stand and fight the advancing Trolls. As the Stag Centaur sounded his orders on his trumpet and the Trolls began anorderly backstep, he saw advancing out of the darkness a huge column of grey figures. Apollo blinked, and realised he was looking at a force of Trolls many times larger than his own.

"We may be in trouble," he growled.

HOLDING ACTION

*"Sometimes in war, all you can do is hold your ground. You can't
advance, you can't retreat, all you can do is stand."*

Kye to Lor, the Wereding Chronicles.

They stared at the spot where the bridge had been, and slowly
the realisation that the river had taken the bridge away sank
in.

"What happened? Why did the river surge?" Lea asked.

"Did you see the form the wave took?" Kye asked in a hoarse
whisper.

"No, why?"

"It was a winged wolf," Silver Skin answered, though there were
tears on her cheeks.

"Our house sign," Lea exclaimed. "You mean Great Mother made
the river do that?"

"She was a high member of the druids," Eloo said.

"But doing that with the river..." Lea was unable to finish the
thought. "Did she survive it?" he asked, looking hopefully at Silver
Skin.

Silver Skin closed her eyes and turned a full circle. Her pendant
glowed in her hand and Lea knew she was searching magically for
Great Mother.

"I cannot find her," Silver Skin said, when she finally opened eyes
brimming with tears.

"She has gone to join Flash in the other world," Kye said, his face
a stone mask.

Lea and Lor flung back their heads and howled long wails of pain
and grief. Kye did not appear to react. Eloo, who could read him,
knew he, too, was shocked to the core.

"Now is not the time to grieve."

"Are you made of stone, Kye," Lea snarled at his taller brother.

For a moment Kye lost his iron control and his eyes flashed. An animal snarl rolled out from him, quieting everyone near. "I, too, feel grief, Lea, but we are at war! Fight first, grieve later. If you want a focus for your anger, find it out there amongst the Orcs."

Lea could find no answer to this, so he just nodded.

"But without the bridge they cannot get across," Eloo broke in, attempting to change the subject.

"Think again, Eloo," Silver Skin said, turning their attention to the opposite bank of the gorge.

On the other side the wall of Trolls were manoeuvring a massive bulk of wood into position. Its wide bulk would fill the gap between the damaged spans.

"Notch," Kye cried in a voice suddenly loud, possibly powered with his grief.

Bows creaked as Lea repeated Kye's order to draw. "Loose."

Kye and the rest of his archers dropped a sheath of arrows on the Trolls, but even when the giants fell to the vibrating arrows the tree trunk moved forwards. Before they could stop them the enemy had bridged the gap and small rat like Goblins were scrambling along the trunk.

"Focus on the bridge," Kye ordered, shortening his own aim to drop an arrow at the bridge. Then the Goblins were on their side of the gorge and were running up the slope to where Kye and the others stood.

Kye dropped his aim so that his arrow would not fly high, but would rather hit the Goblin twenty feet before him. His arrow slammed into the Goblin's throat and sent it flying back, its gurgling form knocking over several of its kin who were trying to follow it. But it was not alone, and though Kye felled two Goblins with one long arrow, there were hundreds of the small rat like men flowing across the bridge.

"Eloo, Silver, can you do something about that log?"

Neither answered him, for they were both in the midst of casting.

Kye grunted and fired a fifth arrow into the advancing wave. He was considering whether to withdraw to the second line when Eloo and Silver's spells made their presence known. Out of the dark clouds there lanced a red tongue of lightning, followed by a column of silver fire that poured down on the bridge, but for some reason neither spells had any effect.

Kye snarled, and releasing his bow slew another Goblin. "Eloo?"

"The trunk may be warded. Our spells aren't having any effect."

Kye grunted and fired another arrow, but as the next Goblin fell a larger Orc leapt over the piles of bodies and sprinted up the hill, its large hide shield giving it some protection from the storm of arrows falling about it. Kye saw him coming, and with a snarl fired his arrow into its dog like face. But this Orc must have had some protective magic about it for the arrow fell short, its force spent on some invisible shell surrounding the Orc. Kye growled and reached for his short sword.

* * *

Lightning swooped low over the gorge, his claws only a spear length above the bridge although as Rose took in a brief glance of the battle ground, she saw the rope and wood bridge was gone, replaced by a great hulk of wood which Goblins and Trolls were scrambling across to reach the other side. Rose did not have time to see how Kye and the others were as Lightning swooped up towards the river's head.

"Lightning, I didn't see Kye. How are they doing?"

"Well enough, but as you probably saw the enemy is across the river."

"We have to stop them. Can we do anything about the bridge?"

Lightning grunted, and smoke curled from his nostrils. "Use your bow to clear it, and I will see how flammable it is."

"Yes," Rose shouted with joy, feeling the lust of battle grip her.

She took from its holster her bow, and stringing it drew from its quiver on the opposite side of the saddle an arrow. She fitted it to the string and by then Lightning had wheeled and was flying back down the river's course and the makeshift bridge was before them. Rose saw a large Troll on the broad trunk, a hatchet held high as it roared in defiance.

"Cry at this," Rose said, drawing the bow string to her ear.

Below her she felt Lightning swell as he drew in a great lungful of air. Then he breathed out a huge gout of fire that washed over the bridge, covering everything in red flames. Rose let fly her arrow as they flew past the now torch like figure of the Troll. Rose's face was covered by her mask, but still she felt the intensity of the heat of Lightning's fire as they flew over it. When she looked back, she saw the Troll had disappeared and so had the trunk in an inferno of red flames that danced and spun like living demons.

"By the gods," Rose breathed, taking in the thirty foot span of bridge that blazed with fire.

"Is it gone?" Lightning asked, wheeling around to face back the way they had just come.

"I'm not sure," Rose squeaked, for in truth she was dizzy from Lightning's quick turn. "It's burning."

"But not down," Lightning growled, and he swooped at it again.

Rose saw a Goblin aiming a crossbow at Lightning, and without thinking fired an arrow at him. She watched, shocked to see him blown back fifty feet when her arrow slammed with a shower of sparks into his leather breastplate.

Lightning roared, and as they swept over the burning log he snapped his tail down at the bridge. Rose felt the vibration of the blow as his tail connected with the wood. But the bridge held, for when they wheeled it was to see a large Goblin dowsing the flames with water from a beaded and feathered water skin, his voice screaming into the air. A score of his Goblin followers chanted behind him.

"Who is he?" Rose asked as they passed over the bridge once more.

"A shaman, I would guess."

"Well, he's raining on our parade."

"Not for much longer," Lightning said, and diving at the bridge he gripped the tree trunk in his front claws. With a huge flex of his shoulders he tore it loose and with a beat of his wings he was carrying the tree away.

"Lightning, what are you doing? Where are you going?"

"Just returning a gift," Lightning snarled through gritted teeth as he carried the trunk just above the heads of the Trolls looking up at them with obsidian eyes and stony faces.

"Lightning, we are too close!" Rose's point was made clear as a spear leapt up at them.

Lightning changed that as he beat his wings with huge effort and rose several feet above the enemy. Once he was out of range he let go of the log. Rose watched as the huge tree fell to crush a line of Trolls who were aiming ballista sized crossbows at them.

"Yes," she cried, watching the huge trunk smash the statues to the ground.

"One good turn deserves another," Lightning said, and with a beat of wings he turned back towards the gorge.

"Die," Rose screamed in a mixture of hate and joy as she fired an arrow down into the hordes which boiled beneath her. She did not know if her arrow hit or killed anyone. She did see a shower of sparks, but did not really care, so long as she could strike a blow at the enemy preventing her from reaching Robin. That was all she cared about, that and helping the people like Kye who had promised to help her in that quest.

* * *

Kye snarled as he reached for Wolf's Fang, his short sword. He did not want to fight at closequarters, but the Orc was too close. As he reached for the blade the Orc lunged at Kye with a broad bladed short spear. Kye used his black bow to sweep the spear wide at the same time ripping Fang from its sheath and plunging its point into the Orc's boiled leather covered chest. Kye heard Fang's growl of pleasure as he drank the Orc's bloodover the Orc's cry of pain as it felt its life drain away.

"Is there anything more tasty than Orc blood?" the sentient sword growled in Kye's mind.

Kye did not respond to the sword's mental comment but snarled as he tore the blade free of the Orc's dying body. He wiped it clean on the Orc's armour and thrust it back into its sheath. Then he tore an arrow from the tube at his hip, and notching it fired it at the nearest Goblin. The rat like man fell screaming, but there was another and another behind it. Hundreds of the monsters must have swarmed across the bridge.

"Kye, we can't hold against such numbers!" Lea cried, firing his own bow.

"We will hold," Kye snarled, drawing and loosing again and again, his movements almost mechanical as he notched, drew and loosed in fluid motions.

What Lea might have replied to this was never heard, for with a scraping of wood on stone a great shudder went through the ground. Kye looked towards the bridge, to see the fiery form of Lightning lifting away the log and flying with it towards the enemy lines.

"We are not alone, it seems," Silver Skin said from behind Kye.

Kye grunted in answer as he released his bow and another Orc fell, but there were still hundreds of Orcs and Goblins on their side of the gorge.

"Silver, can you thin the tide?" Kye asked, drawing his last arrow from the tube.

"Perhaps, but it may not be enough."

"Do what you can," Kye said, and fired the arrow to see a tall Orc fall, his arrow through its shoulder.

Silver chanted behind him, and seconds later a wall of ice sprang ten feet tall into the air, cutting off the two enemies from each other. The wall was a pale mirror which blurred but did not prevent each side from seeing the other.

"Nice one, Silver," Lea wheezed, leaning on his bow.

"It will not lastfor long," Silver said, eyeing the wall.

"Arrows," Kye shouted, and runners appeared from the cover of the trees to bring fresh arrows to the exhausted, and in some cases bloody archers.

"Kye, are you hurt?" Eloo asked anxiously, a stoppered flask in one hand. Kye had no doubt it held a healing potion which she would thrust upon him if he said yes.

"No, I am fine, my love, but if you or Silver can spare the magic please see if any are hurt and heal them."

"I will see what I can do in the little time we have," Silver said, eyeing a particularly large Orc wearing a great feathered headdress and waving a shrunken head about on the other side of the ice wall. "If I am any judge that Orc is a shaman, and he may dispel my wall at any moment."

"Then be quick about your healing and let *me* worry about the dog."

"As you command, Alpha," Silver said, and her voice rang with power.

Kye took a step back, his face shocked as if Silver had slapped him.

"Why do you call me that?" he snarled, a look of panic on his face.

"Flash is dead, you are his eldest son," Silver said, her voice as hard as stone, and as cold as ice. "You are the Alpha now. You are the leader of our clan, and a General of the Silver Shield. If you do not leadus, who does?"

Kye lowered his head as if in shame or acknowledgement of her words. He raised his medallion and looked at it. The disk had only been partly silver before. The top right quarter had remained black metal, but now it turned silver so Kye's pendant was now a silver disk.

"Go, Silver, and return to me quickly."

"As you command, Alpha," Silver said, and Kye nodded at her words.

When he turned back to face the ice wall it was to see it crack down the middle, then shatter into a hundred pieces as the Orc shaman's magic overwhelmed Silver's. The Orcshaman's cry of triumph was turned into a gurgle as Kye's arrow took him in the throat.

FIRE AND LIGHTNING

"Fire and lightning clash, when opposing forces come together."
Takana to Lightning, the Wereding Chronicles.

Rose looked down at the bank on the Kings side to see a wall of black bodies stretching from the edge of the gorge to where Kye and his people were attempting to hold it back.

"Lightning, can we help them?"

Lightning did not reply in words but flew over the fighting. Wheeling at the trees, he faced back the way he had come. He flew low over the defences and breathed his killing fire into the enemies' faces. Lightning's flames withered the Orcs and Goblins, who had nowhere to go to avoid the onslaught. Kye and his thin line of defenders raised their weapons and cheered when they realised Lightning had decimated a force which was about to wipe them out. However, no sooner had the defenders cries of joy died when the sky was filled by the roar of a huge beast. The sky appeared to split apart, to reveal a vast red scaled form that looked down at them with baleful ruby eyes.

"Another Fire Drake," Kye growled, regarding the scarlet form.

"That one looks familiar," Eloo said, as she too gazed up at the huge beast hovering like a red thunderhead.

"That is because he is," Silver Skin said.

"It's the same one that faced us at the Citadel," Kye snarled.

"Then we can assume he's not friendly," Eloo said, her words confirmed as from above the new dragon there fell a bolt of lightning that stabbed at Lightning below it.

* * *

Rose's cry of victory died in her throat as the roar washed over her. Looking up she saw the vast bulk of the dragon hanging above them, like a scaly mountain that might fall upon them.

"Lightning!"

"I see him," Lightning replied, his voice remarkably calm.

"What do we do?"

"We...Rose, your shield," Lightning's answer was changed, as a flash of light fell from the dragon.

Rose grabbed the shield from where it hung on the front of Lightning's saddle and raised it before her. As she raised it to shield her face, she realised why. Like a discharge from a thunder cloud, a bolt of lightning stabbed down at them from the dragon. The bolt would have slammed into her shield but as the bolt shot down the rune embossed on her shield flashed into Rose's mind. Her lips formed a word she did not know, and a disk of red energy formed a few inches before the shield to intercept the lightning. The impact of the bolt as it discharged against the shield with a crackle and burst of sparks rocked Rose back in the saddle. She was only just trying to adjust when a second stroke of lightning stabbed down at them. Lightning lurched to one side and the bolt slammed into his right wing, but appeared not to affect him as he wheeled to his left.

"L. it's raining lightning!"

"I know, hang on," he shouted, flying back toward the trees.

Rose thought at first he was running, but as they reached the trees they turned in ever increasing circles as Lightning wheeled up into the high airs so he could face the dragon rather than be below it.

"Rose, remember the protective spells, I taught you?"

"Yes."

"Then cast them. You will need all the protection you can."

Rose focused on the diamond ring on her hand, and repeating the words she had learnt summoned the dark cloud about her that should protect her from physical attack.

Soon they were on a level with the giant dragon and moving towards it. Now Rose could see past the great horned head and massive shoulders to see this dragon also had a rider, or was it more than one person crouched on the dragon's neck.

"L. there's someone on the dragon."

"I see them. Watch out, your shield is failing."

Glancing down at her shield she saw its red disk was dimming. She spoke the word of power again but stumbled over the pronouncement, and its light all but winked out.

"More clearly," Lightning said, though how he knew its light was dimming Rose did not know because he did not take his glowing eyes off the huge dragon before them.

Rose tried again and must have said it right since the disk of energy created by the shield brightened. Its glow still allowed her to see the figure astride the other dragon. As Lightning flew near to his opponent she was better able to make out the detail of this rider. It was a figure dressed like her in bright red, though it had only a short cape instead of a great cloak like Rose, but unlike Rose this figure wore a great helm, its red armour completely concealing its wearer's face, the helm crested by a red dragon, its wings spread to shelter its shoulders.

"Who is that, Lightning?"

"I do not know, Rose. I have not heard of such a rider."

As they neared the dragon the rider raised its right arm and Rose saw it was holding a javelin in its hand.

"Lightning, watch out, that's a javelin."

Lightning beat his wings and they rose above the aim of the rider. The cast missile fell past them.

"Lightning, give me a shot at him."

"As my lady commands," Lightning answered, speeding up his wing beats. They shot past the red on its left and Rose, who had replaced the shield on the saddle before her fired an arrow at the javelin thrower. The arrow exploded into sparks just inches from the dragon and its rider, making Rose realise they too were magically shielded.

However, as they swept past, Rose saw the dragon did indeed

bear two riders. A smaller figure, dressed in black, crouched behind the rider, facing backwards, and this smaller rider bore a bow of its own. As Lightning swept past this black archer fired its own shaft at them. Rose felt a blow on her side and glancing down saw the arrow protruding from the folds of her cloak.

"Rose, are you hurt?"

"I feel no pain," Rose said, plucking the arrow from its position, to see no blood on its barbed head.

The shaft didn't get through she realised as she felt her side and found no breach.

"It seems that neither we nor they can arrow each other."

"Then let us see what magic can do."

Lightning had flown past the large drake, and whenhe turned found the larger dragon had turned to follow them. As they faced one another, the huge dragon opened its under slung jaw and vomited out a cloud of what appeared to be brown sand. Lightning tried to avoid this sandstorm, but he was not quick enough and his head was engulfed by it. Rose did not understand what happened next, nor why, but one moment Lightning was quivering beneath her like a huge horse, the next he was gone as if he had never existed. Rose was astride a non-existentsaddle, dragon and saddle vanished beneath her as if they had never been there. For a long time she just hung there as if gravity had not realised what had happened, and then as the world caught up with her Rose found herself falling at great speed.

THE DYING OF THE LIGHT

"Before the dawn, darkness."
Apollo, from the Wereding Chronicles.

Apollo's forces slowly withdrew to the ford, but before he left the prince called two of his fellow priests to his side. With their help he prayed to their fiery god. Calling down his power, they burnt off a large swathe of the cloud so that between the fords and where they stood there was now sunlight which they hoped the Goblins would not cross. They had only just done this when the edge of the Trolls reached them. A large Troll in the lead raised a ringed hand, and mutteringa dark spell shot a black beam at Apollo who blocked it with the mirror of his shield and reflected the beam back at the Troll who was reduced to dust in the blink of an eye. This sight stopped the column of Trolls for an instant and allowed Apollo to turn and gallop back to where the White Which stood in the shallows. However, as Apollo glanced over his shoulder he felt as much saw a shadow pass above him. Looking up, he saw to his anger some unfelt wind or will had drawn the black cloud across the sky and where there had been blue sky, there was once more black thundery clouds.

"Curse this ink," Apollo spat at Aleena, splashing up to her.

"Not for much longer," the white which said, gripping a medallion about her neck and chanting.

As her eyes began to glow and then turn solid white, a wind snatched at her long snowy mane and cloak. Apollo would have asked her what she was doing but he would have had to shout above the gale which was suddenly around them. Wind tore at his cloak and he felt as if a giant was standing behind him as the wind pushed at him. He would have told her to stop, if he could, but it took all his strength to stay in his seat as the great stag snorted and bucked.

But then the wind was gone, and silence descended on the area. Then Apollo was dazzled as bright sunlight beat down on him. When his vision cleared he saw the sorcerer's magic had blown all the dark veil away. There was only a remnant of dark cloud, and that was flying at great speed into the south.

"Thank you, my Lady."

"We are not out of it yet, my lord," Aleena purred, pointing with her staff to the still approaching wall of Trolls. "The sun will quail the Orcs and their spawn, but Trolls march in rain or sun."

"What of fire?" Apollo asked, clasping his sun like medallion. Praying to his horned god he summoned power which shot in a golden ray from the pendant to draw a line of fire before the advancing Trolls. The beam made the ground smoke and then a wall of fire leapt ten feet into the air, springing up between them and the Trolls.

"How long?" the White Witch asked.

"Only a few minutes, but it should allow us to prepare for them."

They retreated over the ford and waited for the enemy to come to them. The wall of fire snuffed out and the Trolls advanced on them, but they were not alone. Swirling around the edges of the great block of Trolls were many small clusters of Orcs and Goblins milling around battle standards.

"How are they able to withstand the glare of the sun?" asked Thorn, Apollo's standard bearer.

"The standards must be enchanted, look, they cast more shadow than they should," Aleena pointed out.

She was right. The standards, many of them spears topped with animal or human skulls, or shrunken heads, were casting pools of shade that spread over the groups of Goblins in wide pools that did not correspond to the rays of the sun.

"I can take care of that," Apollo said, glaring at the dark clouds that hung around the Orcs.

"Then I suggest you do so quickly," Aleena said before launching into a spell.

Apollo and his fellow sun priests cast magic that dispelled the Orc shade pools. As the pools of shade disappeared the Goblins screamed fell onto the ground prostrate, or turned tail and ran. The Trolls, however, came on, not dissuaded by the Orcs' flight, but marching over anything in their path.

Apollo's stag, Dawn Tredder, snorted and shied away from where Aleena stood. Apollo realised moments later why, as the temperature around the tall, white clad sorceress dropped. Ice crystals forming in the air as her voice rose in volume. Moments later new clouds appeared over the Trolls, but this time they were grey and white. From them there fell snow, sleet and lightning. The forks of lightning smote the leading Trolls, knocking down at leastthree in the first line, and those behind them fell over them and fell to their knees as they slipped on the now frost covered ground.

"Again, my lady, you have my thanks," Apollo said, giving the order for his archers to fire.

The sky was suddenly full of snow, sleet, lightning and hundreds of arrows. Amongst the rain of arrows fell the spear long bolts of the two ballistas standing on the entries of rock which bracketed the gates. The archers' withering fire fell like rain on the Trolls, but their numbers seemed endless. The steel rain stopped to reveal many Trolls still coming. Apollo grasped his golden medallion and began to chant. When his spell died on his lips, a look of disbelief came on his face.

"My power is gone."

"My lord?" Thorn asked.

"My power from the Horned God, it is gone! I feel no connection."

As Apollo and his fellow sun priests realised their link to their god was severed the world went dark.

* * *

High on his balcony overlooking the battle ground Tristian felt a vast shadow pass across him. Looking up, he watched as something crept across the sun, its bulk cutting out the glow.

"An eclipse," the White Wolf hissed, as if the word was a curse. "Silver Lady, how can this be?"

* * *

Apollo stared at the shadow of the moon and gasped as the sun was completely covered, plunging the plains into the dimness of twilight.

"The Orcs will not be stopped now," he breathed, his voice full of shock.

"Lord, what can we do?" Thorn asked.

Apollo looked out at the horde of Trolls and the many Goblins now appearing behind them and snarled his reply. "We fight!"

THE FLIGHT OF THE EAGLE

"Magic can achieve great wonders, but one of the most joyous is the power of flight."
Eloo to the Red Wizard, the Wereding Chronicles.

Rose still did not know what had happened to Lightning, but she knew she was falling to her death. Then something sparked in her mind and she remembered that strapped to her back was an Eagle Sword, which according to legend should grant her the power of flight. She grasped the hilt of the sword and felt a tingle pass into her flesh. She did not know how to activate the sword's magic, but when she drew it forth the stones in the golden bird's head were glowing. Rose realised she was no longer falling, but hanging in mid-air, neither falling nor rising, but simply suspended. Rose felt a wild animalistic scream rise up from deep inside her, and when it tore loose it filled the world with her anger.

* * *

The cry made Kye glance up from where more Trolls were placing vast slabs of stone across the gap. When he saw Rose hanging there he gasped, realising. *"Tristian's vision!"*

Eloo turned to ask him what he said but saw that his eyes had rolled back in their sockets, revealing their whites. "Kye?"

"She is in chains of darkness," Kye's voice whispered, though whether he was talking to Eloo or himself not even she was certain.

"Kye, the Trolls are coming," Lea shouted, looking to Kye for leadership.

"Kye, come back to us," Eloo said, stroking his arm beneath the leather of his bracers. "We need you here, not in the other lands."

* * *

Rose hung there, the light gleaming dimly on the steel of the blade. A world filling roar made her look up from the metal to see the vast bulk of the dragon bearing down on her like an avalanche of red scales. Rose stared at them and saw the red figure on its back holding up something in her hand. She guessed it was casting some destructive magic. Rose wanted to cast something back at them but she only knew a handful of spells and most of them were fire based. She remembered what Lightning had told her.

"Fire Drakes are immune to fire; they can walk through infernos and love heat."

Still, she could not just hang here and wait for lightning or fire to rain down on her. As she glared at the figure casting she felt the fires within her rising. She tried to hold them back. Part of her, she realised, did not want them to stop. She wanted to unleash her fire upon these monsters who had killed Lightning or taken him away from her. As she felt the fire rise she felt herself float downwards an inch and as she did her elbow nudged something protruding from her belt. Dropping her hand to it she realised it was one end of the long rod that was the wand of Wisdom. As her hand touched it, she felt its many rings writhe against her, and words of magic appeared on the mirror of her mind. Her mouth formed the words she did not understand, and as they did the fire that rose from her core shot out of her mouth, the words empowering them. From Rose's mouth there billowed a huge cloud of fog which washed over the red dragon and its riders, concealing them from her, and perhaps more importantly, hiding Rose from them. Out of the cloud lanced a red beam that would have hit Rose if she had remained where she was, but as she cast the spell the sword jerked in her hand and she floated up beyond the cloud. The ray streaked under her feet, to hit nothing. The dragon roared, and seconds later the cloud was lit from within by the dragon's breath. Rose felt the heat through her boots. The dragon's breath was so intense it boiled off the fog and left the air between them clear.

Rose found herself looking down into the huge beast's glowing and angry eyes.

* * *

Eloo turned from Kye to see dozens of Trolls tramping across a makeshift stone bridge. Turning back to a staring Kye, she leapt into the air and smacked him across the face. When she landed back at his feet Kye's eyes were no longer showing white but were staring at her.

"Kye, the Trolls are coming, snap out of it!"

"I have, but it is worse than that."

"What could be worse?" As Eloo asked the world dimmed, and dusk fell in the middle of the day.

* * *

Apollo watched as the Trolls moved like a wall towards him. He ordered his archers to open fire but their rain of arrows were either turned aside by magic or the stony skin-armour of the Trolls.

"Holly, you are a moon priest, will your magic help?"

"No," the tiny woman said, tears in her voice. "The Lady will not answer me."

"Perhaps," Aleena hissed, "but my magic is not granted to me by a god."

She spoke words of power that chilled the air they passed through, and moments later a wall of hail stones were falling on the front line of the Trolls. The white frozen chunks were as large as Apollo's fists, and although some of them were turned aside by their protective magic, many smashed the Trolls to the ground causing their fellows coming behind to trip over them. Others slipped on the suddenly slippery ground. They quickly covered themselves with shields but the clatter of ice on armour and shield rose to a roar, and in moments a wall of ice had built up before the Trolls. Apollo, staring at the falling hail, realised not all magic was removed. Raising the ring to before his eyes he saw its large ruby glowed with an inner light. When he reached out with his mind to it he felt within the stone's heart the magic he had stored there over many years stir in response. Apollo watched as a Troll wielding a long metal wand melted the ice with a ray of heat. He aimed the ring at the Troll, and speaking a word of power he unleashed the ring's energy which blasted the Troll with a ray of ruby light, burning a hole through the giant's chest.

"Stored magic still works," he cried to his troops. "If you have a ring or wand it will still work."

"Good, because here come the Goblins," Aleena shouted.

Even as her warning came, from either side of the wall of Trolls there streamed a screaming cloud of Goblins brandishing fire hardened spears, stone mauls and bone saws.

∗ ∗ ∗

Eloo stared up into the darkened sky. "What is it?"

"An eclipse," Kye said, his voice making the words a curse.

"My link to the Silver Lady," Silver cried, holding her pendant out before her, "is broken! I cannot feel her!"

"She is being held in chains," Kye whispered.

Eloo reached for her own pentacle and tried to tap into the magic energies, but she too felt her reservoirs drained.

"I too cannot feel the Goddess's magic." She looked to her wand of lightning, and reaching into it summoned its powers. Its tip flared with light. She spoke the command word and a bolt of energy shot thirty feet into the approaching wall of Goblins. "Some magic still works."

Kye, giving the order to "loose," fired an arrow at the Goblins. Then raising his hand, he looked at the moonstone on his ring. Summoning its power, he fired a ray of cold at the nearest Goblin.

But the realisation that the moon and sun priests amongst their ranks had lost their connection to their gods had shaken many of the defenders, who now believed their arrows were not enough to hold the hordes back. Kye realised, as he fired another ray, the time to fall back had come. "Withdraw, and quickly."

Lea passed the order down the line, and after launching a last volley the archers broke ranks and ran back to the next position, reforming to fire at the horde with fresh arrows. Kye and Lea held till the last archer had passed them, and only then did they turn and run, but not before Lea had played his own trick. He had cast a spell on his horn, for being a Bard he drew most of his power from the magic of music. When he blew it, it issued a roar so loud it acted like a wall of sound into which the enemy ran, and came to a halt as if they had run into a solid wall of stone, instead of sound. Lea's magic held the Goblins and Trolls back for a moment, but more came on. Kye and Lea turned back just as they reached the low barrier of stone and earth behind which the archers hid. A Goblin came at Kye, a Troll behind it. Kye used his bow like a staff and swotted the leaping Goblin aside. His voice snarled out a spell, and from his ring hand there grew an icicle like blade. When the Goblin came at him with its bone dagger Kye drove his ice dagger through its throat. The Troll behind it raised its club above its head, but staggered as over Kye's head there lanced a stroke of lightning, and Kye knew Eloo was supporting him. Kye drove his ice dagger into the statue's stomach. When the ice struck the stone of its flesh it shattered into several shards but still had some effect. The stone skin cracked and a dark liquid oozed from the wound. Kye reached for his short sword, but he knew he would not be quick enough.

* * *

Rose watched as the dragon almost lazily flapped its wings to lift it to her level. As she watched, his great chest swelled as he drew in air for a fiery breath. Although she knew her clothing was fire resistant she did not believe it could withstand the fury of his furnace. As she stared into the jaws of death she remembered she had been here before. Then the magic within her had provided her with protection, but Rose did not feel it rising now. Its fire, too, had been for the moment drained. As she resigned herself to her fate, the vast dragon unleashed his killing breath. Rose closed her eyes, expecting the heat to slam into her like the punch of a giant. But as she heard the roaring whoosh of the drake's breath, it was counterpointed by a ripping sound, and a roar that was not the drake's but another's. What was more, the killing blow did not come. Rose's eyes snapped open to see hanging before her and between her and the drake, the large saddled form of a fire dragon who could only be Lightning.

THE RIDE OF THE WHITE WOLF

"Fear the riding of the White Wolf. If he should come forth with spell and sword, be afraid. For it is the coming of death."

A saying in the north.

Kye knew he would be dead before he could draw his short sword. The Troll would kill him, but he went for it anyway. He would have fallen then if Lea had not attacked the giant with a sword that screamed through the air, its very shape blurring as it vibrated in his hands. When the sword struck the giant's shield arm it sent cracks shivering up the stone limb. When Lea struck it again the stone like armand the sword shattered. The giant roared, and would have struck Lea instead if an arrow had not struck it in the face, blinding one of its coal like eyes. The Troll bellowed in pain and when Kye plunged his own sword into its chest the blade, now sheathed in ice cold flames, slid into the flesh as if it was butter, not stone. With a gurgle of fluid the Troll died on the blade.

But there were a hundred more of the stone men behind him, and thousands of Goblins behind them. Kye looked beyond to where the rain of his archers were keeping them back, but he knew that even his archers, led by Lor, could not keep it up enough to take them all out. He was wondering what he should do next when from the slightly higher ground to the west there sounded a horn. From that higher ground there swept the battering ram of Wind Fist and his Centaurs, their lances driving into Goblins, their blades rising and falling. Their charge came as a complete surprise, and they were able to turn the flank of the enemy, but the Centaurs swift strike could not cut through to the main body. As crossbow bolts began to fall among the Centaurs and a phalanx of Trolls marched to face them, Wind Fist realised he had outstayed his welcome, and ordered his men and women to draw back.

Kye, realising they could be overrun, sent half of his Trolls out to drive the horde back. But although they were able to hold the enemy long enough for Wind Fist to disengage, they were not enough to stop the enemy's advance.

"My captain, you should pull them back," Dancing Falcon said from Lea's side. Her short bow covered him as he climbed over the low wall.

"Thank you for your advice," Kye said, taking the arrow Eloo held out to him. "I was about to do exactly that."

Lea, understanding what Kye required of him, used his bard powers to enhance his voice and ordered the retreat. As Kye observed his Trolls retreat he watched the many monsters milling before them.

"We need more men," he whispered to Eloo.

She gently turned his head so he could look over his shoulder, to see emerging from the woods the white heads and standards of the Whitehead clan.

"It looks like White Mane has joined the fight."

Eloo was right, and seconds later the tall, blonde form of Starsheen was at Kye's side, her long bow firing an arrow into the enemy as they tried to gather another charge.

"What kept you?" Kye asked, as he too fired an arrow into the sky.

"Waiting for things to get interesting," shot back the young Werewolf, turning to watch as twenty of her archers bolstered Kye's lines.

"Better late than never, Kye," Lea pointed out, leaning on his bow to accept more water from Falcon.

Kye turned to count heads and assess if the new reinforcements would be enough. Starsheen had brought him twenty more archers, another company of Trolls, and the black Centaur and probably half his Centaurs.

"Where is...?"

"He is leading the bulk of our force to reinforce Apollo."

Kye grunted his acknowledgement, but did not say that it was not enough; he was not going to get any more. Eloo had watched his eyes and the cogs behind them. "Can we last?"

Kye gave her a look which said, "I do not know."

"Here they come again," Dancing Falcon shouted, firing her short bow at the nearest Goblin.

Kye grunted and drew his own. As he did, he wondered how many arrows he could fire before the Darklings rode over them.

* * *

Rose stared in disbelief as Lightning spread before her. He had been gone, vanished, never to return she thought, but he was here now. He roared again, and spat a flash at the dragon. Rose wanted to see better and the sword, appearing to hear her thoughts, allowed her to float up over Lightning's back so she could look down at both the dragons. From this angle Rose could not but help compare the two dragons and note the differences between them. For a start, the opposing Fire Drake was probably twice the size of Lightning, its form bulging with muscle, whereas Lightning's frame was covered in lines of wire thin cords. Lightning was more like a great cat in form and action, and the larger dragon was all spikes and horns jutting from every angle, his many horned head protruding from massive shoulders giving him a crouching appearance. Even their scales were similar, yet different. The larger dragon's scales were a ruby red which made it look like the dragon itself was a huge coal. Lightning's scales were lighter, more a pale rose, and almost rusty on his lower jaw.

As she watched, Lightning spat another stroke of lightning at the larger dragon which shrugged the effects of the spell off, although from the look of it the two figures on its back had felt something of the shock. The figure on its back in the dragon crested helmet screamed, and raising its hands sent a blast of magic back. Lightning dodged it, and flying to the dragon's left, swooped in to claw at its great wing. The large dragon snarled, twisted its long neck and bit at Lightning. This fuelled Rose's rage, and not even thinking about it she swooped in at the dragon from the other side. Her sword slashed a long cut into the smoky membrane. The Dragon roared, and pulling its wings closer into its body it swung them at Rose, attempting to strike her with the huge hooked claws studding the appendages. Rose gave him another slash for his trouble.

Then the air she was hovering in was full of tiny metal blades that spun through the air like metallic hail. The rain of blades cut at Rose's clothing and scratched her skin. Watching the dragon crestedrider, Rose saw her draw from a back sheath a great flame bladed sword that she lifted over her head and swung at Rose. Rose was a few feet away from the red figure and out of reach of the blade although she still raised her blade. When the blow slammed against her own sword, jarring her arm, she was shocked. It was as though the wavy sword had a ghost blade that reached out far beyond the edge of the metal.

Enraged by this, Rose without thinking drew upon her fire ring and sent a handful of flames flying at the helmeted figure. The flames broke over the figure and appeared to do nothing at all. The figure appeared to be warded against fire. The burst did have one effect, to dazzling the helmeted figure. Rose grabbed at the chance to swoop in and stab at it with her sword. But as she did the drake half turned towards Lightning and swotted Rose aside with a vast wing. The scaly mountain fastened his fangs on Lightning's forelimb. Rose, however, did not realise this at first. Not until she had recovered from the stunning blow did she see what was happening. She screamed and flew at the huge dragon, slashing at his wing. She was nearly smashed aside by the huge dragon's mace of a tail but spotting it at the last moment dodged it. Suddenly the dragon howled, and like a dark comet began to plummet towards the ground.

* * *

Apollo called upon the magic of his mace and turned it into a torch, its golden light forming a beacon for his troops. "We hold or die."

As he cried this a Goblin leapt at him, its stone axe aimed at his chest. It might have dealt a deadly blow but his great stag tossed its head and the Goblin was sent flying back, its body ripped by the deer's crown of horns. A spear slammed against his shield and flint headed arrows fell about him. At his side Thorn used his axe to protect his general's flank. On the Weredings other side Aleena fired spears of ice at the Goblins. Apollo looked about him to see he was an island in a sea of grey writingbodies. Anger rose up within him, and like a fire it flared red hot. Not caring who would kill him or what wound he might take he spurred his steed forwards. With a vast bellow the stag lowered its head and charged at the wall of Goblins. He held his mace high and its light blazed like a tiny sun. Its light drove the Goblins back in the face of his and the stag's fury. Apollo, driven by his rage, followed them, leaving the rest of his force far behind, and suddenly the Goblins were gone, and he was facing the wall of Trolls. Apollo raised his mace high and roared a challenge although he was outnumbered many hundred times. But the wall of Trolls did not attack him. Instead, they split in two, and from between their ranks there loped a great grey wolf like beast, and upon its back was the giant form of the Orc general, Cyclops.

From where they still contested with Goblins, Thorn watched helplessly as his commander faced the giant upon a beast that wore the grey pelt of a wolf, but which stood five feet at the shoulder, its head long and lean, great jaws open to display tusks.

"What is it, that beast?" he asked, deflecting a Goblin spear.

"A wolf altered by right and gods," Aleena answered, blocking a Goblin's sword with her long white blade and discharging a burst of cold magic from her staff in the other hand.

"A Warwolf." Thorn snarled, blocked the Goblin's blade with the staff of his standard and cut him down with his axe.

"Yes, and that is Cyclops on it," Aleena said, sweeping her staff in a circle before her, an arc of cold ice sweeping all before her.

"We cannot leave him to stand alone."

"We cannot advance, either," Aleena said, launching into more spell casting. "We must hold the gates."

"I will not let him stand alone," Thorn said, and before Aleena could stop him the young Deer Centaur leapt over the thin line of Goblinheads and galloped to his master's side.

* * *

Apollo, for his part, was not aware of what was happening behind him. He was trying too hard to stay alive to care what his forces might be doing. When Cyclops appeared the Trolls had begun to beat their long spears against their great wooden shields in a challenge to the two combatants. Cyclops had unsheathed a battle axe from his back, and raising it above his head had roared in reply and charged the tall Wereding. Apollo's stag bellowed and bucked his horned head at the huge Warwolf which snarled and snapped at the stag's barded legs. Cyclops' axe flew at Apollo's head, but he countered with his shield. His mace, still glowing like a tiny sun, slashed tears in the Orc's hide shield. The wolf steed whined in pain as a kick from the stag shattered its shoulder. Cyclops' next swing of the axe went wide as the altered wolf reared up to sink its fangs into the stag's neck. The great stag moaned as the beast drained its life blood. Apollo, knowing his faithful steed was slain, killed the wolf with a great blow of his mace which stove the beast's skull in. Both warriors were forced to leap from their saddles as their respective mounts died beneath them. When Cyclops got to his feet he fired a ray of utter darkness at Apollo from a ring on his gauntleted hand. Apollo blocked it with his shield and sent it back at the Orc, but it was absorbed into the onyx stone from which it had come.

"Any other tricks, Cyclops?" Apollo asked, sweeping his glowing mace before him.

"Crow all you like," Cyclops snarled in his deep voice. "The Grim Reaper will not take you. My master will claim your body and add you to his army."

"Over your dead body." With these words Apollo leapt forwards and aimed a huge blow at his enemy's helmed head.

Apollo's blow would probably have killed the Orc if it had reached its mark, but as he made the swing Cyclops' shield rushed him. His great hide shield slammed into Apollo, knocking him back and knocking off his aim, so his mace came down not on his enemy's head but his shoulder, with bone crunching force. Cyclops shoved again with his broad shield and Apollo fell back, lost his footing and fell to one knee. The huge Orc roared with victory as he lifted his axe above his head to deliver a killing blow.

At this moment Thorn reached his lord's side and his axe met and blocked the massive swing Cyclops bore down on his opponent. Cyclops roared in rage and fired another black beam at Thorn who did not have Apollo's shield and was unable to block the ray, and it blew a large smoking hole in the young Centaur's narrow chest. Apollo bellowed in rage, and powering to his feet swept the giant's axe aside and hammered at the Orc's head with his mace, its spikes driving through helm, flesh and bone, to tear great holes in the Orc's head. Apollo drove it into the beast's head, pulled it out and drove it back in. Only when he had reduced the giant's head to a pulp did he turn to the blasted form of Thorn. The young Centaur lay on his side, his hand grasping at the blasted hole the ray had burnt in the middle of his chest. When he looked up at his lord with soft brown eyes, they were brimming with tears. "I am sorry, my lord, I have failed you."

"No, Thorn, you have not failed me," Apollo said, cradling the Centaur in his arms. "You saved my life, Thorn, you have triumphed. In years to come they will sing your name."

This made the young Deer Centaur smile despite the pain. He made to say something but before he could a great pain contorted his face, and his spirit fled him. Apollo bellowed in rage to the heavens as he realised his friend had left him.

He made to rise and carry Thorn's body back to his people, but heard the clack of claws. Turning, he found another enemy had appeared to confront him.

"Apollo, I believe," hissed the cold voice of the Wraith King.

* * *

Aleena cried out as she saw Thorn die, and then cried a warning to Apollo to look behind him as a vast shadow swept over them. A beast, half horse and half dragon landed behind the grieving Wereding lord. The beast had the hind quarters of a horse, but its head was more like that of a Fire Drake. From its withers there stretched vast leathery wings, but despite the horror of the steed the real threat was from its rider. Upon its back there sat a giant armoured figure, which if it stood must have been seven feet tall. But seated or standing, the armoured form, whose great helm was crafted to resemble a crowned skull, radiated the cold power of the grave. Aleena had herself never encountered the Wraith King, but she had no doubt this was who stood before her. "Apollo cannot stand against him."

* * *

Apollo turned to find the huge dragon like mount, and upon its back the giant armoured form. It looked down at him with glowing red eyes from behind the skull crafted great helm. The red coals fell on Thorn's body in Apollo's arms. "Such a brave warrior, he will make a good addition to my bodyguard."

"You shall not touch him," Apollo snarled.

The Wraith King appeared to regard Apollo for a long moment. Then from within the skull there came a gale of laughter that stabbed Apollo's senses like tiny daggers in the mind. "You cannot prevent it."

Apollo drew himself up and faced the giant, anger flaring in his eyes. "We shall see about that."

The Wraith King hefted a long black staff, topped with an onyx skull. The eye sockets of the skull flared with red lights. Apollo tensed himself for an attack but it never came. Both the Wereding Prince and the Wraith King turned their attention to the sound of metal grating on metal. It was not a loud sound, but in the stillness surrounding these two it filled the world. Then from behind Apollo a hoarse whisper broke the silence. "Stand down, Apollo."

Apollo turned, to find Tristian clad in his white wolf furs. In one hand he held a shield bearing his arms of a white winged wolf, and in the other the long white blade that was his signature weapon. The Dragon steed snorted as its large nostrils caught the scent of Tristian's mount, a huge white wolf that stood nearly as tall as Tristian himself and which appeared to be a Warwolf.

"So, old man, you have decided to come out of your sanctuary at last," rasped the Wraith King.

"I have come to finish you for once and all," Tristian said softly, watching Apollo gather up Thorn and run with him to where his own forces stood, now swelled to twice their former size by the reinforcements of the White Head clan.

The Wraith King looked beyond Tristian to the forces before the Kings, then to where the Trolls stood like silent sentinels. "What are you waiting for, bring me their heads."

The Trolls sprang to life as if the Wraith King had turned a key and marched towards the ford. Tristian calmly watched them go, and once they were past spurred his wolf forwards. The Wraith King watched him come, and reaching over his left shoulder he drew a huge sword, a massive double edged weapon as wide as a hand. The sword would normally be held in both hands, but the giant wielded it easily enough with one. Tristian watched him calmly, and with lightning speed stabbed his white blade at the larger man. The Wraith King's huge blade swept down and blocked the stab. As the blades connected sparks of red and blue light flew in all directions and as the combatants clashed so too did the magical fields which surrounded them.

THE FALL OF THE DRAGON

"What goes up must come down, but sometimes what flies comes crashing down. Remember that when you cast your flying spells."

Takana to the Red Wizard, the Wereding Chronicles.

Kye was just wondering how long his forces could hold the dark tide back when a roar from above made him glance up to see the vast bulk of the red dragon falling like a fiery comet towards the ground. He was wondering in a detached way if the dragon would fall on them when it came to a devastating crash on the ground before him, its landing so great the ground beneath him shook, and he was nearly thrown from his feet. However, the great dragon had fallen upon the Trolls and Orcs, and his lines had escaped its devastation. The great beast had crushed many Trolls beneath its bulk, and at the same time impaled itself on many huge spears and swords. It tried to rise, pulling its body off the blades, ripping its flesh even more and pouring blood all over the place. However, Fire Drakes wreakdestruction even when they bleed for as the dragon's blood flowed from its torn flesh it ignited and became a flaming liquid burning everything it touched, melting blades and dead Troll flesh alike. Still, the dragon had been grievously wounded and it struggled to stand, its body bleeding from numerous wounds. Trolls and Goblins unfortunately close to it screamed and tried to attack it, but even wounded the drake was a force to be reckoned with. With a roar it snapped up an Orc in its jaws and bit it in two, spitting the bloody pieces at its fellows. The warning appeared to work, for Trolls and Goblins alike withdrew from the beast, leaving it to try to take flight, but its wings were too badly damaged and it could not seem to find the strength to climb back into the air. Then Lightning, who must have let go of the falling dragon at some point, flew over and hovered above it, challenging him to re-join the fight. Kye wondered if the dragon could stand for much longer. There was a flash of red light and when his sight cleared Kye saw that the great Fire Drake had employed some magic and vanished from the battlefield.

"I will run away, to live and fight another day," muttered Eloo from beside him.

"Perhaps, but what of his riders? Did they go with him?"

Kye was answered moments later. Rose floated down towards the field of destruction as the figure in the dragon helm blazed into fire, her form surrounded in a halo of dancing, red flames.

"A flame shield spell," Eloo exclaimed, watching the figure rush at Rose.

"Does it look familiar?" Kye asked, aiming an arrow at the fiery figure.

"Kye, we must help Rose."

"Perhaps, but Lightning is with her," Kye observed as the great dragon landed at Rose's side and changed into human form.

* * *

As Lightning watched, the helmed figure who had been riding the Fire Drake burst into flames and swung aflaming sword at Rose. "Rose, *LOOK OUT!*"

Lightning cried the warning but he was too late. The burning sword and Rose's Eagle blade clashed, and flames were sent flying in all directions. Rose flung up her arm to protect herself from the flames and began to shout words of power. The red helmed attacker, however, struck at her again, this time sending Rose's Eagle sword flying from her hand. Lightning watched in frozen horror as the red clad attacker lifted its flame bladed sword high in a two handed grip that would bring the sword down on Rose with the attacker's full weight behind it. But if Lightning was frozen in place, Rose was not. She, too, burst into fire, her body haloed in dancing red flames. She had lost her sword, but she still had a weapon in her belt. She tore from her girdle the Wand of Wisdom and drove its three foot length into the attacker's lower stomach. The rod had a pointed tip, and it plunged through the figure's armour as if it were paper.

The figure stood there impaled on the rod, a grunt of surprise rather than pain escaping its hidden lips. It dropped the sword and reached for the rod protruding from its stomach. Rose stared at the figure she had impaled. As she stared at the helmet, a growing horror enfolded her in its dread embrace. She let go of the rod that was once more twisting its rings into new configurations. "I'm sorry."

The figure grunted and reaching out with both arms grabbed hold of Rose by her shoulders and pulled her towards it. Rose tried to pull away, but the figure's strength was that of a giant, and she was pulled towards it. Only as a dagger of pain tore through her belly did Rose realise the dragon crested attacker had drawn her to its bosom to impale Rose on the wand so they were joined in death.

"No, Robin, I have failed you."

The helmeted figure must have heard her cry, and from behind its concealing cage of grill work a voice that was hauntingly familiar asked, "Rose?"

For a long moment Rose could not comprehend what she was hearing, but with a thrill of horror she realised who the voice belonged to. "Robin?"

Lightning was at her side then, his arms around her despite the flames still flickering about her, his voice whispering in her ear, "It's all right, Rose, it will be all right! Just hang on and I'll get Silver. She can heal you."

Rose did not understand what he was saying. She was staring at the face hidden behind the helm. "Lightning, I think she's Robin."

As Lightning watched the figure raised a trembling hand to the helm and swung back the cheekpieces to reveal to Rose's disbelieving gaze the face beneath. The face was Rose's face, red scales and eye and all. The only difference between the two girls was that the helmeted one had close cropped hair, whereas Rose's was still shoulder length.

"Rose, is that you?" Robin asked, a thin trickle of blood creeping from the corner of her mouth.

Rose at first did not understand how Robin did not recognise her, but then she realised she was wearing the mask. Without her concentration on it the mask had turned back to its real form and her face was concealed behind it. She reached up a hand, speedily losing strength, to her face and pulled down the mask revealing her own features now half transformed by the scarlet scales, which themselves looked like some kind of mask. "Yes, Robin, it is me."

A single tear ran from the corner of Robin's normal green eye. "I am sorry, Rose, I've killed us both."

Lightning, hearing Robin's words, staggered to his feet and speaking a few words of magic magnified his voice to be heard over the clash of battle which raged around them, though they stood in the eye of the storm. "Kye, Silver Skin, they're hurt, I need your help."

* * *

Kye, hearing him, looked around to where Silver was using her staff to cast beams of cold at a group of axe wielding Orcs. "Silver, can you oblige him?"

Silver Skin snarled out a word of power, and with a crack of thunder the three Orcs before her turned into solid ice as if she had summoned the ice of the north to freeze them solid. "I can now, though what help I can bring is doubtful."

Kye grunted, and giving his bow to Lea he drew the long sword from his back, its edges gleaming silver, and as he drew it he heard in his mind the yip of pleasure that was the sword's spirit as it scented blood. Kye led Silver Skin and Eloo towards the three at the eye of the storm. Any Goblin or Orc who tried to get in his way was met by an impenetrable net of steel as Kye slashed and stabbed the blade with the grim but deadly precision of the Grim Reaper himself. When they reached Lightning and the two injured girls it was to find the two had impaled each other. Despite a difference in hair, they were the mirror of each other. Kye looked from one sister to the other, an expression of realisation on his grim face. "This is Robin, her sister?"

"Yes," Rose gasped, as more pain lanced through her stomach. "Please, Kye, save her."

"They are twins," Silver Skin said, exchanging a look with Kye.

"Never mind whether they are twins or not," Lightning broke in, "please, Kye, heal her!"

Kye looked from Lightning to Silver and shook his head, a look of pained regret on his face. "I am sorry, Lightning, I cannot."

"What do you mean you can't?"

"My connection to the goddess is gone."

"But you have spell stones, use them to heal her."

"I can try, but I am not sure they will work."

"Eloo, have you no healing potions?"

Eloo pulled from her pouch a vial and pressed it into Lightning's hand.

"Wait a moment," Silver said, gripping Lightning's arm, holding him back. "We must remove the wand before they can be healed."

"That could kill them," Lightning protested.

"It must be done," Kye said, turning to the twins.

But as he turned towards the injured twins events overtook them. The wand had been twisting its rings, and from it there now flared a silver light that mingled with and changed the red flames lingering about the twins, transformed the blaze from red to silver and expanded to twice their previous size. Silver Skin, fearing what this might mean, grabbed hold of Kye with one hand and Eloo with the other and dragged them back. Kye, realising what was happening, reached out a long arm and dragged an unwilling Lightning back from the expanding wall of flames.

"No, Kye, they need my help."

"L. you are not immune to all fire, nor all magics," Eloo reminded him, watching the silver flames grow brighter. "Cover your eyes!"

Eloo had not spoken or acted too soon. As the companions watched the silver glow blazed up to blinding intensity, and even through their hands they could see the glow grow to brilliant levels. Then it was gone, as if a full moon had blazed at them and been extinguished.

"What happened?"

Lightning searched for the impaled twins, but wherever he looked he could find no sign of the girls. They, the wand, and even the blood which had been gushing from their hideous wounds had vanished, leaving not a trace of the twins.

"Where are they?" Lightning wailed, his grief and sanity barely under control.

"Lightning, we cannot stay here," Kye said, spying wary Trolls watching them from a distance.

"Where are they?"

Kye had no answers, so he grabbed Lightning by one arm, and Silver taking the other they pulled him back to the barricades.

"No, she is still here! I must save her."

"Lightning, she is no longer here," Lea shouted into his face, he too trying to calm the crazed Fire Drake.

"You don't know that," Lightning screamed.

"Yes, I do," Lea shouted back. "You were too close to see, but from here it looked as if the silver fire took on the form of a dragon and it flew like some kind of comet up into the sky."

"Silver fire?" Silver Skin asked, a look of realisation transforming her face. "Are you sure it was a silver dragon?"

"That's what it looked like," Lea said, shrugging and staring at the spot where the twins had been.

"What is it, Skin?" Eloo asked.

"The prophecies of the Grey Pilgrim," Kye answered for her.

"Kye?"

"The prophecy spoke of a split mirror and the girls are twins. They are a mirror of each other."

"Then where are they?"

"I wish I knew, Lightning," Kye answered, staring up at the sky, and the moon veiled sun.

THE SILVER FLAME

"The Silver Lady has many forms, and may manifest through her servants;not all are Werewolves."

The Druid Handbook.

The Wraith King's mount roared and reared, spreading its vast wings. Tristian's white wolf lunged, snapping at its underbelly. Tristian ducked low over his wolf's neck to avoid the dragon-horse's forelegs and the great eagle like talons which tipped them. He lifted his sword and slashed the saddle strap spanning the beast's belly. The Wraith yelled in surprise when his saddle began to slide off the creature's back.

"Back, Frost."

Hearing his master's command, the wolf quick stepped backwards just in time to avoid the monster crashing down. When Tristian looked up the Wraith King had dismounted, the saddle hanging from the creature's back. This meant that he was now able to attack his enemy from another direction than his mount which now drew in a great lung full of breath and spat out a cloud of poisonous looking vapour. Tristian, however, recognising this creature was a Hypodrake and knowing it was part dragon, had heeled the wolf in its side so it lurched to one side, just avoiding the cloud of venom. This meant that Frost, his giant wolf, had moved him closer to the Wraith King, who aiming his skull tipped staff at Cyclops' fallen body conjured a black beam, and seconds later the corpse staggered to its feet. The undead Orc was directed by the spirit lord to attack Tristian.

"Silver Lady, if you are watching I could do with a hand here."

The Wraith King gave a gale of laughter that stabbed at the ear like daggers of ice. "Your goddess cannot hear you, Tristian. The Lord of darkness has bound her and her power and yours are lost to you."

Tristian cursed, and lifting his fist high aimed a moonstone studded ring at the undead Orc. A ray of silver light burnt a hole through the zombie's chest filling the air with the smell of burnt flesh. But the undead monster did not fall.

* * *

Apollo was not faring much better. Despite the Kings' ballista hammering the Trolls before they could reach him and his archers' constant rain of arrows, the Trolls were unstoppable, and the two phalanxes came at him from both sides. As if that wasn't bad enough, hordes of Goblins and Orcs bolstered the Trolls flanks. He beat back a Goblin's sword and shield punched it backwards into the incoming Trolls. "My Lady Aleena, can you help us?"

"Perhaps, but then I must go to Tristian's aid. He needs me."

The White Witch plucked from her pouch a crystal that she cast onto the ground before them, and after a mystic couplet brought the butt of her staff down on it. The crystal shattered and completed the spell, summoning a dome of ice which enclosed Apollo and his forces in a protective globe.

"Thank you, my lady."

"It will not hold for long," Aleena said, and as if to mock her amassive blow spiderwebbed the wall as the Trolls attempted to smash their way through. "I am sorry, I would provide more help, but I must go to Tristian."

"I understand."

The White Witch did not answer but made several passes with her staff and with a couplet opened a door in the air and stepped through it.

The portal narrowed as Aleena passed through, but as it did Winter, her Fury bodyguard, leapt through it after her mistress.

"Good luck," Apollo hissed after them.

"Well, Prince," Whitehead asked, coming to stand shoulder to shoulder with Apollo. "Are you ready to die?"

"Not today," Apollo answered, gripping his mace more tightly as the ice wall before them burst into flames and was gone. "Charge!"

* * *

Kye and his companions were being pressed too. They had fallen back to the second line of walls and pits. These walls were taller, and the pits larger, but even when several Trolls at a time fell through the earth, two took their place. Kye had ceased to fire arrows since he had run out of them and was using his swords to hold back the enemy. "Lady, help us."

Next to Kye, Lea fired his last arrow into the face of a great Troll carrying a battle standard, and the giant fell to one knee, the arrow protruding like ahorn from the centre of its face. The giant used the staff of its standard to try to get back to its feet, but Eloo blasted it with a lightning bolt from her rod. From the other side, Dancing Falcon put an arrow into its shoulder. Lea dropped his bow, and drawing his sword spoke words of power. Jumping down to face the Troll he struck it down with a vibrating sword. Kye, seeing a tall Goblin behind the Troll swinging an axe at his brother, leapt down beside him. He blocked the axe with his long sword, his short sword burying itself into the ratman's side. For a moment the two brothers stood shoulder to shoulder against the tide, their eyes glowing yellow at the horde of Trolls, Goblins and Orcs. A moment later Lor appeared on Kye's other side and Silver joined them, followed by Eloo, Dancing Falcon and Willow Skin, Eloo and Kye's daughter. Together these few companions stood between their own handful of fighters and the Darkling horde.

"At least we die together," Lor said, watching the great horde gather itself to attack them.

Eloo was not watching the Trolls, she only had eyes for Kye which was why she noticed the change in his attention. Kye had been glaring at the enemy, but something made him glance up at the sky and so only she was not surprised when he spoke. "Look at the moon, the silver flame."

Eloo glanced up to where the moon still blocked their view of the sun, but now there was a new light. Not the light of the sun, but a portion of the satellite was lit by a blazing silver glow that danced and flickered and was then gone.

"What is it, Kye?"

"The dragon," Kye said, looking back to the enemy before him. "The twins, perhaps."

"It may be too late," Lor said, watching the Trolls marshal into a phalanx and advance towards them.

As Lor said this, the sky was suddenly full of sunlight. When they looked up the moon had moved from before the sun and its full light beat down on them. Kye smiled, as the Orcs and Goblins screamed in pain and fear and their skin began to smoke and char as the sunlight burnt them.

"Thank you, Silver Lady," Kye whispered, seeking and finding the moon moving to the east.

"She is back!" cried Silver, gripping a now glowing silver pendant. "My powers are back."

"It might save us from the Trolls," Lor said, watching the Goblin kin turn and flee, no doubt seeking some bolthole to hide from the light.

Kye grunted, watching the Orcs flee, but the Trolls were waiting for the sun hating Orcs and Goblins to leave the field before they would advance and finish Kye and his fellow warriors off. Kye was about to order a retreat to the trees when Lightning's voice from behind him made him hesitate. "Look, a dragon."

Kye looked up to see a flash of something gleaming in the new sunlight. At first he thought Lightning must be mistaken, for the thing approaching gleamed silver, and he knew of no dragons that particular colour. Then the creature was flying low over the battlefield, and he understood what he was seeing. "A silver dragon."

"A two headed silver dragon," Eloo corrected him.

It was true, the creature flying over the battlefield, and roaring, enveloped the Trolls in a curtain of fire was a dragon the size of Lightning, but it appeared to have two long serpent necks and two horned heads.

"It's the twins," Lightning cried in joy, and rushing past Kye he reached a wide open place where he transformed into his scarlet draconic form and leapt into the air.

The silver dragon, hearing his cry, turned towards him one of its heads and roared back, and then it had turned and was flying towards the Kings. Lightning bellowed and flew as quickly as he could after the silver scaled beast.

"Could the magic have changed them into this?" Lea asked.

"It would appear so," Silver said, making her medallion blaze with light. "Now with the lady's blessing let's finish this."

"Amen," Kye agreed, making his pendant glow too, and sheathed his swords with cold flames.

THE TURNING OF THE TIDE

"The night is dark and deadly, but the night does not last forever."
The Druid Handbook.

Tristian's blade smashed into the Orc's spine and the zombie collapsed to the ground, not to rise again. Even as the undead crumbled to dust the Wraith King's massive sword swept at his head. Tristian only saw it at the last moment and bringing up his shield managed to block the blow, but the force of the attack drove him back. If he had not kicked out of the stirrups of his wolf saddle he would have been dragged along the ground as he fell reeling from the force of the blow which had splintered his shield. Frost turned to bite at the giant spirit lord, but as it snapped at him the dragon beast came at him from the other side, its huge jaws closing on the wolf's large shoulder and driving a whine of pain from Frost. Tristian used his ring to stab a silver beam into the monster's flank and the creature let go of Frost to howl its pain. The two large creatures began circling each other, looking for an opening. While they did this their riders began to do the same.

"You cannot win, Tristian," the giant gloated from behind the skull of its helm. "Without your goddess you have not the power. Your spell stones will run out of power before my magic does."

The White Wolf grimly clenched his jaw and stabbed his blade at the giant's armoured chest. The Wraith King, moving with a speed and agility that was surprising for one of such size and weight, side stepped the thrust and countered with an overhead swing. Tristian moved with inhuman speed and dodged the attack and punched out with his shield, driving it into the giant's chest. The Wraith King grabbed his arm and pushed him back. The strength of the undead master was that of a titan, and Tristian felt himself bending backwards as the giant forced him back. Then his legs gave under him and he dropped to his knees, overpowered by the giant looming above him, his sword rising up above his head to deal the killing blow.

Tristian was enveloped in the giant's shadow, a darkness deep even in this twilight. Then the shadow was gone and he was blinking in the dazzling sunlight beating down on them. "The darkness has passed, and so have you."

The Wraith King glared up at the sunlight. Then with a snarl of defiance he lifted the sword higher to bring its full weight down on the Werewolf, but the moment had passed. Tristian had felt the link with his goddess leave him, but now her cold fire was burning in his veins and he knew she was with him once again. Before the spirit lord had realised the tables had turned, Tristian pushed back against him, his strength suddenly that of his goddess, and many times greater than the undead master. Tristian did not just stand up, pushing back against the wraith's iron grip, but straightening and lifting the giant one handed, hurled him from him. The giant landed in a heap, unable to collect itself. Tristian would have strode to it and finished the matter then and there, but the hypodrake turned from Frost to stand between Tristian and its master. Tristian reached to his medallion and was about to unleash the lady's silver fire upon it when a shadow passed across the sun. A huge glittering form dropped out of the sky to snatch the hypodrake up in its own huge talons and tear it to pieces. Tristian stared at the huge beast before him. It was a dragon or he was an elf, but it was unlike any dragon he had seen before. For a start it was a gleaming silver, and what was more it had not one but two heads. The heads were similar, but not the same. One of the heads was cat like, but had a mane of spines, like foot long rose thorns. The other head looked more like a bird's, its long jaws almost a beak, its head topped by a high crest. Tristian faced this dragon, not certain at first whether it was friend or foe, but as he looked on it he saw the light of the Silver Lady glowing around the creature and through its scales. "You have come from the Silver Lady?"

"We have come to finish this," the dragon said in two voices that were one.

"The Wraith King?"

"His head is ours," replied the dragon, and it turned towards the undead giant.

The Wraith King had recovered from Tristian's cast and was standing in a circle made of the dust which had been Cyclops. Lifting his staff above his head, he began to chant. As Tristian watched a dark mist sprung up around the giant and thickened until his form was barely visible through the dark cloud shrouding him.

"I am not sure we should touch it," Tristian said.

The twin headed dragon flung back its long, sinewy necks, and roared a sound which was earth shaking in its volume. The next second the twin heads uncurled like striking snakes to unleash twin streams of silver fire upon the mist shrouded form. Tristian blinked, dazzled, but when his vision cleared the shroud still hid the giant and from nowhere a pair of large Orcish zombies had appeared. Their flesh looked as dried and leathery as their armour. "Beware his undead."

The dragon roared as the two undead lumbered towards it. The undead reached for it with claw like hands, but the dragon held its ground and as Tristian watched in amazement it closed two pairs of eyes and began to hum, of all things. As the tuneless sound rose the silver light which appeared to pour through its scales like light through a lantern grew brighter and brighter. When the undead reached the dragon and laid hands on its scales, silver fire burst from its body. The zombies crumbled as the silver fire boiled them away.

"You are indeed a servant of the lady."

The Wraith King must have been aware of what was happening beyond his mist shroud for no sooner had the undead been destroyed than a stroke of black lightning forked from the cloud. The bolt slammed into the halo of silver light surrounding the dragon and the black energy was either absorbed by the silver fire or vanished like mist. In reply the dragon snarled words of power, and a wind sprang from nowhere and blew the mist away, revealing the Wraith King, casting more magic. The dragon roared, and springing forwards brought its tail around in a great swing. As Tristian watched, the tip of the tail, as long as a sword and many times sharper, punched through the chest of the giant and out the backplate. The air was filled with a scream that came from the hells and which chilled Tristian to the bone. A great wind passed through him and the armour was suddenly a crumbling collection of rust on the end of the dragon's tail. Then the giant silver creature spoke in a familiar voice. "Now it is over, and we are found and whole."

"Rose. is that you?" Tristian asked, realising who the dragon's voice was.

The twin headed dragon might have answered but at that moment a shadow fell across them. Fearing some new attack Tristian glanced up to see Lightning hovering there.

"Rose, is that you?"

The twin headed dragon craned its necks to look up at him. Then with a thrumming growl it sprang into the air and flew north.

"No, wait," Lightning cried, and shot after the retreating silver dragon.

"Good luck, my friends," Tristian said, looking about him.

The dragon, who or whatever it had been, was right, the battle was over. With the coming of the sun the Orcs and Goblins had fled, and Apollo had held off the Trolls until the Wraith King died. As if the undead lord had controlled the stone men, with his death their will to fight crumbled with his body and they had fled. As Frost limped up to his side a door opened in the air before him. He raised his sword, ready to defend himself against a new attack, but lowered his guard when he saw it was the White Witch, closely followed by Winter, who stepped from the portal. Without a word, he wrapped her in a huge hug.

EPILOGUE

"Only gods can see the full tapestry of the future. They may know what the future holds, we mere mortals cannot."
Selene to the Red Wizard, the Wereding Chronicles.

Kye looked out over the battle ground and wondered what had happened. One moment they were being overrun by Trolls, the next the stone men had throwndown their weapons and turned tail to flee. He turned to where Eloo was forcing vials of healing potion down the throat of one of his archers. Beyond her, Silver Skin was bathing another casualty in the healing light of her medallion. Kye went to Eloo's side, looking down at the Wolfblood man she was trying to heal and his stomach wound. He pulled bandages from a belt pouch and began to bind the now staunched wound. Eloo's healing potion had stopped the wound from bleeding but was not powerful enough to close it entirely. That would take time and better tending than they could provide here, but at least Kye could bind the wound and prevent it from becoming infected. Eloo wiped a bloody hand across her face and gave her lover a tired but grateful grin. "Thank you, love."

Kye grunted as he used his teeth to tie off the knot. As he finished Silver Skin joined them and looked out at the mass of dead, scattered weapons littering the field. "So much wasted life!"

"War always is a waste of life," Kye grunted, looking at the sky.

"The crows may not agree with you there," Eloo said, watching as a cloud of carrion crows fluttered amongst the many corpses.

Eloo, noticing his glance to the clouds, spoke the words they were all thinking. "Do you think it was the twins that were that dragon?"

Kye shrugged noncommittally, but Silver answered Eloo's question. "Anything is possible."

"But how is it possible? The twins can't have done it themselves, could they?"

"I do not know, Eloo," Silver said, suddenly looking and sounding very tired. "If you were to ask my guess, I would say that the rod had something to do with it. It appeared to emit the silver light."

"It changed their fire silver," Kye whispered, turning to give Eloo his water bottle.

"Then where are they? Where did they go, and where did Lightning go?"

"Eloo, you always had a quick and enquiring mind," Silver said, accepting Kye's water bottle. "But not every question has an answer."

"If you are asking questions," Lor said joining them, his arm in a sling, "then perhaps you could ask why the Trolls turned and ran when they had us on the ropes."

Kye took one more long look to the sky, and turned back to where the rest of his forces were waiting for orders, and hopefully others to relieve them. "Some questions do eventually answer themselves. We simply have to wait for them, but for now let us see to bodies and let time take care of the rest."

THE END

ABOUT THE AUTHOR

Christian Boustead is a blind author who lives in Hanley, Staffordshire. *Dark Tide, Book Three of The Wereding Chronicles* is his most recent novel. He has also written:
Awakening of Magic, Book One of The Wereding Chronicles;
Dragon Games, Book Two of the Wereding Chronicles and
The Voice of Nature, a collection of poetry.

Next in the series:
The Silver Twins, Book Four of the Wereding Chronicles

If you wish to learn more about him and his works you might like to visit his website.
https://findbooksinside.wordpress.com/
or you could sign up to his newsletter and learn more about his books at: http://eepurl.com/c3sup5

THE AWAKENING OF MAGIC
BOOK ONE OF THE WEREDING CHRONICLES

"The curtain was swept aside, to reveal a figure almost as startling as the wolfman ...

... she seemed to fill the space she took up with a whirlwind like presence and when she grinned at Rose, Rose couldn't help but smile back."

What is the magic changing her into?

After losing her mother as a child, Rose has been raised as a human without useful magic, but while in pursuit of her father's murderer she slips through a portal and is transported to the Wereding woods. Plunged into a world of magic, dragons, werewolves, elves and more, Rose is surprised to discover that she has magical blood and that her sister Robin is in grave danger.

Rose has no knowledge of her magic powers and cannot control them, but the magic breaks out of her when she is threatened, leaving changes to her body behind. What is the price of her magic? What is it changing her into?

Forced to work with a cat-like elf, Eloo, and a bestial Werewolf, Kye, Rose must learn to accept creatures she has been raised to abhor and master her magic before it consumes her.

Can she save her sister from the dark magic users before they turn Robin into one of their own? And as if that wasn't enough for the young girl to manage, Rose will have to fight a dragon before she even starts her quest!

A treat for Game of Thrones fans. This is epic fantasy at its best!

DRAGON GAMES
BOOK TWO OF THE WEREDING CHRONICLES

... When Robin opened the heavy cover of the book, it was to find it was a dictionary of the old tongue, the ancient language used in the mists of time and which was sometimes used by the noble houses to embellish their coats of arms. Robin knew a few words of this language, and she had been taught her own family motto by the late Scholar Galmor years ago, so many of the symbols and words before her felt familiar even if she could not actually recognise or interpret them. Her own motto, "Rosa ess Swarvace, bet Falcos fallow laz t'e dona balt," meaning, *The rose is sweet, but the eagle falls like a thunderbolt*, helped her to pick out the words that made up this motto, but other than that she found most of the rest of the words unfamiliar. She glanced across at her two fellow students who sat on either side of her at identical desks, studying, from what Robin could make out, the same books as her own, although by the look of it they were both further along. Robin was about to turn her attention back to the book when Calador, who may have spotted her glance, decided to test her.

"Canduss, the words for the four elements?"

"Terra, Ventus, Insendium and aqua," Robin heard herself say, almost amazed that she knew the answer, but she did.

"It seems we have a prodigy." Calador sneered at her and Robin was not sure if he was pleased or angry. "Perhaps she can give me the words to the ignite spell."

Robin, of course, had no idea what the master was talking about, though she felt she could tell him given a little more time. She had been surprised she could tell him the names of the elements and realised that she suddenly understood many of the characters that had, until that moment, mystified her. It was as though a window in her mind opened and showed her some hidden key. The key was not revealed to Robin, but somehow it gave her the understanding to interpret the complicated symbols, and she knew what the word was and how she could take individual characters and make them words that were now clear in her minds-eye. It was as though the words were written in fire across her mind.

"Incendium..." Robin heard her own voice say, the words escaping her lips before she could stop them. The effects of these words were remarkable. The tall man narrowed his eyes and staring coldly at her, turned away and left the room.

"We may all pay for that," Alfred whispered.

"I'm sorry! I didn't mean to say it," Robin whispered back.

"It doesn't matter, Robin," Cara said softly. "If you can read, you will soon please him."

"I don't want to please him," Robin spat. "I want to cast magic."

"You will, you will," soothed the other girl.

"But it was another two days before she was allowed to cast a spell. She had gone leaps and bounds with the old language and before very long Calador was speaking to her in the old tongue and Robin, who had grasped an almost magical skill with the language, answered him easily, as if she had been speaking it all her life. This meant that he was, by the third day, willing to let Robin practise a spell. She and her fellow students were gathered into the central courtyard that formed a well around which the tower circled. This lesson took place at night and the moon, just past full, shone down on the small pool that sat at the centre of the paved yard. Robin felt a thrill anticipating the upcoming magic, although Calador had not told them what he would be teaching them. She wondered if it would be some kind of elemental spell, as he had talked about the manipulation of fire with an almost loving tone in his voice. That thought, however, made her frown as she stared down into the almost mirror calm waters. If he wanted to teach them about fire magic, wouldn't they have been better practicing that in one of the magically protected chambers that Cara and she had cleaned out once.

"Do you see anything in the water, Canduss," Calador's voice whispered in her ear, making Robin jump, for she had not heard him approach. "Do you intend to learn the lesson without me?"

Robin bit back a retort, and managing to control her anger and gather her courtesy, spoke in a voice devoid of a tremor. "Master Calador, how can I learn a lesson without you, when I don't even know what the lesson is?"

Her only answer was one of his cold, enigmatic smiles that Robin found infuriating.

"What are we here to learn, master?" Alfred asked, switching his gaze from Calador to Robin and back again.

"We are here to learn how to scry," Calador said, standing on the opposite side of the pool from the three students.

"Scrying, what shall we see?"

"That depends, Alfred. What is your heart's desire? What would you wish to see? Who do you seek?"

Robin suddenly thought of Rose. This would be her way of finding her, but even as she thought this she was distracted as the desire to see Luna almost drove Rose from her head. Both their faces were driven from her mind as Calador's cold voice cut into her thoughts.

"Canduss, perhaps you would like to join us."

"I am sorry, master," Robin apologised and averted her eyes from his cold gaze.

"Concentrate," the master said. "I am about to teach you something important, so watch me carefully or you might miss a vital component."

Robin watched, as from a belt pouch the black master removed a small leather bag, from which he took a pinch of dried leaves.

"This is dried rosemary," he said, sprinkling it over the pool. "Now, remembering to summon the power from within you, visualise what you wish to see and speak the words of power, Speculum revelum."

As he said this, the mirror of the lake seemed to mist, as if a giant had breathed on a mirror. Then the mist cleared to reveal to them all an image of a high mountain pass, silvered by the moon. Then the image was gone and the pool was a blank silver disk.

"Very well, who wants to go next?"

Alfred accepted the bag of rosemary next and when he cast the spell an image of a young girl lying in a bed appeared, but the image only lasted a second before a single tear fell from Alfred's eyes to send ripples spreading across the image, distorting and then shattering it.

"Control," Calador snapped at the little boy. "You will never gain mastery, if you let your emotions rule you, boy."

Cara's scrying was misty and seemed to show a castle tower, but either it was surrounded by fog or for some reason the casting was not working. "Did I do something wrong, master?"

"Uncertain," the master sighed. "Something may be interfering with the scrying."

Cara did not respond to that, but passed the bag to Robin. Robin hated herself for doing it, but she thrust all thoughts of Luna from her and summoned Rose's face before her mind's eye and spoke the words. She watched as the water clouded and could not believe it when the mist cleared to show her sister lying in some grey room, was it a cell? Robin thought that Rose was dressed in strange leathers, but the image was not clear and as she watched a curtain of clouds rolled across it. Robin felt the power coiling inside her as she commanded the magic to show her Rose. The cloud cleared, but the image that appeared suddenly was not her sister, but a large horned, reptilian head covered in bright red scales. Robin felt its glowing red orbs meet and lock with hers. She heard the beast roaring in her ears and then all was black.

* * *

Blood and flames are what you get, when dragons play their games.

Who is the mysterious sorcerer Luna, and what are her designs for Robin?

THE SILVER TWINS
BOOK FOUR OF THE WEREDING CHRONICLES

... "So does that mean his power is broken?"

"I cannot say," replied the White Wolf, his gaze going distant, as if he were staring into an unseen world beyond Aleena's sight. "But he is defeated. His spirit was forced to flee and with it whatever hold he had over the darklings was broken."

"So that is why they fled the field?"

Tristian's attention appeared to return to the moment and his lady. "It would appear so, or that is at least my guess."

"Then what is your guess to why your power failed ... and who or what was the silver dragon?"

"Those are questions I do not have answers for."

"But what do you *guess* my love?"

"Not now," Tristian said, his gaze lifting to the sky, "Something is coming."

As Tristian spoke, a shadow swept over them and a great feathered form dropped out of the sky to land before them. Winter, the white haired woman with the lower body of a snow leopard, leapt in front of Aleena, rearing up before her mistress, short sword drawn and four claws raking the air ...

CPSIA information can be obtained
at www.ICGtesting.com
Printed in the USA
BVHW040019110221
599727BV00012B/448